THE SYZYGY EFFECT

Georgia "Rainy" Keating had a full house for the first transmissions from the Newton-8 spacecraft. Senators, Congressmen, newspeople, fellow scientists.

"On the screen at the top of the console," she began, "you're going to see the first pictures of Jupiter as it crosses in front of the sun."

Suddenly the technician was signalling distress. There was a sound coming from the speakers like nothing the spacecraft had ever produced before. It was as though an animal cry had blended with the whines and rumbles of a machine on the verge of breaking down.

"We're getting overloads on the solar energy systems, Rainy. Maximum tolerance and still climbing!"

Then the signal cut off as if a switch had been thrown.

SYZYGY
BY FREDERIK POHL
Author of JEM and MAN PLUS

SYZYGY

FREDERIK POHL

BANTAM BOOKS
TORONTO · NEW YORK · LONDON · SYDNEY

SYZYGY

A Bantam Book / January 1982

ISBN   0-553-20527-7

Published simultaneously in the United States and Canada

Bantam Books are published by Bantam Books, Inc. Its trademark,
consisting of the words "Bantam Books" and the portrayal of a
rooster, is Registered in U.S. Patent and Trademark Office and in
other countries. Marca Registrada. Bantam Books, Inc., 666 Fifth
Avenue, New York, New York 10103.

PRINTED IN THE UNITED STATES OF AMERICA

0   9   8   7   6   5   4   3   2   1

ARECIBO

Because Jupiter is the greatest of the planets, it is named after the greatest of the Roman gods. As a god, Jupiter is known as Fulgurator, the thrower of lightning; Imperator, the ruler; Optimus Maximus, the best and most high. As a planet, Jupiter is all of those things. Its swirling atmosphere is lanced with lightnings. Its huge mass, outweighing all the other planets combined, rules the orbits of a thousand lesser worlds. And it is indeed Maximus. If it were any larger, it probably would not be a planet at all. It would be a star.

Wednesday, December 2d. 9:45 PM.

The party was beginning to slow down, but then it had never been a high-speed party. It was not meant to be. It was meant to mix the people who wanted money with the people who could give it to them, and the predominant mood was Cover Your Butt. The scientists had to be careful of the senators. The politicians had to be careful of the people from the news media. The news media people had no one to worry about, except perhaps each other. But they all had deadlines to make, because of the differences in time between Puerto Rico and wherever their home bases were, and early sessions in the morning to wake up for. Ancient old Senator Bielowitz was the first to go, before ten, and some of the newspersons hitched a ride with him to the motel at the bottom of the hill. It was a terrible waste of a good party, Tib thought, considering that it was out of doors in the warm Caribbean night and the sky was a glory, but then he wasn't here to have fun. One more drink, he told himself, and then I too will walk over to the Visiting Scientists Quarters and read myself to

3

sleep with the reports on the tilt rate of the Salton Sea.

As he was building himself a weak Canadian Club and ginger, the chairman of the meeting climbed on a stone bench. "Gentlemen!" he called. "Ladies. Can I interrupt the fun for just a minute?" The chairman was a Florida meteorologist and, Tib thought critically, a bit of a butt-kisser. But maybe that was because they were always under the gun with their forecasts. He waited a second, until a majority of the faces were turned more or less his way, and said, "Miz Georgia Raines Keating, our representative from the Jet Propulsion Laboratory, has something to tell you. Here you go, Rainy." He offered a hand to help her up.

Space scientists and weathermen, what the hell was he doing here with them? Tib took an angry swallow of his drink. They got all the money they needed! They had everything going for them, including a rub-off from the military budgets, because everybody knew that space rockets and nuclear missiles were first cousins, and weather was itself a kind of weapon. But everybody was quieting down to listen—partly, and there was another unjust thing, because the scientist from JPL was a very good-looking young woman who wore her jeans very tight. "Thank you, Dr. Zinfader," she called, and then, to the audience, "I've got good news. Our course corrections were optimal! Around two PM tomorrow—that's year 81, day 337, time 1613 in Universal Mean Time—Jupiter, the sun, and Newton-8 will be in syzygy. That means that, from the Newton-8 satellite, Jupiter will appear to transit the sun. Just as promised," she added, beaming. There were a few polite handclaps. "I'll be telling you more about it during the coffee break tomorrow morning. Right now I'm going to send it a message to tell it how to deploy its instrumentation to observe the transit, so if any of you would care to accompany me to the mission control . . .?"

Most of the twenty-odd people left at the party were looking at their watches, and only about half a dozen took her up on the invitation. Tib, finishing his drink, decided to be one of them; it was on the way to the V.S.Q. in any case. What surprised him was that so few persons joined her. And none of them of any real importance. Two of the observatory scientists and their wives; one young woman who turned out to be Rainy Keating's assistant; himself. And the senators and the congressmen who were supposed to be here to learn everything they could learn about the science they were spending the taxpayers' money for? Not one!

Shocking, Tib thought to himself, though he was not really shocked. It was only what he cynically expected. He only half-watched while the young research assistant sat down at the keyboard of the mission control console and did not even half listen while Keating explained what she was doing. It was such a waste to fly three thousand miles to this place! His work interrupted, his time taken away from him, and for what? Only so that he could beg a few more dollars from the politicians, to do the things that every thinking human being knew absolutely had to be done anyway!

Still—speaking of things that had to be done—his slides were still in the car, and so was the easel for his charts. As long as he was here, he might as well set them up for his presentation, he thought, since he was speaking in the morning. As he came back into the little meeting room with the folded easel under his arm he discovered that everyone else had gone, and only Rainy Keating was standing by the doorway, looking lost. "Hey," she said. "Dr.—?"

"Sonderman. Tibor Sonderman."

"Right, you're the geologist. I wonder if you could do me a favor? I missed my ride down the hill. It's only about a mile, but at night—if you wouldn't mind—"

"Mind? Why should I mind? I've got a car right outside." But of course she knew that; she'd seen him go out to it. And of course she had no compunctions about imposing on him! If she had been a man, even if she had been an older woman, then there would have been quite a different thing. It would not have been a *sex* thing. Tib Sonderman's perception of sex things was that he was always on the losing side. The better the woman looked, the smarter, the more amiable, the more certain he was that the cards were stacked against him. "Let me help you with your things," he said, picking up her briefcase.

5

"Thanks." She gave him a quick, uncertain grin that faded when she saw his expression.

Outside again, in the damp, lush Puerto Rican air, she was making conversation about the stars and the radio telescope, and he was responding, but neither of them was making much of an effort. It was only a short drive, through the parking lot and down the looping road that descended the mountain to a white house with a solar roof, set back among trees at a bend in the road. Tib drove with great concentration, like someone who had never learned to drive until he was in his mid-twenties; he drove as though he were following a memorized checklist of instructions.

He drove as though he were in a hurry to get it over with and get rid of her, Rainy Keating thought. What an awkward person he was to be with! Good looking enough—not very tall, and maybe a little heavy, but he had a nice face. He even had a sense of humor, because she had been listening to him talking to one of the newsmen early in the party. But he didn't seem able to relax with her. And when they got out of the car and walked up onto the breezy porch of the house she had been allowed to stay in for the meeting, he almost blundered into the blown-glass mobile that hung near the door. "Oh, watch out," she cried, and he ducked just in time, grazing it and making it tinkle gently.

"I am sorry," he said. "I hope I haven't damaged your wind-chime."

"It's an orrery. I got it in San Juan, and I think it's all right—I'm sorry I shouted at you." And then there seemed nothing to do but to add, "Would you like to come in for a drink?"

He thought it over for a moment. "Thank you, yes," he said, but she had had time to get annoyed at his hesitation. And he still didn't come in, even after she had unlocked the door and held it. He said uneasily, "Do you hear voices? Your family, perhaps?"

"I don't have any family here. It isn't my house; the people who live here are on sabbatical, and they let me borrow it."

6

"Perhaps I was mistaken," he said, following her in and looking around the room as though he expected to have to write a report on it.

Rainy Keating felt that she, at least, had a really good sense of humor, and the way she diagnosed that was that she saw a lot of comedy in herself. For instance, it was funny that she had let what she called her "dating skills" get rusty. She had had plenty of practice, after all, and not *that* far in the past. And anyway, dating lore was all high-school stuff, passed from sophomores to freshmen around the time of the menarche, and all simple. Lesson One: Talk about what *he* is interested in. So she finished turning on the lights, set out a tray of glasses and said, "What do you think, Tibor? Does this kind of circus do any real good?"

He smiled suddenly and sat down, seeming to relax. "Good? I don't know. But I am sure that to stay away from it would bring ultimate harm."

"Meaning no money?" She brought him a whiskey and soda—not very large, because she wasn't having so much fun that she wanted to protract it indefinitely.

"Exactly no money. These senators and congressmen are important people. They would tell you that they do not want to be flattered, and that's true. But it would surprise them so if we did not, that they would be quite unable to vote our appropriations. Are you married?"

Sitting down near him, Rainy was startled enough to misjudge and bump into the arm of the chair. "What kind of question is that, right off?"

"I just like to know, since you wear no ring."

"I used to be married. What about you?"

He nodded, as though it was the answer he had expected. "I used to be married, too, but now I'm divorced. For six years—no, this is December already. For six years and two months."

"And two weeks and three days and five hours and twenty-two minutes? Oh, wow, Tibor, you know what I bet? I bet the divorce was your wife's idea." He shrugged. "And you didn't want it to happen, right? And you're still not happy about it."

7

He said stiffly, "If I said something that upset you, I'm sorry."

"Why should you upset me? I'm used to it. My ex-husband knows exactly how long it is, too."

"And he didn't want the divorce either?"

She laughed, relenting. "No, he didn't. Let's start over, okay? I'm not divorced—yet. I've been separated four months, and as soon as it's a year I'll get the papers, and, yes, my ex-husband didn't want it and he still hassles me about it . . . and I'm not usually so touchy." He had gulped his drink; penitently, she freshened it and tried again. "Are you worried about losing your funding?"

"Not me personally, no." He hesitated, then let her add ice to the glass. "There is a great need for more observation stations all over the United States—particularly in California. There are thousands of square miles that we cannot monitor at all. We had the funds for expansion, but NSF has cut back—I have been asked to testify about the importance before these politicians, hoping they will restore the money. I do not, honestly, have much hope. I suppose it is the same with you?"

"Well, not really," she said with a touch of pride. "I'm JPL's pet exhibit of economy, because my own project is pretty nearly all pure profit. They sent me here to tell the committee that, so they can see what a good investment space missions are. There are some big ones that need funding—a Venus radar orbiter, a cometary mission. Some really nice ones."

"They will get the funding, of course."

There was an edge to his tone that made her look at him curiously. "Why do you say that?"

"Oh, space, you know. It is the glamor department of science, after all—and very close to rockets and missiles."

"I don't have anything to do with missiles!"

"Not directly," he conceded, and then spoiled it by adding, "perhaps. But it is all much the same thing."

"The hell it is, buster."

He looked at her in astonishment, then scowled. "Well, Miz Keating," he said with heavy irony, "I have enjoyed this little talk. I apologize for touching so often where you are so touchy."

She stood up with him. "I am not in the *least* touchy about my work," she corrected him angrily.

"Oh, you feminists!" he exploded.

"What do you mean, 'feminists'?"

He had an infuriating smile, she realized. "After all, you play both sides against the middle, do you not? When you want a favor, all sexual and sweet. When you discuss your work, hard-nosed, all men together—"

"Hold on a bloody minute. Where did 'sexual' come into this?"

"At the very beginning, of course, are you denying this? The scenario is obvious. You ask me to drive you home, and of course there is the implied possibility that you will allow me to kiss you at the door, yes?, and then perhaps to go farther, even in the direction of your bed, all according to expectation."

"*What* goddamn expectations?"

"The expectations of the whole world! They are very clear. If a woman indicates to a man that she does not dislike him, the world expects him to make an advance—it is his obligation; he must spare her the embarrassment of making sexual overtures herself. Even if he does not particularly wish to! And if he fails in this he has insulted her—he has indicated she is not sexually attractive; what rudeness!"

Rainy Keating was holding the heavy tumbler in her hand; to her surprise, she realized she wanted to throw it. "You've got hell's own nerve, fellow! If I wanted to go to bed with you I'd let you know!"

"You see how angry you are?" He nodded. "Because I have not picked up my cue properly. Listen to me, *Missus* Keating, you're right, I did not want my wife to divorce me. But I accepted her decision, because that was what was expected of me. Now what is expected is that I must accept the decision of every woman I hand a drink to at a party! How ridiculous! The unpleasant mornings I have spent, waking up after a night with some wholly unacceptable woman simply because I could not offend her by failing to make the overtures—"

"Get the hell out of here, Sonderman!"

He blinked. "Did I say something offensive?"

"Get out of here!"

He did, with dignity. Outside the door he said severely, "You have taken this in quite the wrong spirit."

"God," she cried, and slammed the door in his face.

In the early Eighteenth Century Charles Boyle, the fourth Earl of Orrery, was known as one of England's most enthusiastic amateur astronomers. An inventor named George Graham made, and gave to the earl, a clockwork mechanism that represented the course of the known planets around the sun. The device did not show the moons of Mars, because no one knew they existed, but neither did it show Jupiter's Galilean satellites, though they had been seen by everyone with a telescope. Perhaps the mechanism was not delicate enough to deal with things so tiny and so remote. The earl enjoyed the device. He liked it so well that he permitted it to be called an "orrery", after himself. The feelings of George Graham about this are not recorded.

Thursday, December 3d. 7:30 AM.

The house that Rainy Keating had borrowed had a back lawn enclosed in a stone fence. Two young people finished the first joint of the day and rolled up their sleeping bags; they had spent the night in the shelter of the wall. "Eat first or haul tail first, Dennis?" the young woman asked.

Dennis Siroca put his arms through the straps of his pack frame. "Let's get out of here before the people wake up. We'll eat up the hill a little." He shrugged the pack into position uncomfortably. It was warm enough, but damp. "Maybe we'll smoke a little more dope first."

"Now?"

"Up the hill, Zee." He helped her with the bedroll, and then stood waiting while she methodically snapped the harness and fastened all the ties on her quilted jacket. Siroca was a tall man of about thirty. His full beard was sulfur yellow, and so was his hair, which he wore pulled to the back through a leather thong. He inspected the little house with approval: the solar panel meant the owners had respect for the ecology (though maybe that didn't matter any more). As they started across the front yard he glanced at the porch, and something made of bright glass caught his eye. It hung like a Calder mobile, and when the crystal globes touched each other in the morning breeze they tinkled. "Hey, that's pretty," he said, pleased. "You go ahead, Zee. I want to take a look."

He climbed the steps and reached out to touch the bright-colored spheres, smiling. Then he heard a sound from inside the house, and turned quickly to look in the picture window.

Inside the house Rainy Keating heard the phone ring, jumped out of the shower, grabbed a towel and ran for it. Too late. The ringing stopped just as she reached for the phone. She glowered mistily at the thing, fuzzy because she hadn't put her glasses on; Rainy was a telephone addict, and a missed call was more than an irritation, it was enough to spoil a day. She swore softly, and turned around just as something crashed with a terminal sound on the porch.

She snatched the towel around her and raced for the bathroom and her glasses. By the time she was peering through them around the bathroom door, what she saw was the ruin of her orrery dancing crazily from its hook, and the shape of a man disappearing down the steps— there were Peeping Toms in Puerto Rico, too! Really, it was too much. That insufferable grubby Cossack last night, and this interloper this morning. She had not been entirely pleased to come to Arecibo anyway, because its research in communication with extra-terrestrials was a little too close to the indiscretions of her youth. That gut feeling was now validated.

She dressed quickly, the bloom off her morning. In the shower she had been singing, but she didn't want to sing

11

any more. Her mood had turned sour, quite unusual for a healthy young woman who knew she was good-looking and, usually, knew she was the luckiest person in the world. How many women in their mid-twenties—well, their latter twenties—had their own careers, and even their own spaceships? But Rainy had hers. Old, second-hand, lingering on by chance and the luck of the draw, but her own special project. It was what she had wanted since she was a little girl. Even if she hadn't known she wanted it, exactly, at first.

When Rainy was ten years old an aunt told her she was a Pisces. Little Rainy immediately perceived that a Pisces was about the best thing you could be. And all you had to do to be it was to be born at the right time of year! Her aunt had gone on to explain the influences of the planets to the alert little girl, and how important it was to understand them—not to change them, because you could not do that, but to guard against the baleful portents and enhance the good. For a whole year Rainy studied the astrology columns of the Los Angeles newspapers. She spent long hours calculating when she would allow herself to become pregnant with her first child, assuming she got married as planned at twenty-one, in order to bear the baby at the most favorable possible moment. It was of no small help to her grades in arithmetic.

Then, one day when she was eleven, the television was full of shocking news.

A spacecraft called Mariner had flown by Mars and photographed it at close range. It had transmitted pictures of a dry, empty landscape pocked with craters.

That was a moment of wrenching disillusionment for Rainy. The planets were not mystic flashlight bulbs in the sky, set there for the purpose of bathing the Earth with occult rays that seeped through clouds and storms, through the roofs of hospitals—even through the bulk of the whole Earth itself—to reach into each delivery room and mold the minds and destinies of squalling newborns. Mariner showed they were nothing of the sort. And as mission followed mission, the story grew always more grim. Mars was a rusty rock, airless and cold. Venus was hot poison gases smothering stone, Jupiter a dense swirl of refrigerating fluid, Mercury a cinder.

At first Rainy was furious. Then the sense of betrayal began to dissolve in wonder, then fascination. Astrology dropped out of her mind without a trace. But the planets themselves! The stars! Before she was fifteen she could pick out Orion's three-jeweled belt, the Pole Star, the great Summer Triangle and a dozen other asterisms. The Christmas of her sixteenth year was a great disappointment. The presents under the tree were well enough, but in the skies the comet Kohoutek was a washout. In her senior high-school year she dated the ugliest boy in class. He was the only one who owned a telescope, eight-inch mirror, hand-ground. When she lost her virginity it was in the hills of Griffith Park, to the only boy she knew who shared her every-week addiction to the planetarium.

At no time after twelve did Rainy doubt what her career would be—at least, not after discovering that she would have to wear glasses for most things, most of her life. NASA had this terrible bigotry which said that astronauts had to be able to pass pilot's vision tests. So that was out. Astronomy remained. If she couldn't go to the stars, at least she could devote her life to looking at them.

She got her B.Sc. at UCLA and her master's at Caltech in Pasadena. Her doctorate, or most of it, was also at Caltech just before she got her job, right up the hill at the Jet Propulsion Laboratories. Of course, her job had nothing to do with jets. Neither did JPL itself. What it had to do with was space. *Deep* space. The kind of space that the Mariners and Vikings and Explorers went out to touch, and smell, and listen to. The information they sent back came to Jet Propulsion Laboratories, and JPL monitored it and translated it and passed it on to the world.

Then the week Rainy was supposed to start her dissertation, one of JPL's principal scientists totaled himself on the Golden State Freeway. Her dissertation advisor sent her up the hill as soon as he got the news, to see about a part-time job as the scientist's replacement's assistant, and when she came dazedly down to say that she herself was the replacement her advisor was as astonished as she, and almost as thrilled.

But she had her own spaceship!

Its name was Newton-8, and it was a veteran of a highly successful mission. True, it was pretty well used up by now. It had done its basic program long since, flying by Jupiter and the asteroid belt and faithfully tattling what it saw. Now it was old. Parts of it were worn out, and it would never again, not in the billions of years of time before the Sun burned out, come close enough to a planet to use most of the instrumentation it still possessed.

But it would not die! It was still sending back reports. The one-millimeter radio transmitter still fed telemetry into the Deep Space Network. The meteoroid detector still picked up an impact every day or so. The helium-vector magnetometer, the flux gate magnetometer, and the imaging photopolarimeter had long since stopped recording, but where Newton-8 was there was not much for them to record.

And yet its fading vision continued to see radiation and dust clouds and it continued to report them to Earth— long after its life was supposed to be over. Its solar array still collected the dwindling, distant sunlight and transformed it into electricity to supplement the output of its aging nuclear power pack. Newton-8 was about the least of all possible spaceships to own. But it was hers, and that was what made her the luckiest person in the world—hers, at any rate, provided this joint committee of Congress allowed her to keep it.

But of course they would—she was JPL's prize exhibit, after all. Her mood improving, she picked lint off the lapel of her three-piece gray suit, squirted a dash of cologne on the white shirt under her tie and reached for the handle of the door, just as the phone rang again.

This time she didn't take a chance on missing it. She clutched it before the second ring, trying to see her watch at the same time because she was running close to critical for getting up the hill. "Oh, hell," she said, "it's only you, Tinker."

Her husband's—her *ex*-husband's!—distant voice was honeyed. "I'm sorry to bother you, love. I just wanted to know how you are."

"I'm fine," she said crossly. "I'm the same as I was yesterday afternoon when you called, and yesterday morning, and that's not what you called about. You called to tell me how important the family is and why we should get back together again and, Tink, I'm not going to do it."

Pause. Then his soft, troubled voice, trying to patch things over one more time. "I know how you feel, Rainy—"

"Hey!" She looked at her watch again. "It's four in the morning in L.A. What are you trying to do, Tinker?"

"I can't sleep," he said sadly.

"Oh, God," she said, as he began the same old thing again. The cat had got out and the car wouldn't start, and he was losing weight; and she was never more glad to hear her ride honking outside the door. "Got to run, Tink—you hear the horn blowing?" She hoped he had. But she didn't wait to find out. In the Jeep, winding up the narrow road, she wished with all her heart that Alvin Keating would find himself a new girl.

Just as they turned into the parking lot she saw an unkempt man and woman sitting up on the side of the hill, passing a suspicious-looking cigarette back and forth as they gazed over the vast radio-telescope dish and the blue-gray hills around it. Rainy glared at them. She was sure that the man was the Peeping Tom who had broken her orrery.

Yugoslavia is one of the world's most seismically active areas, because it lies where two giant tectonic plates crunch together. The continent of Africa tries to close the Mediterranean Sea like a door, with its hinge at Gibraltar. Yugoslavia is where the edge of the door slams. It shares its distinction as an earthquake center with Iceland, Japan, and nearly all the western coast of North America.

Thursday, December 3d. 9:20 AM.

Rainy slipped into the auditorium as inconspicuously as she could. The meeting did not seem to be going very well, at least not from the viewpoint of a scientist getting ready to hold out her own begging bowl; the particle physicist before her was sweating as he tried to explain why two hundred million dollars was not much to pay for a new accessory that would smash a handful of tiny bits of matter at very high speed into a handful of others. A freshman senator from one of the industrial eastern states was giving him a hard time; this same Senator Marcellico, along with two or three others, had already savaged the first presenter of the day, from Arecibo itself. The animals smell blood, Rainy thought to herself, trying to look both alertly attentive and impartial.

But they were taking a long time about it! She looked furtively at her watch. Did they understand that her next appearance had to be no later than 10:40 AM, no matter what?

The elderly blonde congresswoman from the farm belt took up the attack on the physicist. "Dr. Vorwaerts," she called from the back of the room. "I understand the Russians have an even bigger machine. Can you tell us why you want to spend all that money to build a second-best?"

The scientist nodded excitedly. "Ah, theirs is quite a different thing! It is the *kind* of particle here that is most important; ours will be at least five years in advance of anything they have!" The congresswoman sank back in her chair, satisfied, and Rainy filed that in her mind. The economy-minded legislator had not blinked an eye at two hundred million, as long as it looked like it was going to outdo the Russians.

Just as the physicist was finishing explaining why particle accelerators always seemed to be built in New York, Illinois or California—to a congressman from South Dakota— and Rainy was beginning to steal looks at her watch again, the chairman stood up. "If you don't mind," he said, "we're due for a coffee break in just a minute— and first, Miz Georgia Keating has thirty seconds for something that just won't wait."

"Thank you," she called, walking up to the command console on the side of the platform. "As you may remember, last night I sent an instruction to the Newton-8 spacecraft. It was rather a long one—eight hundred and twenty-five words. Now I am going to send the enabling command." She turned and pressed the glowing red button at the corner of the keyboard. "That's all there is to it," she said. "The message has now been transmitted to the Deep Space Network, and relayed from Canberra, Australia, out to the spacecraft. At a hundred and eighty-six thousand miles a second, it will take about an hour and fifty-two minutes to reach the spacecraft. At that point Newton-8 will deploy its instruments and cameras in the direction of the planet Jupiter—or the sun, which will be essentially the same thing at that time. A few minutes later it will observe the transit of Jupiter and relay the pictures and telemetry to us. And we will, of course, begin to receive them an hour and fifty-two minutes after that—at which time I will be here for my presentation. Are there any questions?"

Senator Marcellico called, "Just one, young lady. Are we going to see any little green men?" He was grinning, but the question left a bad taste in her mouth.

During the coffee break the senator was huddled with one of his aides, but as soon as the last morning session started again he was right there. It was Tibor Sonderman's turn, and Rainy observed that the geologist was as tactless with the legislators as he had been with her. He started out by saying that the really basic need was for fundamental research, and immediately Marcellico interrupted. "Is that going to find us any oil?" he called.

17

"Oil? No. Of course not. Our greatest need is to observe what is happening under the crust—way down, thirty or forty kilometers down—"

"Excuse me, Dr. Sonderman." It was Senator Townsend Pedigrue, from California, with his brother and chief aide whispering in his ear. "Dr. Sonderman! You're not trying to revive the Mohole program, are you?"

Sonderman said stubbornly, "I do not think you will support drilling to the Mohorovicic layer, no, but it should have been done. Down there is basic knowledge, which we need, to understand what is going on in plate tectonics. It is too bad that former President Johnson involved it in Texas politics, so that we missed that chance. But the layer is still there. However, in more immediate terms—"

It looked rather doubtful that he was going to get a chance to tell what the immediate terms were, because Marcellico was upon him again like a ferret. Rainy slipped out of the room. She wasn't fond of Tib Sonderman, but she didn't want to see his blood spilled.

She walked over to the little garden where a buffet table was being set up for lunch, hoping to get a cup of coffee out of the kitchen without the necessity of talking to any senator, congressman, aide, or newsman. She failed on two counts. The coffee wasn't made yet, and one of the TV newscasters was sitting on a stone fence, having failed in the same errand. "You're Dr. Keating, right?" he asked, beckoning her over.

"Ms. Keating—A.B.D., not Ph.D. That means 'All But Dissertation'," she explained. "The dissertation is going to be based on the results from Newton-8."

"So you have a personal interest in your spacecraft?"

A little alarm went off in her brain, and she said, "Every good scientist does, Mr.—" she peered at his name tag— "Altonburg. By the way, did you know you were missing some excitement in the meeting?" She told him about Sonderman and the hard questions that were being thrown at him. The newsman looked concerned, then relaxed.

"My cameraman's getting the whole thing," he said. "Is this your first trip to Puerto Rico, Miz Keating?"

"Afraid so. It beats the hell out of Los Angeles right now."

"Don't think the senators don't know that—it isn't any accident they scheduled this meeting for here. Last week it was life sciences and, just by luck, that happened to be in St. Thomas—so they could check on marine biology, of course. Will you tell me something, Miz Keating? What was Marcellico on you about?"

"Oh, that." She would definitely have preferred to talk about the weather, but it was a reasonable question. It deserved an answer. "It's about my master's thesis, I suppose. My subject was the impact of extra-terrestrial events on life on Earth. There weren't any little green men in it. That was just the senator being nasty. It was about things like the Tunguska event, and the Barringer crater, and the hypothesis that the mass extinctions of living species in the Cretaceous were caused by some astronomical event. I was hoping no one would bring it up." She sighed and looked around at the tropical paradise. "I was even a little sorry the conference was being held here, because Drake and Sagan and so on talk so much about communication with extra-terrestrials with this instrument."

The man said diffidently, "You know, that would make a more interesting story than budget figures—"

"Oh, no! Please!"

He changed the subject gallantly. "Are you going right back from here?"

Unfortunately, she was; all the same, she couldn't help contrasting his style with Tibor Sonderman's. Sonderman might be a hell of a fine geologist, but as far as getting along with people was concerned— "What's the matter?" she asked, startled by the expression on his face as he looked past her.

"What do you suppose *that* is?" he asked.

She turned and heard a distant, angry yelling down by the great radio-telescope dish. At this distance, the figures were tiny, but there was no doubt of what she was seeing. Halfway out the catwalk, almost to the receiver pod, a man and a woman seemed to be taking off their clothes and throwing them out into three hundred feet of empty space.

"Good heavens," she said.

The newsman glanced at her, then back at the scene in the great round valley. The strippers were not without opposition. There was not much of a security force at the Arecibo observatory, but three men in green suits like army fatigues were out on the catwalk with the struggling couple. It was unclear whether they were trying to get the rest of their clothes off, or to keep from being dragged back onto solid ground. The skinny wire catwalk shook and plunged wildly.

The newsman said, "Excuse me, I'd better get my cameraman!" And he was running down the hill, along with half a dozen others who had appeared from nowhere.

Rainy knew what she *ought* to do, but human curiosity was overpowering. You didn't see a suicide attempt every day—if that was what it was. She hurried after. It was a considerable distance to the base of the walkway, down hill and up again, and by the time she got there the couple were in custody, back on solid ground. They were standing by themselves, leaning against the huge cement holdfast that anchored the catwalk, with the biggest of the men who had gone after them ominously close. At their feet was a pack, its contents spilled on the ground—hash pipe, a couple of books, canned food, and a few other odds and ends. A few yards away, the director of the observatory and a few other men were trying to decide what to do with them.

The couple seemed serene enough, gazing contentedly at the excitement around them. The woman had been made to put a sweater over her bare upper body. She still wore her jeans, perhaps because they were too tight to get off while holding onto the gyrating rail. The man had got all the way down to swim trunks, and was still that way. He was shivering—not with cold, surely, in the muggy Puerto Rican heat. He looked up at Rainy as though she were a friend. "Tell them to let us go back and soak up the vibrations, please," he said politely.

"It isn't up to me," she said. "Why were you out there?"

"Why?" he repeated, as though it were some foreign word he could not be expected to understand. Tardily Rainy realized that both of them were stoned blind.

"Well, why anything, lady? Are they going to put us in jail?"

"I don't know that either," Rainy began, and then realized who she was talking to. It was the creep who had broken her orrery! "I wish they would," she said angrily. "Peeping in windows and smashing things up!"

"Did I break something? Hey, I'm real sorry. But I hope they don't put us in jail, because my old lady's got a job to do, and she needs the bread."

The woman giggled. "No, we don't, Dennis."

His expression clouded. Then he nodded, enlightened. "Oh, sure. What would we need it for, right? We're all about to be aced by the Great Conjunction, and what's money going to be good for then?"

Rainy looked puzzled. "The Great Conjunction?"

"When old Jupiter pulls hell and crap out of the sun and dumps it on the planets," the young man explained. "What's a few bucks going to do for you then, lady? So please, can't we go back out there and soak up some rays while we still got time?"

Because the earth is spinning, it is thicker through the equator than through the poles. It is as though the planet had a spare tire of fat around its waist. Calculations show how great the difference in diameters should be and, curiously, it is substantially greater than the facts permit. Perhaps the earth's crust "froze" at an earlier time, when it was spinning more rapidly. All that heaped-up mass around the equator represents stored energy. If, through some immense crustal movement, it relaxed to its proper dimensions, it would liberate enough heat to raise the earth's temperature by hundreds of degrees and boil away the seas.

The planet Venus, whose rotation has been slowed by the sun's tidal forces, is almost a perfect sphere. It has almost no equatorial hump. Its surface temperature is hundreds of degrees hotter than Earth's, and if it ever had liquid water it has long since been boiled away.

Thursday, December 3d. 12:15 PM.

Almost, the buffet tables revived Tib's spirits. Sliced ham, fried chicken, salad materials and—what?—yes, some sort of fried bananas, and of course large trays of fresh fruits.

Tib Sonderman was a man who appreciated food, having missed a lot of it as a child. But he couldn't take full pleasure in it. Bits of dialogue kept coming back to him—

"You mean, *Doctor* Sonderman, you want to dig this damn hole when you don't even *know* what you're gonna *find?*"

"If we knew what we were going to find, Senator Marcellico, we wouldn't have to dig the hole; that is what basic research is all about. In any case, I am not asking for funds for the Mohole at this time—"

All he wanted was funds for an expanded network of stations to report crustal movements. Who could be against that? The very survival of southern California, to name but one area, might depend on it! And even so, that other congressperson had affected to misunderstand: "You want, what is it, twenty-six million dollars a year so you can carry out your figures a couple more decimal places?"

"Mr. Congressman, that is only a drop in the bucket, compared to, say, the cost overrides on one new overkill weapons system."

Well, that had been a mistake. Gloomily, he knew it had been a mistake, but what was one to say? Gloomily, he carried his plate to the very end of the long table and tried to take pleasure in the food. As the table filled beside him, he responded politely to observations about the beauty of the view and the warmth of the day, but he was still replaying his presentation in his mind. They spoke so glibly of saving the taxpayers' money! But what were there here? Perhaps forty persons, coming from twenty states—how many thousand gallons of jet fuel so that the senators might conduct their business in a nice warm place? Assume each came in a 727. Assume a load factor of 80%. Assume an average flight of, be conservative, eight hundred miles to get here. What did a 727 get, three or four gallons to the mile? One hundred people divided into eight hundred miles, times 3.5, times the forty persons here—yes, perhaps a rough-cuff ballpark estimate, doubling for the round trip and adding in the extra energy cost of climbing to 30,000 feet or so for cruising altitude . . . not less than three thousand gallons of jet fuel. For this one meeting! Which was meant to save money, i.e., energy for everyone!

As Tib Sonderman had been taught in his first months of life to conceal emotions, no anger showed on the bland face he raised, from time to time, to glance around. But the anger was there. The average American expended thirteen kilowatts of energy, day in and day out—more than a hundred thousand kilowatt-hours a year. Sonderman made a serious effort to stay below that national average, and it angered him when he couldn't do it—because he worked in Los Angeles, and how could you not drive a car several hours each day? because he was required to fly to attend meetings like this, and how could you avoid it? Three thousand gallons of oil—enough to heat a whole block of homes through a winter, enough to—

"I beg your pardon?" he said, startled. The observatory man across from him had said something.

The man repeated, "I thought as a geologist you might be interested in this part of the world, Dr. Sonderman."

"Oh, yes?" Sonderman looked around. The bright hills stood sharply defined in the crystal air. Down below them, the great spider of the radio receiver hung from its three-stranded web over the big dish. "Eroded caves, that is what these valleys are, is that right?"

"Exactly. The mountains are honeycombed. And that is why this telescope was such a bargain. It's a great bubble in the rock with the top eroded off. All we had to do was line it with antenna wire and put in the instrumentation; the rest was a gift from God."

A couple of places down the table one of the newspersons laughed. "All you scientists are real budget-balancers, aren't you?" she asked good-humoredly. "What do you say, Senator? Have they convinced you?"

Senator Townsend Pedigrue was sitting, democratically, with the common people, his wavy brown hair blowing in the breeze, his jaw muscles senatorially tight. He relaxed them in a smile. "Now, you know I'm not hard to convince, Doris. I've surrounded myself with good, science-based people—there's my brother Tommy right over there; he's got a science degree himself, and that's probably what he'd be working at if we didn't need him so badly in Washington. Look at the record. You'll see I've sponsored twenty-two separate bills, just in this session, where we've recommended more funding, not less."

"You sure have, Senator," the woman called. "And, if I remember right, about forty recommending cuts."

"That's what I'm after, Doris, saving the taxpayer money. I'm not the big bad wolf, you know; I'm the woodsman with the axe, and I use it as gently as I can—"

Farther down the table, Sonderman saw Rainy Keating looking curiously toward him. When she saw that he was seeing her she smiled forgivingly. Tib did not smile back. What right did she have to forgive him? For what? For speaking candidly? Let her go on stimulating the testosterone flow of the young men who had clustered around her, the senator's brother and three or four others. She had not even stayed for his presentation! And that was a violation of the unwritten rule of academia; you sit through my dull paper and I'll help swell the audience for yours; otherwise everybody would be talking to empty rooms! Of course, she was not the only one, he acknowledged justly; a third of the audience had crept away to stare at the hippies who were making fools of themselves—

With surprise, he saw that one of the hippies was quietly eating from the remains of the buffet, at a little private table a few yards away. A security man stood guard over him, but he didn't seem to need much guarding.

Sonderman inconspicuously left the table for coffee, and when he returned others had spotted the bearded, slim young man. Rainy Keating was talking to him; he seemed to have come down enough to be intelligible.

"Oh, sure." He looked up at Rainy and grinned. "We didn't mean no trouble. Zee and I were just coming up to look, you know, and it was all so beautiful we just sat down to mellow out. Next thing you know we felt the need to get naked out in the middle of it."

"Is that why you broke my orrery?"

He looked at her in dismay. "Oh, shit, lady, was that thing yours? I'm really sorry about that. It was pretty." He accepted a glass of orange juice, originally intended for making screwdrivers, and swallowed it uncritically.

The geologist from the morning session watched him swallow the vitamin C and said,

"Do you think you can answer a few questions now? I'm interested. What did you hope to accomplish out over the dish?"

The young man selected a cold chicken leg, took a delicate bite, and shrugged. "We just wanted to feel the rays, man."

"What rays? There aren't any more 'rays' over the telescope than there are right here."

"That so? Well, what would I know? I was a music major. But I'm sorry I caused you trouble, Dr. Sonderman." He licked his fingers and grinned at the expression on the geologist's face. "You don't remember me. But we met at the San Onofre nuclear protest. My grandmother was there, too. I was playing lead guitar in the group right before you spoke. You were pretty good," he said, nodding. "All about tectonic faults and all that, so how come you're not doing anything now?"

"About what?" Sonderman demanded.

"Why, old Jupiter. It's all laid out in the book, man. Even my grandmother knows about it."

"I do not care about your grandmother," Tib said irritably. "What book are you talking about?"

"All the books! Cayce talked about it years ago, and now you scientists are just catching up, right? Mount Saint

Helens. Naples. All that stuff—and now the planets are getting together, and when they're all lined up just right they're going to suck some kind of rays out of the sun and into the earth's atmosphere. No, no shit, man!" he said, looking defensive under Tib's scowl. "It's all right there in that book, *The Jupiter Effect.* Then the like air gets all charged up, and it swells up and rubs against the ground—and, *pow*, there goes the old San Andreas fault. God's sake, man! You're a geologist yourself, aren't you? How come you don't know all about it?"

One of the tiniest of the asteroids—less than forty feet across—passed between Earth and the moon. No one saw it. It was too tiny, and it did not come close to the earth. Many had come closer. On August 10, 1972, one very much like it actually entered Earth's atmosphere and became an astonishingly bright meteorite. Because it passed through only the outermost, most tenuous layers of atmosphere, its speed was not slowed enough to prevent it from passing on through and out into space again. If it had approached at a very slightly different angle and struck the surface of the Earth at, say, latitude 41.53 N and longitude 87.38 W, the city of Chicago would have ceased to exist, and Lake Michigan would have had a quite circular new bay at its southern end.

Thursday, December 3d. 1:15 PM.

Senator Pedigrue's kid brother tucked Rainy's arm in his to lead her back to the meeting room, and Rainy made no protest. Young Tommy Pedigrue wasn't all that young—his hair was a good deal thinner than his brother's, and he was known to be the senator's consigliore and, occasionally, hatchet man. He could do her a lot of good. Also she was annoyed. That graceless geologist had been positively rude.

She was as much sorry for him as angry, though; the poor man simply did not know how to protect himself.

"Overkill" indeed! The Department of Defense was represented there too, and the DoD had a long memory. Some congressman somewhere, with a couple of airfields and an electronics plant fattening payrolls in his district, was going to pay off his IOUs by pulling a few feathers out of one of Sonderman's projects some day. Whatever the project was. It was too bad, but that was the way the game was played.

The other way the game was played was that you took advantage of any breaks you could get. Tommy Pedigrue's squeezes on her forearm were definite pluses. Rainy had no objection in the world to taking advantage of the fact that she interested men; it was the little extra vigorish God had given her. If she had been born male, no doubt she could have had a different kind of edge, like the kind you got from mingling with the mighty in saunas and whorehouses. God had denied her that, but given her sexual attractiveness instead. Rainy did not feel it demeaned her status as a scientist to accept Her gift. It was not her fault that Sonderman didn't use his assets—whatever they were. Good heavens, he had an easy job! All he had to fund was geology! Geology was how you found uranium ore and oil domes and all those good things that everybody not only wanted but knew they wanted. Not like astronomy!

They were at the meeting building now, and she had not really heard a word the man had said. A quick look at her watch showed that she had five minutes leeway; she excused herself by pointing to the ladies' room and escaped to freshen up and get her act together.

She left Tommy Pedigrue looking a little surprised, because he had just been telling her about the current international crisis. But the nerve endings in her crisis centers had long since been anesthetized. Not just in hers. In her whole generation's. To the young people born in the 1950s, the world had cried wolf one time too many; they no longer heard the alarums.

Rainy Keating had been born in the year when Eisenhower was re-elected and John Foster Dulles began easing troops into Vietnam. She lived through fallout-shelter drills in nursery school. She reached menarche the day of the riots at the Chicago Democratic convention. That night she saw a face she recognized on television: it was her cousin Ron, clubbed bloody in Grant Park. She was eighteen when the Palestinians shot up the Munich Olympics and twenty when, every day in the newspaper, she studied pictures of starved babies in the Sahel. The father of her best high-school friend was hijacked to Cuba, and the Iranian mobs swarmed over the U.S. Embassy while she was on her honeymoon. It had all been like that. It was too much. Ayatollahs and Nixons and Idi Amins came and went, and after a while Rainy—and her generation—simply looked away.

Or looked into the mirror, to make sure she was ready for the big event. The hair was all right. The eye makeup still fine, in spite of the muggy heat. The three-piece suit, though—no. It was a little too much, even for a pretty young female astronomer who wanted to be taken seriously. She took the necktie off, opened the top two buttons of the shirt and then, satisfied, entered the meeting room to check her equipment.

She still had a few minutes. She spent them worrying.

The messages from Newton-8 should be coming in right now. They were the most distant messages ever received on Earth; every second they grew a few thousand yards more distant still, as, far away, that half-ton chunk of metal called Newton-8 was taking its slow departure from the Sun.

It had come a long way. It had left the east coast of Florida, just over the horizon from where they were now, on a plume of thundering fire a few years earlier. It had slipped through the dust storm of the asteroid belt, taken aim at the planet Jupiter, and sailed among its brood of moons. The powerful tug of that giant planet whipped it into a new orbit that grazed Saturn; then Saturn, too, contributed some of its own immense momentum to speed the spacecraft outward. At each point it had done all of its jobs. It had returned thousands of pictures from each, taken in blue light and in red, narrow angle and broad, along with temperature readings, charged-particle counts, magnetic field intensity measurements, and scores of other data.

Then its assignment was complete.

Newton-8 had added a fraction of a percentage point to the growing store of human wisdom, at a cost about equal to one week's production of nuclear missiles. The spacecraft was through—but it didn't die. With most of its instruments powered down forever, since there would be nothing near enough for them to observe for a good many millions of years, it climbed toward the wide, empty spaces between the stars. In another decade or two it would pass the orbit of Pluto, the outer limit of the solar system.

But Newton-8 had had an unusually lucky flight. Its first course approximations were almost dead on the money; mid-course corrections were infrequent and small. It came to the end of its planned life with a substantial store of propellant still unspent. It was still receiving inputs from its radio and optical eyes, and so the engineers at JPL coaxed it tenderly, and it lived on. Its targeting systems could still find the planet Earth, and its attitude jets could still point its transmitter right on target. It continued to trickle information back to the great listening ears of the Deep Space Network, three posts on three continents that among them girdled the world. Then they became the property of a doctoral candidate named Georgia Raines Keating.

And the telemetry on her control equipment showed that they were doing it faultlessly still. Supremely confident, Rainy turned from her assistant and faced the audience.

She had a full house—every one of the senators and congressmen, most of their aides, nearly all of the newspeople. Tommy Pedigrue, sitting between his brother and fat, moonfaced young Senator Marcellico, winked at her from the front row. Rainy took a deep breath—partly for air, partly to give those top two buttons a chance to do their work—and nodded to her assistant. As Marguerite pulled back the drapes from the old model of the Newton-8 spacecraft, Rainy began.

"That's my baby. Its name is Newton-8, and it is right now—mark—" she raised her hand and leaned forward to read the counter over the keyboard—"one billion three hundred sixteen million sixty-four thousand and about two hundred miles from us—*now.*" She dropped her hand. "We have about eight minutes before it observes Jupiter transiting the sun, so I'd like to tell you a little about it. What you see is a quarter-scale model. That long thing sticking out is the magnetometer—the important one, that is still working; with that one we expect to be able to measure the sun's magnetopause, which is to say to find out just how far the sun's magnetic influence extends into space. The round thing sticking out on this side, that looks like a wok—that's the little brother to the big dish outside here, the parabolic radio transmitter. On the real spacecraft it's about eight feet across, which gives you an idea of size. The whole thing weighs about as much as a motorcycle, say five hundred pounds plus, and it is the farthest outpost of the human mind right now." She thought for a moment and added, "The Russians have nothing like it. All the data they have on transmartian space they get from us, and a lot of the best of it is what we get from Newton-8."

They were quiet, and seemed attentive. She paused for a moment, to let the people absorb the faint trills and clicks and peeps from the instruments and to see the wave forms displayed on the CRTs. "Over here at the console," she went on, "that big screen at the top is going to show us the first pictures ever of the planet Jupiter as it crosses in front of the sun. No human being has ever seen that before. We in this room will be the very first—yes, Senator Marcellico?"

The plump little man stood up good-humoredly. "What about those little green men?" he asked.

Rainy almost dropped the pointer she was holding. "I beg your pardon?"

"I'm sorry. I guess I'd better speak up," he grinned. "The thing is, all this morning we were listening to Dr. Sonderman over there telling us how lucky we were we didn't have Mount Saint Helens blowing up in our laps every other day, and then those young people came and entertained us with some other stuff about how the world was coming to an end, and, well, I just wondered if you were going to cheer us up some more."

There were a few smiles in the audience, but more scowls—unfortunately the scowls all came from scientists. Rainy managed a smile of her own. "Not at all, Senator," she declared. "Newton-8 is purely a science experiment. We are simply now in a position to see the planet Jupiter—"

"Yes, I know about Jupiter," he said courteously. "But aren't you the young lady who said that little men from space were coming to call on us any minute?"

"Certainly not, Senator! I—"

He persisted, "But I have right here—" he fished a paper out of his briefcase—"a copy of a document that p'ports to be your thesis for your master's degree." He put on his spectacles and studied it. "Uh-huh, your name's right on it—of course, it was just 'Georgia Raines' then, but that's you, isn't it? Let's see, here. The title says, *A Numerical Estimate of Intervention Events from Extra-Terrestrial Sources*. Seems to have a whole lot of troublesome things in it, Miz Keating," he added, flipping slowly through the pages.

Rainy laughed shakily. "Oh, that," she said. "Yes, that's mine, Senator. Of course, I had to write something to get my degree, and I was more or less limited by what my degree advisor would accept. But there certainly aren't any little green men in it. The paper is an attempt to quantify the probabilities of some event outside the earth that will affect humanity deeply. There have been many such in the past, as I'm sure you're aware. For example, there was the Lower Cretaceous episode, when apparently almost all higher life forms on Earth became extinct at once and—"

"Lower what was that, Miz Keating?"

"Lower Cretaceous, Senator. That's a geological term. It refers to a time about sixty-five million years ago, when apparently some great disaster—"

"Miz Keating," the senator said good-humoredly, "it's that word 'apparently' that does me in every time, not to mention that other word 'sixty-five million years ago'. You ever hear of the Golden Fleece award, Miz Keating?"

She saw Tommy Pedigrue nudge his brother, who took pity on her. "Bert," he said, reaching over to touch the other senator's shoulder, "that's all very interesting, but as I understand it there's a very important event coming up in just a few minutes—"

"That's all right, Towny," said Marcellico, chuckling, and sank back into his seat. "I don't want to miss that. Please accept my apologies and go on, Miz Keating. I was only trying to clarify something in my own mind."

Rainy glanced at her watch, biting her lip to regain control. She smiled politely. "Just above the monitor," she said, "you'll see a drawing of the position of the sun, Jupiter, and Newton-8 as they are right now. It's not to scale, of course. As you can see, our spacecraft is rapidly approaching its rendezvous point, the position from which it will observe the planet cross the disk of the sun. Please give us the pictures as they are received now, Marguerite." The technician nodded. The screen went to black, with a very bright spot the only thing visible in the center of it. Rainy went into her pitch.

"What I'd specially like to emphasize," she said, smiling warmly at Senator Marcellico, "is that this is like being given a whole new spacecraft free. Newton-8 finished paying for itself when it exited the Saturn system. Every bit we get now is pure profit—Senator?"

Townsend Pedigrue was leaning forward for attention. His expression was amiable enough as he said, "Please feel free to interrupt me whenever you need to for this demonstration. Like Senator Marcellico, I always worry when I hear certain words, and one of them is that word 'free', Miz Keating. Isn't it so that we still have to pay for the radio receivers, and all this fascinating looking hardware, not to mention a salary for your own good self?"

Rainy maintained her smile. "That's right, Senator, the ground support still has to be maintained. But the spacecraft itself is worth three hundred million dollars. That's paid off. We're getting information from a volume of space never before explored, and it's on the house. Let me show you some of it."

She nodded to Marguerite, who turned up the audio gain. A soothing hiss came from the loudspeakers. Rainy listened for a moment and said, "That's the sound of neutral hydrogen. Newton-8 is programmed to scan a whole band of frequencies, something like those radios that zip through the police and fire frequencies and only stop when there's an actual transmission. Newton listens to each signal until it can match it against its data store. If it is something already on record, like this neutral hydrogen emission, it will drop it and go looking for something else. Give it a second—"

On track, the sound changed.

"There it goes," she said, satisfied. "Let's see what it finds next."

There was a staccato *teep-teep-teep* from the audio speakers, the hunting cry of the frequency scanner as it sought a new source. Then it locked and delivered a warbling hiss which Rainy quickly identified as the song of the hydroxyl radical; then another, then another. Rainy watched the audience carefully. She had made her main points already, and it was only necessary to let them sink in. Maybe to reinforce them from time to time? She focused her attention on the row of other committee aides and said, "I think you'll be interested in the way Newton-8 deals with emergencies. For instance, we had a failure in the radioisotope thermoelectric generator, so we're limited to solar power. At Newton's distance from the sun, there isn't much of that. But we managed to command an extension of the solar electric panels—the things that look like wings on the model. We get about twenty-two watts, which is enough to run the important instruments full-time and the rest when they are needed."

"That doesn't sound like enough for a radio broadcast from, what did you say? Two and a half billion miles away?" It was one of the women whom Rainy had not met, an aide to the minority leader of the committee. At the last moment Rainy came up with the name.

"We don't need much, Miz Landro," she said. "The data transmission only takes eight watts of radiated power on the one-millimeter wavelength. At that rate, we expect to continue data acquisition and tracking capability for an indefinite period—maybe another twenty years."

Eve Landro said frostily, "Does that mean you want to

spend the next twenty years on the public payroll?"

It had been a mistake to open those top two buttons after all, Rainy realized. "Well," she said warmly, "there's the information, Ms. Landro. We can take it, or we can let it go to waste— What is it, Marguerite?"

The radio technician was signaling distress, and Rainy could hear why. There was a new sound coming from the speakers. Rainy frowned, trying to identify it. It was at the threshold of hearing, and quite unlike anything her spaceship had ever produced for her before. "Turn up the gain, Marguerite!" she ordered. But even at maximum amplification there was more background noise than signal.

Once Rainy had heard a Moog synthesizer concert in which the human voice had been superimposed on the frequencies of a rock band. What she heard now reminded her of that—though what she heard could not be human language, or even any language at all, considering where it came from. It was as though an animal's cry had been blended with the whines and rumbles of a machine on the verge of breaking down. "Check the telemetry!" she cried to Marguerite; and then, collecting herself for the sake of her audience, "Either we're getting a new kind of signal that's right outside of my experience . . . or there's a malfunction of some sort."

Eve Landro looked almost pleased. "Twenty years went very quickly, Miss Keating," she observed.

No one laughed. Rainy said honestly, "I have to think you're right. Something has gone wrong. But that's happened before, and the chances are we can clear it up."

"Rainy?" It was Marguerite, from behind her; but Rainy went on.

"The difficulty is distance. Newton is nearly two light-hours away. That means what just happened happened two hours ago, and any commands we transmit won't get to it until two hours from now—and we won't know the response until two hours after that. Then—"

"Rainy."

Marguerite could no longer be ignored. Her face showed dismal news. "We're getting very strong inputs in the solar electrical generating systems, Rainy. Close to maximum tolerance, and still climbing."

"Solar energy? That can't be, Marguerite! If there were a solar flare or anything we would have known!"

Wordlessly, Marguerite pointed to the oscilloscope trace above the instruments. It was surging higher, so high that the top of each new wave was off scale entirely.

Everybody's face was turned toward her. Rainy caught at the buttons on her shirt, twisting them while she tried to think. The Newton-8 electrical system had automatic surge controls, to limit damaging inputs—but they had been programmed out of circuit more than two years earlier to save power. But there was no need for them! There was absolutely nothing anywhere near the spacecraft that could provide damaging radiation! And yet—

The gabble of noise, fading in and out of the background static, was getting on her nerves; but when it stopped it was worse.

The signal cut off as though a switch had been thrown. Rainy waited, afraid to ask, while Marguerite checked the parallel control circuits; and then she looked up and shook her head.

"Telemetry's gone too, Rainy. Nothing's coming in to the DSN. The system's crashed."

Rainy stared emptily at her audience. After a moment Tommy Pedigrue cleared his throat. "Would you say the free ride is now over, Miz Keating?"

"Not necessarily," she said quickly, out of instinct. "We'll certainly try to re-establish contact. We've had temporary interruptions before and cleared them up—"

But not like this. Whatever she told the senatorial committee, inside herself Rainy had no doubt. Her spacecraft was dead.

LOS ANGELES

In California, half a dozen earthquake engineers were playing a board game. The board was a motorized table twenty feet square, with a model of an office building in the middle of it. The table team were trying to shake the building down. The building team, by tightening and slackening steel cables inside the model, were trying to save it. So far the building team had won three times in a row, all the way up to a scale equivalent of a 7.0 Richter shock. But the table team had timed the building's sway. On the next trial they reduced the shock to Richter 5.5, but slowed the shaking to match the toy building's natural frequency.

They won that game. The structure collapsed in upon itself. It wasn't a surprise. Sooner or later, the destruction team had won every other game, too.

Friday, December 4th. 8:20 PM.

The plane was two hours late out of O'Hare, because there had been a bomb scare. No one believed the bomb was real, but no one would take the chance, either. So they all marched out of the plane into one of the already overcrowded passenger lounges, their belongings on their backs and in their hands. Then they all marched into another plane, but as it was a DC-10 instead of an L-1011 the seat configuration was all different, and Tib lost his place by the window. That was taken by a black man with a face like Eldridge Cleaver, with a little black girl on his lap. On the aisle was an elderly woman who began calling for Bloody Marys before the plane had reached the runway. As soon as they took off Tib, despairing of getting back to his straingauge reports, pushed his seat back and closed his eyes.

"Are you sleeping?" the little girl said. Tib opened one eye enough to glare at her as she added, "Because that man wants to talk to you." Her father glared at Tib and began whispering in the little girl's ear, and from the aisle, holding on to the seat back, Tommy Pedigrue said, "Dr. Sonderman? Thought I saw you aboard. Have you read this?"

He was holding out a paperback book. Tib reached carefully over the woman's tray of two glasses of tomato juice, two tiny bottles of vodka, and a bag of peanuts to take it from him. It was called *The Jupiter Effect*. "Ah, yes," he said. "That crazy hippie."

"Well, I don't know if it's all crazy," Tommy Pedigrue said uncertainly. "I was sort of hoping you could tell me. I picked it up at the airport, but it's kind of out of my line—I had a double major, biology and pre-law. Want to give it a quick look?"

Tib turned a few pages, glanced at the introduction, shrugged. "Yes, why not?"

Pedigrue nodded, started to turn away and checked himself. "Uh, there's a seat open next to me in first class," he said. "My brother decided to stay over in Chicago. So if you'd like to—?"

Tib frowned. "Surely there is a regulation against that?"

Tommy Pedigrue grinned. "Not if you're a senator's brother," he said.

"Well—thank you. But no." Certainly not! It was bad enough he should have to read what this man gave him. It would be far worse to have to talk to him for two thousand miles. "But perhaps this little girl would be more comfortable—" he suggested, dead-pan.

Her father, who had not appeared to be listening, jerked around and said, "No way!" Pedigrue retreated, his face scarlet, and Tib Sonderman, feeling more cheerful, opened the book.

He read it straight through, all across the continent, and then he closed it and sat back.

It was not hogwash. Forget about Edgar Cayce, forget about that stoned young man. This was not astrology, it was science.

Wrong-headed science? Maybe. That didn't mean much.

A lot of theoretical science was false. That was what science was all about: forming theories, many of which were bound to be wrong, and then attacking them as hard as possible. A theory was no good unless it was falsifiable. If it could not be subjected to an experiment that could show it to be wrong, then it was merely a speculation, not a theory.

The book, to be sure, was *speculative* science. Much of what it suggested rested on presumptions and inferences. There was much in it that was unproved. But nothing that struck him as wrong.

The argument came in a number of steps. The first was that the sun and all of its planets, and every atom of each one of them, were a single system, and that each part affected every other.

In strict theoretical terms, there was no argument there. In strict theoretical terms you could go a lot farther. Every atom in the universe was tied to every other, by a sea of photons and a network of gravitational force. The practical fact that the ties between a hydrogen atom in the center of the star Betelgeuse and one in the melting ice cube in the plastic cup before him were terribly tiny in comparison with those that linked nearer particles did not make the statement untrue.

According to the book's authors—their names were not wholly unfamiliar to Sonderman; Gribbin he had heard of, of Plagemann he was less sure—in the spring of 1982 a somewhat unusual event would take place in the solar system. All of the major planets would be on the same side of the sun. Not for long. Just for six or seven weeks, but for that little while the solar system would be asymmetrical, as happened from time to time but not very often—once every 179 years, the authors said, and Sonderman could see no reason to doubt them.

The next step in their paper chase of logical sequences was less certain. According to them, there was some sort of connection between the position of the planets and the activity of that boiling, burning hurricane of hot gases that was the sun. They conceded the effect was not large, and that it wasn't very obvious, and that there was not any good theoretical basis for understanding why it should be there at all. But they claimed it existed. Sonderman was willing to suspend disbelief—at least until he checked it out.

The third step in the chain was much firmer. There was a definite cause-and-effect relationship between solar activity and the Earth's weather. That Tib accepted; it was close enough to his own specialization that, as a matter of course, he had more or less kept up. He knew that changes in activity on the sun were followed by changes that could be measured on the earth—in the aurora, and even in the intensity and distribution of highs and lows. Among these weather effects, the book said, was an increase in ionization and heating of the air, which appeared to have the result of causing the ocean of air to expand a tiny bit.

He frowned. That seemed reasonable enough, although he had never thought of it in those terms. But yes. That was why Skylab had come crashing down early, because of atmospheric expansion and—

"Is that a good book?" the little girl asked him.

He saw with dismay that she was leaning over, staring at the pages. Tib was fairly sure she couldn't read, because her father had been dutifully reading to her the words on the cover of the airline magazine and the descriptions of ditching procedures from the safety instruction card. But now the man was asleep and the girl was bored.

"Yes, thank you," he said heavily.

"I didn't think it was," she said, "b'cause you were making such faces."

He smiled. As detached and discouraging a smile as he could manufacture. "It's a very good book," he said, "and I really want to go on reading it."

"Do you want to read it out loud?"

"I don't think so," he said. She nodded without surprise, peering at the cover.

" 'Trig-gers of dev- dev- devastating? earth- earthcakes?' "

"Earthquakes," he said. " 'Triggers of devastating earthquakes.' " She was older than she looked, he saw, and much, much smarter.

Sonderman was saved from continuing the conversation, as the father woke up enough to sit up, nod neutrally at

Sonderman, pick up the little girl, and turn her toward the window before he fell asleep again.

Sonderman returned to the book. The next step: The earth's rotation is not perfectly smooth. Every now and then it slows down or speeds up unexpectedly—the changes are called "glitches"—not much, to be sure. (Sonderman nodded.) And there was some reason to suspect that changes in the atmosphere caused the glitches. (He scowled at that. What reason?) The basis behind the suspicion lay in the conservation of angular momentum—in, in lay terms, the same effect that made an ice skater whirl more slowly when she extended her arms. (Sonderman made another mental note to check further.)

Next to the last step: Plate tectonics.

Sonderman frowned thoughtfully. These people seemed to have quite a reasonable layman's understanding of the basis for crustal geology. The theory of plate tectonics was not yet twenty years of age, at least in any form except an amusing speculation. Not everyone understood it. For him, of course, it was the core of his specialty. But Plagemann and Gribbin, he saw by skimming, were pointing out that the surface of the Earth was made up of "plates"—hardened rock "skin"—which float on the molten rock inside the globe. The plates move. They rub up against each other, like floating slabs of ice on a freezing stream. And where two plates rub together there is a break, called a "fault line" . . . and all of that, Sonderman saw, was as close as anyone needed to get to the basics of the theory. But the part that came next—

"My name is Afeefah."

Sonderman jerked his head to the right. "What?" The girl was looking at him again, and, studying her narrow face under the tight corn-rowed scalp, Tib was sure she was not two years old or less, as she was meant to be to ride free on a parent's lap.

She said quite clearly, "Afeefah means 'chaste'." Did children talk that well at two? Not bloody likely.

"I need to read my book, Afeefah," he said. It did not turn her gaze away. He thought of the snack untouched before him and broke open the cardboard box. "Do you like cookies?" he asked.

She neither answered nor took them from him. He sat there, half turned toward her, the plastic package of Oreos extended.

"Don't do that," her father said without changing position. His eyes were half open, looking at Sonderman.

"I was just—"

"Don't do it." This time he didn't move the girl on his knee, he just continued to watch Sonderman, face impassive, eyes still not wholly open.

Tib shrugged, dropped the cookies back in the box and turned again to his book. The next part he did not need to read at all, since it was all his own domain and he knew it better than the authors. California's great fault line was the San Andreas. The huge North American plate, the one they had been flying over for two hours without covering half its breadth, was trying to move one way. The even huger Pacific plate was trying to move a slightly different way. The edges rubbed together. Friction made them stick for a while—perhaps for fifty years at a time, or a hundred. Then they would slip. And that slip was, for instance, the great San Francisco earthquake of the 18th of April in 1906. The rubbing movement was very slow, but it was very strong and it never stopped. And between slips the shearing force was building up all the time. When it got big enough, even some quite small force could trigger it and release all that energy. And then you had your earthquake.

And all that was very true, but what Plagemann and Gribbin added was that the Jupiter Effect—the unbalance in the solar system, tugging at the core of the sun, increasing its activity, warming up the earth's atmosphere, slowing it down by a microsecond—would be the small force that could trigger it. They didn't mince words or pull back from the conclusion of their train of logic. They said it loud and clear: "A remarkable chain of evidence . . . points to 1982 as the year in which the Los Angeles region of the San Andreas fault will be subjected to the most massive earthquake known in the populated regions of

44

the earth in this century. . . . in 1982 'when the Moon is in the Seventh House and Jupiter aligns with Mars' and with the other seven planets of the Solar System, Los Angeles will be destroyed."

Sonderman slipped the paperback book into his pocket and leaned back.

Was there any truth to all of this?

There was some. He had to agree there was some. The San Andreas fault was surely an earthquake waiting to happen. One of the sources of energy that drove the slowly boiling mass of anger that was always inside Tib Sonderman, waiting to erupt, was that not one in ten thousand of his fellow human beings seemed willing to look that fact in the face. Gribbin and Plagemann had at least done that much.

But what about the rest of it?

As far as his own knowledge was concerned, he could only grant that their statements *might* be true. The position of the planets *might* affect the core of the sun. The enhanced radiation *might* cause changes in the volume of the earth's atmosphere. The extra moment of inertia *might* trigger crustal events.

But they were all mights; did three mights make a right? At this point Tib reached for his pocket calculator. He set minus 179 as a constant, since the authors had said that this position of the planets recurred every 179 years, and punched in the date 1982. As fast as he could copy them down he had a series of dates: 1803, 1624, 1445, 1266 . . . at that point he stopped, because the records were not likely to be very complete that far back. If they were even in 1624. As soon as he got back to his computer he would start a search to find out if those dates were associated with abnormal earthquake years. If they were, the theory deserved investigation. If they were not—well, that was just one more example of the sort of thing Tib hated most.

"Can I play with that?" Afeefah's father was dozing again, and the little girl was gazing covetously at the TI-55.

"I don't think your father would like it, dear," Tib said,

putting the instrument back in his pocket. The man opened his eyes.

"You *know*?" he drawled. "You *right*." He sat up straight and turned Afeefah around in his lap again, facing away from Tib. Tib glowered and stared down at his notes, but the subdued giggling from Afeefah made him steal a look. Her father was searching through her corn-row hair, nipping at invisible things with his fingernails, inspecting them and dropping them on the floor. Sonderman was shocked and repelled. Then he saw the strain of a suppressed grin in the man's cheeks and realized that that was what was intended.

What a surly brute! He closed his eyes and allowed himself to feel the anger that was always inside. Such mean-hearted people there were in the world, and such stupid ones! This man was a symptom, just as the stoned young hippies at Arecibo were symptoms, of what he disliked most in the world he lived in. He could not define it exactly, but it included violence and carelessness and stupidity and ugly behavior in public places. He responded to it as he had practiced to do; he closed his eyes and pretended to sleep.

His expression was placid enough, but that was an artifact. Tib Sonderman was rarely placid. He would have spent half his life gnashing his teeth if he had allowed the internal rages to reach the surface. He had given up anger. Or thought he had; he rarely allowed his internal fury to erupt into flame. He had learned that lesson very young. When Tibor Sonderman was a newborn in the "resettlement" camp in Hungary, the thing his mother feared most was that her baby would cry. As the wife of a known partisan, fighting the Germans somewhere out in the gorges, her life balanced very precariously in the camp. If the baby cried the guards might hear. And be annoyed. And move them one step closer to the gas ovens. She had taught him self-control, and he had never forgotten.

Near a spot on the surface of the sun a surge of great heat released a burst of X rays. The source itself was tiny—it was no larger than Australia—but its fierce explosion was

only the start of a huger event. An immense plume of hot
gas sprang up from the sun's surface, tunneled through
the diffuse bright gases that surrounded it, and flew out
into space. On Earth, astronomers recorded a minor solar
flare.

Friday, December 4th. 8:22 PM. PST

Saunders Robinson, later Khalid Mustafa Muhammad, later
still (and at present) Saunders Robinson again, carried his
daughter off the plane and put her down on a bench near
the phone booths. "You go to sleep a minute, Feef," he
ordered. Obediently she squeezed her eyes shut, the corners wrinkled with the effort. "No foolin', now! And don't
talk to nobody."

"Specially if he's white," she nodded, the eyes still tightly
closed.

"No matter who he is! Yeah, specially if he's white,
though." He tucked her sweater under her head and raced
to the phone in time to beat an elderly black woman into
it. He grinned at her in a brotherly way as he dumped a
handful of change onto the counter and began the job of
finding him and his daughter a place to stay. He dialed a
number and smiled widely into the telephone. "Jesty!
What's happening? What do you mean, who's this? It's
Rob!" The smile faded as he talked. "Yeah, later, man," he
finished, pushed down the phone hook and tried again. In
the first five phone calls the best he did was the suggestion that he go to the mosque for help. But he didn't want
to do that. He owed something to Al-Islam. When he got
out of CMR-East he found they'd taken care of Afeefah for
him—not Afeefah's mother; she'd sloped off somewhere.
But owing them something and getting tight with them
again were two different things; he couldn't hang in there
with Allah. It took twelve phone calls, and almost all the
change he'd saved up, before he got an offer. Some kind of
ashram, way down off Wilshire. No money. But he could
crash there, and maybe get something to eat. The good
thing about it was that the airport limos went to the big

hotels across the freeway, and then it would be only about a ten-minute walk. He picked up the five dimes remaining of his change, investigated the coin return for mistakes, and went over to wake Afeefah up. He almost bumped into a very young-looking man with a fretful expression, heading for the men's room. Robinson recognized him without being sure where he recognized him from, and then put it together. It was the honk from the first-class section, the one with his hand over his nose to keep out nigger smell. Most of the passengers were gone now, and Robinson thought for a moment of following Mr. First Class into the toilet to see what he might have in his pockets.

But he'd given all that up. "Come on, Feef," he said. "We got to go on home now."

The Santa Ana had been blowing for two days. Down in the canyons the chaparral was dry as matchwood. When it caught a spark or a cigarette butt it burned, and kept on burning.

Friday, December 4th. 8:25 PM.

First class wasn't really first class as long as you had to fight everybody else for the exits. Tommy Pedigrue had learned how to deal with that. You sit back and chat up the stewardesses while you wait for the traffic jam to end, because you don't have to worry about getting out fast since your driver will be right there waiting for you.

The other thing wrong with first class these days, however, was that all those affirmative-action and sexual-discrimination lawsuits had resulted in putting the most senior stews in the most attractive jobs, instead of putting the most attractive stews in with the most senior passengers. There was only one who was really worth hitting on, and she claimed to be happily married. That was okay, though. Tommy Pedigrue expected to bomb out now and then. When you counted up for the year, his batting average worked out pretty high, though not as high as his brother's.

What wasn't okay was that his driver wasn't waiting for him. Worse. He needed to pee. He didn't like to pee in public washrooms. He wished he had thought to go in the airplane, but who knew the driver wouldn't be there? Now if he ducked into the toilet it was just as likely as not that the driver would come running in, not find him, and tear-ass off in some other direction and they'd never get together.

Tommy fumed, standing indecisively in the middle of the lounge. He couldn't try calling the car; the phone booths were all filled. Probably he would have to take a taxi all the way out to Hidden Hills. Probably he would have to find his own baggage, and schlep it out to the curb. Probably—probably the driver would hear about this, he thought grimly, marching toward the john.

His first thought was that the men's room was empty, which was a whole grateful surprise. Then he saw he was wrong. A young boy, thirteen or fourteen at the most, was standing in front of the full-length mirror by the door. He was sloppy-looking, sullen-faced, not, evidently, recently cared for by a mother; and what he was doing gave Tommy Pedigrue a brisk electric shock. The boy's fly was unzipped, and his penis was in his hand. He was not looking in the mirror. He was looking at Tommy Pedigrue, with an unwinking, uncommunicating stare.

Damn the little pervert! Pedigrue stalked past him, to the very end of the long row of urinals. He turned his body as much away as he could.

What a downer this whole trip had turned out to be! Those spacey kids at Arecibo, the delayed flight, the middle-aged stewardesses, the missing chauffeur. Now this! It was a considerable nuisance. Sometimes Tommy couldn't get going when people were looking at him. He could almost feel the boy's on him clear across the empty room—

It was worse than that.

The boy moved up to the urinal right next to him, his face absolutely blank, looking straight at the wall, slowly stroking his penis.

For a moment Tommy Pedigrue felt as though he were exploding with rage. Then he felt as though he wanted to cry. Why me? he asked the universe. The caution signal in the back of his brain was flashing furiously. What was the use of being careful with everybody you met, limiting yourself to two or three drinks on the plane, watching your mouth when you talked to the stews, if you then walked into something that, if it went the wrong way, might mean the worst kind of scandal? What if someone walked in right then—someone who recognized him—and saw the two of them there, like that?

Although Neptune is an immense planet, seventeen times the mass of the earth, it is so far away that it is invisible to the naked eye. It is a curious and poignant fact in the history of astronomy that—with all the vast sphere of the heavens for it to hide in—the first human being who could possibly have seen it, the inventor of the telescope, Galileo, was in fact the first person who did, in the year 1612. He did not know what he had seen. The notion of planets even farther from the sun than Saturn had not yet occurred to anyone, even him. He took it for an ordinary, if somewhat perplexing, star.

Friday, December 4th. 8:38 PM.

It was nearly nine o'clock, but Wes Grierson was a late person. Tib Sonderman checked his watch and saw that, because of the plane's lateness, he had nearly half an hour before he could get a bus to Studio City; it was worth trying to reach the information-retrieval man.

Grierson answered the phone himself. "Wesley? This is Tib Sonderman. I'm sorry to bother you so late, but I want you to dig up some papers for me. Are you taping this?"

"Of course I am, Tib." His voice was almost offended.

"I want everything in the last five years that references a book called *The Jupiter Effect*, by two people—I'm not sure of their names—"

"Gribbin and Plagemann. That's easy if you've been reading the papers. What else?"

"That's it for now. Send the list through to my home, you've got the number?"

"Of course I do, Tib." Grierson's specialty was information retrieval; it was almost insulting to ask him if he had a computer terminal number, or a Social Security number, or the number of the hotel you stayed in in Philadelphia last time you were there, eighteen months ago; that was his *business*. "I didn't know you were into astrology, Tib."

Sonderman scowled at the telephone. "What are you talking about? I read the book. It's got nothing to do—"

"Not the book. The people who're taking it up." Grierson chuckled. "I guess you're not one of them, but you had me worried for a minute."

"It's just something I need to know about."

"Sure, Tib. At this time of night. I'll get the stuff out to you. . . . Oh, Tib?"

Sonderman stopped, just about to hang up. "What?"

"Did you know Gribbin had recanted?"

"No!"

"I'll send that along too," Grierson promised, and broke the connection, laughing.

Sonderman grinned too, after a moment. So he had wasted a couple of hours on somebody's pipe dream. Well, he had wasted more on less. Now he could face the long drive home with one fewer thing on his mind. Which reminded him; he backtracked a few steps and pushed open the door to the men's room.

For a moment he felt a sting of shame, as though he had accidentally pushed open a bedroom door in someone else's house. Although the man at the far end had his back turned, Sonderman recognized him easily. Townsend Pedigrue? No, the kid brother, Thompson. And his back was eloquent. The ragamuffin next to him was easier to recognize. Maybe not by name, but for what he was.

It was evident that Pedigrue was not molesting a minor, as Sonderman had thought at once. He was still good-humored from his talk with Wes Grierson, so he said easily, "Son, if you're still in here one minute from now I'm calling the Juvenile Division."

The boy turned unhurriedly and looked Sonderman up

and down. Then he shrugged and walked to the door, rearranging his clothes only as he left. He paused as the door was closing to say, "Fuck you."

Tommy Pedigrue's face was scarlet as he turned away from the urinals to wash his hands. He waited until Sonderman had joined him at the air-dryer to say, "Jesus! What was that all about?"

"That's just one of our famous Los Angeles chickens, Mr. Pedigrue. He was just showing you the merchandise."

"Disgusting," Pedigrue said with indignation. Away from the presence of his brother and the stimulus of an audience, he was a much quieter, less confident person. He stayed close to Sonderman as they walked along the people mover toward the main terminal, as though he expected the young boy to solicit him again. But they were almost alone on the moving belt. Overhead the ceiling speakers murmured reminders: "—and stand to the right. If you wish to pass, please do so on the left. . . . Please hold handrail—"

"I forgot to say thanks," Pedigrue said suddenly, as they came to the end.

"You're welcome." Getting on the good side of somebody like Tommy Pedigrue was as important, in its way, as setting strain gauges across Palmdale. Sonderman was unskilled in this operation, but knew that the best way to press an advantage was to leave it alone and let it ripen. "I guess we'll be running into each other now and then, Mr. Pedigrue," he said.

Pedigrue grinned. "Next time we have a funding hearing, you mean. Tell you what. We'll have a drink somewhere, before that, and you can give me the off-the-record stuff, what's important, what we can get along without—Oh, there you are!"

He broke off to scowl at a middle-aged black man in a chauffeur's uniform, standing worriedly just outside the anti-hijack checkpoint.

"I'm real sorry, Mr. Pedigrue," the chauffeur began at once, "but they wouldn't let me in because of, you know—" he touched the bulge under his armpit—"and I tried to have you paged, but—"

Sonderman nodded politely, and moved on. He stood on the sidewalk just outside the door, and he could hear, over the new set of speakers that were telling him that the white zone was for the loading and unloading of passengers only, Tommy Pedigrue's voice raised in anger. He was glad when his bus came. It was just as well to be somewhere else when your potential benefactor was losing his temper. It didn't much matter at whom the rage was directed. It took only a small splash-over to cost you an inflation increase, or even a whole project.

Sonderman's house in Studio City was tiny, and it clung to a hillside. Directly behind it was a sheer face covered with chaparral. If it rained, the mud might slide into his back yard; if it was dry, the vegetation would die and it was likely to burn. And then it would slide into his back yard. Living there was a constant challenge.

Since he had slept on the plane, he was not ready for bed when he got home. He left the door open and slid two windows up to air it out, and then went at once to his basement, past the bumper-pool table and the stationary bicycle, and opened the door to his workshop.

The workshop did not look like a workshop. For that matter, the door didn't look like a door. It looked like a bookshelf, and was, except that the rows of books just next to the wet bar were not books. Sonderman reached up to the top shelf and hooked a finger to the top of the binding of the fattest of the fakes. It gave under the pressure of his fingers, unlatching the door, and he pulled the whole thing open.

The hidden entrance wasn't Sonderman's idea, but it had appealed to him. He was away nearly half the time, and there was no one to watch the house when he was gone. Although there was not a great deal of crime in Studio City, there were neighbors who had come home to find their TV sets and stereos gone. Sonderman didn't worry about that. There was always insurance. But insurance did not cover his papers, his instruments, his little computer; so, when the woman he was dating for a while, an interior decorator, had offered to put the secret door in, he was delighted. The woman was long gone, like all the others he had gone with after the divorce. But the door remained.

The room behind it, as always, looked like a mess. The every-Thursday cleaning service never entered this room. They didn't even know it existed. Every flat surface was covered with books and papers, and folded lengths of computer printouts were on the floor next to his desk and behind his chair, convenient to reach when he wanted them. His small seismograph was slowly turning its paper roll beside one wall; his file cabinets stood against another, half the drawers partly open and papers protruding from cocked folders. Sonderman sat down before his terminal, picked up the dedicated phone, dialed a number, heard the computer squeal that said he had a connection, and placed the handset in its acoustic coupler. A green light went on next to the keyboard, and he typed:

LOGON
330105056
ARCHIMANDRITE

Having given the machine the information that he was ready to receive mail, his numerical address, and the code word that said he was really himself, he got up and began to unpack his briefcase.

At this time of night there was seldom much competition for the shared-time services of the net. The terminal began to deliver his messages at once. Sonderman let them accumulate on the cathode screen until it was full, then decided to get them all at once and punched out a set of instructions. The machine responded immediately by printing out hard copy on a long roll of paper.

Sonderman thumbed through his mail. His pay check. A handful of bills. A postcard from his ex-wife—this time she was in Nogales, Mexico, doing heaven knew what and with heaven knew whom. A set of admission badges and speakers' instructions for the forthcoming American Scientific Federation meeting. (Did that mean his paper had been accepted? Or was it just that one hand of any bureaucracy never knows what the other is doing?) Four journals, six offprints of papers, and, of course, the usual dozen or two advertising pieces.

He sorted it out while he waited for the printer to finish his electronic mail. The junk mail he simply tipped into the brown-paper supermarket bag he used for a wastebasket, except for one that bore the return address of Danny Deere, Ltd., a real-estate agency. The little house that he had paid thirty-eight thousand dollars for nine years before had been going up in value ever since, and one of the amusements of Tib Sonderman's life was to look at the blind offers from realtors that came every week or so—fifty thousand, sixty thousand, eighty-five thousand; the last one he had seen had offered a hundred and fifteen thousand dollars. Almost, he had been tempted to sell, but in this mad Los Angeles real-estate market what could he buy? But there was a limit to resisting temptation.

As he started to open the envelope the printer announced it was finished, and Sonderman ran through the paper printout.

The thing that had taken the most time was a lengthy report from the U.S. Geological Survey on earth movements along some of the northern branches of the San Andreas; nothing important, but he clipped it and carefully folded it for the pile behind his chair. There was not much else except for chatter—people on the teletype net calling him for transient errands, none of them seeming important—until he came to the last item. Wes Grierson must have got right to it, and his computers must have been hunting all the time Tib was en route from Los Angeles International. There was a list of twenty-six citations for *The Jupiter Effect*. Sonderman clipped the paper roll and was about to throw it in the wastebasket; he had lost interest in the subject when Grierson told him the principal author had changed his mind. Then he caught sight of a postscript from Grierson:

DID YOU EVER FIGURE OUT WHAT WENT WRONG WITH YOUR GIRL FRIEND'S SPACESHIP? SEE SCIENCE V 84 P 506.

Sonderman hesitated. He probably had that issue somewhere in the house—volume 84 was probably only three or four years ago, and he kept nearly all of them. But Rainy Whatever-her-name-was was certainly not his girl friend, and he had relatively little interest in what had gone wrong with her ship. Sonderman dropped the whole wad into the waste bag and stood over it, with the ad from the real-estate company, ready to do the same with that as soon as he had satisfied his curiosity about the offer.

It wasn't an offer, however. It was a little note, and all it said was,

Dear Mr. Sonderman:

Because of the softening of the home market due to apprehension over the possibility of a major earthquake within the next few months, we regret that we must withdraw the offer we made recently for your property.

Very sincerely yours,
DANNY DEERE LTD.

How very strange! Didn't these people know that the whole thing was some sort of mistake? Was it possible they were still taking it seriously? Sonderman shook his head, and tossed the realtor's letter after the citation list.

Then, thoughtfully, he bent down and took them both out of the trash again.

In a grassy river valley in southern Washington State, a young woman heard her husband calling. She ran to join him at the end of a long trench, with Mount Saint Helens looming above them. They had dug every inch of it themselves, over a period of nearly a hundred weekends and two summer vacations. He had just uncovered the license plate of a car. It was the one her parents had been in when they disappeared after the eruption.

Saturday, December 5th. 2:20 PM.

The airport was hung with wreaths and Yule bells; the stores along Century Boulevard had their Christmas decorations up; even La Cañada High School had a Christmas

56

tree. Rainy could not make herself feel Christmasy. She drove straight through to the laboratory, flashed her badge at the guard, parked at the far end of the employees' lot, and slipped in to her office. Nobody saw her come in but department secretary doing some overtime word-processing. That was the way she wanted it. She was feeling threatened and harried.

There was a thick sheaf of pink telephone messages clipped to her desk blotter. It was a measure of Rainy's mood that she didn't want to look at them. She knew what they would be. The pressure had started right after Newton-8 had gone silent. Every newsperson in Arecibo crowded around, the whole afternoon session interrupted; it had been pure hell. The most she could say was that she had managed not to cry. Apart from that, total loss, and it didn't get better. The next morning, when everyone else was getting ready to leave, more reporters arrived and she had to hold a news conference. When she finally tore loose from the observatory, it was too late to make her plane. So she got a ride into San Juan and checked into a motel. She spent the whole afternoon in the pool, gloriously; nobody knew where she was. Then she sneaked onto the first flight the next morning—

"Rainy!" Her boss burst through the door. "Sheila said you were here! I've been trying to call you all over the place!" He mopped his forehead. "What a mess," he moaned, his plump face filled with worry.

"I'm really sorry, Dr. Teppinger—"

"Oh, hell, Rainy, it wasn't your fault. I mean— No, of course it wasn't. But you wouldn't believe the heat we're getting!"

"Yes I would."

He blinked. "Well, anyway," he said, "I'm glad you're here. Listen. You're just in time. The Lab's going to have a news conference on the Newton-8 at four o'clock. They've been praying you could get there."

"Another news conference?"

He shrugged. "It seems to be big news," he said morosely. "God knows why. Spacecraft stop functioning every day and nobody pays any attention." He scratched his bushy moustache. "Maybe it wasn't such a good idea to build our presentation around a spacecraft on its last legs," he said.

Rainy kept her mouth shut. It had been his idea, after all. "Uh, Dr. Teppinger? How's this going to affect me?"

"Oh, God, Rainy, who knows about that?" He considered for a second. "As far as your grant's concerned, of course, well, that's just out the window. Of course, you'll get severance pay."

"Dr. Teppinger! I just bought three rooms of furniture!"

"I'm really sorry, Rainy. Listen, you'll connect somewhere—I tell you what I'll do. Were you going to the ASF meeting next week? Well, I think you ought to; it's a pretty good slave mart, especially if you make yourself visible. I'll see if I can get you a spot on the program, although it's the last minute. . . ." His voice trailed off and he sat on the edge of her desk, staring unseeing at the launch photograph of the Newton-8 on her wall. "Rainy? What do you suppose did happen to the son of a bitch?"

"I wish to God I knew," she said.

By the time she finished discussing that with him, they had gone over every possible disaster that either of them could imagine, and there were only twenty minutes left before the news conference. Rainy sighed, pulled a yellow pad toward her and began to make notes on what she should say.

At approximately 1830 hours on Wednesday, December 2d, Universal Mean Time—that would have been about ten-thirty AM, Pacific time—the spacecraft Newton-8 abruptly ceased transmission. The spacecraft had already completed every scientific mission for which it had been designed and budgeted. It was functioning normally until—

Rainy's phone rang.

For a moment she wished she dared not answer it, but the habits of a lifetime won out. Of course, it was Tinker. His soft, melancholy, undertaker's voice said, "Rainy, I've been trying to reach you for hours."

"I know that, Tink." At least five of the phone slips had been from him. "Tink, I'm really busy—"

"I know that, honey. Have you seen the paper?"

Had she not! Someone had carefully folded back the late edition to display the headlines. "Oh, yeah," she said, reading. "Let's see. 'Hippies Frolic at Space Mirror.' 'Gang Boss Indicted in Conspiracy Trial.'"

"No, no! I mean—"

"Tink, I *know* what you mean." Her story was right between them, and the biggest of the three. "It's been rough, and thanks for calling."

"It's been rough around here, too," he said mournfully. "The garbage disposal broke yesterday. I just turned on the dishwasher and water spouted out through the sink. The repair man said he'd never seen anything like—"

"Tink! For God's sake, have mercy! I've got the most important meeting of my life coming up!"

"And what's my life, Rainy? There's only half of me here. I'm not complete without you—wait a minute," he added quickly, hearing her intake of breath. "Don't hang up. I'll let you go in a second, only there's something I want to ask you."

"Ask, damn it!"

"Aw . . . you know."

"Tink," she cried, "you're just not to be believed! You want to know if I'm screwing around, right?"

"I want to know if you've kept our agreement," he insisted.

"Yes! To the letter! Now, good-bye!" Shaking, she slammed the phone into its cradle and reached again for the pad; but there was no time. "Oh, sweet God," she moaned, jumped up, glanced at herself in the mirror, gave up and half-trotted down the hill to the Von Karman Auditorium. A few days ago it would have been a pipe dream to think of herself as the central figure in Von Karman . . . but a few days ago the world had been entirely different. In the sweltering Santa Ana she could feel her blouse sticking to her; what a mess she was going to look!

But that wasn't the thing that bothered her most.

What bothered her most was a little voice in the corner of her mind that kept pointing out to her that, if only she went back to her husband, she wouldn't have to worry about her professional reputation, or rent, or car insurance, or meeting the payments on all that furniture.

She was braced for the press conference; she didn't panic, she didn't lose her voice, she didn't fumble for words; all the same the questions astonished her. Such questions! "Do you have any reason to believe the Russians sabotaged your spacecraft?" "Can the space shuttle get a crew up to repair it?" "What would you say the cash value of the spacecraft is—I mean, how much has losing it cost us?" And the worst one: "According to reports, you have believed for some time that we were in danger from space. Is that in any way connected with the loss?" But she had hung in doggedly, and had managed, every time, to be polite.

And at least it was over. Or almost. On the way to the door she was stopped three times—a picture; questions about her childhood and her reasons for becoming an astronomer—even her sign of the zodiac. By the time she got out of the room it was almost empty, but two men were waiting outside. She had seen them during the news conference, in the back of the auditorium. They had been listening intently and apparently taping every word, but they had asked no questions. "Oh, gee," she said, "haven't I said enough on the subject yet?"

"I'm afraid not, Mrs. Keating," the taller one said. He flipped open a wallet. "We're from Air Intelligence. Let's go to your office for a minute."

The kind of nuclear fusion that keeps the sun going produces neutrinos. Neutrinos are so tiny and so lacking in electric charge that detecting them is very difficult. A neutrino "telescope", typically, consists of ten thousand gallons of cleaning fluid at the bottom of a gold mine in North Dakota. The earth above the mine filters out all other particles; atoms in the cleaning fluid react with the neutrinos. Strangely, all the neutrino telescopes consistently report fewer neutrinos than the sun's core should be producing. One possibility is that the theories are all wrong. Another is that the sun has begun to grow colder.

Tuesday, December 8th. 8:40 AM.

Danny Deere stopped in his breakfast room on the way to the front door. "Jesus, Manuel," he cried in disgust, "you got the son of a bitch crooked. Has to go up on the left. You blind? *Up.*"

The handyman hopped off the stool to take a look. The painting was a Reginald Marsh, just promoted from the basement. It clashed violently with the violently bright Leetig it faced across the room, but the handyman never expressed an opinion about art. "Oh, sure, boss," he agreed, smiling and bobbing his head. "Way up."

"Not *way* up, goddamit, maybe an *inch* up, and don't drop it." He turned to the door, accepting his raw-silk sports jacket from Manuel's wife. "Keep an eye on him," he ordered, slinging the jacket over his shoulder.

"*Si, señor.*" She also gave him a giant smile, which he did not return. His chauffeur opened the door of the Mercedes as Danny approached the terrazzo driveway; he didn't smile, but then he was the one who actually liked Danny Deere.

Danny's morning paper was neatly folded on the white leather seat, open to the real-estate section. The car was freshly polished, the stereo was whispering the morning news, the day was warm but not yet hot from the Santa Ana; and everything considered Danny Deere was in about as good a mood as was possible for a person like Danny Deere. But he knew what he would see as soon as he got out of his driveway. Halfway to the gate he found what he was looking for, an excuse to blow off steam. "Jesus, will you look at that?" he cried. "Joel! You run in the gatehouse and tell those kids they got to cut down their marijuana. You can see it from the road, for Christ's sake!"

"Okay, Danny." Joel de Lawrence stopped the car gently

in front of the house occupied by Danny's peons. Although he was nearly seventy, he was sprightly as he hopped out and rang the doorbell. Danny Deere glowered for a moment at the teen-ager who came to the door but did not deign to listen to the exchange. He popped the paper open to the classifieds and began running down them with his thumb.

When Joel was back in the car, pressing the button that activated the gate, Danny ordered, "Don't take the freeway right away. I want to look at some houses."

"Okay, Danny." Joel de Lawrence knew why Danny didn't want to take the freeway. But he didn't say anything. He didn't even look at the great sprawling skeleton of steel that was going to be the biggest condominium in Southern California, and was also going to spoil Danny's view of the Pacific.

When Danny Deere was six years old he was famous. Between 1935 and 1942 he made fifteen movies, and every one of them made money for the studio, if not an awful lot for the kid star. When he got too pimply and awkward for kid roles he decided to become a millionaire and show them. He did. He persuaded his stepfather to put the money that was left into Los Angeles real estate. By the time he was thirty he had his million. By the time he was forty his ex-wives had most of it, but Danny had learned that you didn't have to actually own the real estate to get rich from it. He opened an office, and in the explosive market of the 70's he was Southern California's fastest-moving dealer.

When he drove downtown, which was only when he had to, Danny Deere stayed off the freeways as long as he could. His driver knew what to do. He took all the winding roads through the areas the developers had never been allowed to touch, passing the homes of the movie stars and oil sheiks and political exiles. Every big estate was an old acquaintance to Danny Deere, and he took note of every change he saw. This place's royal palms were looking yellow at the crowns. Damn shame, that was fifty thousand off the price, at least. That one was building something—what? A greenhouse around an indoor pool? He paid conscious attention for a moment. Interesting idea. The investment couldn't be more than sixty, sixty-five thousand at the most, and it might raise a one-seven house past the two million mark, if you found the right buyer. Not that all those one point sevens wouldn't go to two anyhow, sooner or later—two? In ten years, who knew? Maybe three million. Maybe anything you cared to mention. There were just so many square feet of land in California, and nowhere for prices to go but up.

Unless a smart operator could bend a little downturn into the curve.

The big Mercedes came to a decision point, and the driver turned around. "Danny? If you want to get to that place by ten AM, I better take the freeway now."

"So take the goddam freeway, Joel, do I have to drive the goddam car myself?" Danny wasn't angry at the old man. He always talked to him like that. He always talked to everybody who worked for him like that, but it gave him the most pleasure when it was Joel de Lawrence. For the twenty minutes that it took to run the Golden State Freeway to the Hollywood, and the Hollywood to the Santa Monica, and the Santa Monica to the Sixth Street exit Danny didn't bother looking out the window. He lay back on the doubly upholstered seat, thinking about his little plan, and the various other little plans that filled his days, and smiling quietly to himself.

He came to as they jolted off the freeway and made a sharp turn. For a moment he couldn't remember what he was doing way the hell downtown, so far from his office on Sunset Boulevard and even farther from the real action, and then he saw the public library on his right and the entrance to the hotel just ahead.

"Hot damn," he said, surprised.

"What did you say, Danny?" Joel half turned to listen, keeping his eyes on the traffic.

"Just pay attention to your goddam driving." But Danny wasn't angry; he was pleasantly astonished. There was a thin loop of marchers outside the hotel entrance, carrying placards.

"Drive right past," he ordered. "Slow. No, don't make a U-turn. Just keep driving, slow."

He peered at the signs and placards as they drifted past, scowling a little. Christ, they had everything in the world on them! *Fluoridation Is Poison. Remember the Shah.* But there were two or three that said things like *California Is Doomed* and *Beware Jupiter.* He sank back as they passed, then called to the driver, "Pull over. Let me out here."

"I can make a U-turn, Danny—"

"If I wanted you to make a goddam U-turn I'd tell you to make a goddam U-turn. Just let me out. Then swing around the block and wait for me at the Figueroa Street entrance. Then I'll tell you what to do next."

"Sure thing, Danny." Deere hopped out at the intersection and trotted across Flower Street against the lights. There were no more than a dozen people in the picket line in front of the hotel, and they seemed to represent every shade of kookery in Southern California. A tall, skinny young man with a blond pigtail was having a desultory argument with the doorman. He wore a sandwich board which said *100 Days to Doom.* Danny stood at the doorway for a moment, watching with interest, then pushed on inside.

The lobby of the hotel was spectacular at any time, with its brightly lighted elevators running up and down immense columns in the hundred-foot lobby and its pools and pods of lounge seats cantilevered out from the upper levels. With the ASF convention in the hotel, it was a madhouse. Every person he saw wore some kind of a badge, most just the plastic clip-ons with a name and an affiliation, but others marked *Speaker* or *Staff* or other, more cryptic designations, and all of them seemed to be in a hurry. They also all seemed to have programs, which Danny Deere did not. He saw a knot of people standing by a display counter and headed toward it, but it was not a registration desk. It was a glass case that contained a model of a new apartment condominium, six arcs of high-rise buildings that climbed a gentle green slope. It looked rather pretty in the model. Actually, it was one of the running sores that spoiled the course of Danny Deere's life—not least because he could not get a piece of selling it. He scowled and snapped his fingers at a hurrying bellman. "Where's the registration desk for this thing?" he demanded.

"Two flights up. You can take the escalator over there—" The man waved toward a string of moving lights across the lobby, and then did a double-take. "—Mr. Deere," he finished. Danny smiled and patted the bellman's arm before he headed through a sort of random cocktail lounge toward the moving stairs. Being recognized was never unpleasant. In his late teens, suffering the humiliation of watching his old films beginning their endless television reruns without getting a penny out of it, nobody had wanted to know him; he could stroll Sunset Boulevard without attracting any attention except from cruising johns. But since his real-estate career had blossomed, he was a familiar face again on TV commercials.

But as he reached the registration area the good feeling evaporated. There were long lines waiting to pick up the badges without which you couldn't get into any of the meetings, and Danny Deere was not a person to stand in line. He weighed the possibility of a bribe to one of the registrars, gave it up, and moved thoughtfully away.

The cantilevered pods on this level had been taken over by TV crews. Deere dawdled past one of them, where a stocky dark man with a Russian accent, no taller than Danny himself, was explaining how glad he was to be in America and how much he hoped for friendly cooperation in the peaceful exploration of space, and another where a rather good-looking young woman with a set smile was waiting for the cameraman to get his act together. Deere recognized her after a moment; whatever-her-name-was, the one who lost her spaceship at the same place where the kid had taken all his clothes off and first called Danny's attention to this Jupiter business. And then, with a delayed flash, he realized that he had just seen that kid talking to the doorman outside the hotel.

He found a staircase and headed for the Figueroa Street entrance, where Joel de Lawrence was waiting with the limousine. "Dummy! You didn't park the car!" Danny greeted him.

"You didn't tell me to—"

"Do I have to tell you everything? Here's what you do, dummy. First, go around to the other door. There's a skinny young guy there, blond beard, long blond hair, carrying a sign. Find out who he is and where I can get in touch with him. Then go up to the registration desk and pick up my credentials. Then just wait there till I get there."

"Sure thing, Danny. What'll I do with the car?"

It was blocking the interior lane meant for arriving guests, and already a taxi driver was leaning out his window to yell.

"You'll leave it there, what else?"

"I could put it in the garage on the way, Danny, that's right next to—"

"Would you quit arguing, for crap's sake? You know what they charge in that place? Go on, I've got something to take care of."

He turned his back on de Lawrence and headed back for the TV crews. It had just occurred to him that one of them might recognize him and ask for some kind of comment and then he could be on the six o'clock news. And when did a little extra exposure ever hurt?

The American Scientific Federation was no better than Number Two in scientific professional groups. The hoary old AAAS had twice the membership and five times the muscle. Still, ASF had pulled more than three thousand scientists to its annual meeting in Los Angeles, physicists and archeologists and mathematicians and economists. It was not the kind of place where you would expect to find the Danny Deere kind of person. So the first thing the reporter would ask him, Danny calculated as he moved genially toward the floodlights, was what he was doing there. Right. He began rehearsing answers. Maybe even a truthful answer. It struck him as strange, but it almost seemed as though the best thing he could say would be to tell them that he was interested—no, concerned; *deeply* concerned—in the serious threat that seemed to be confronting the city we all loved so—

No. Not fancy; just concerned. Maybe even scared?

It would come to him when the camera was on him, he thought comfortably, and assumed the expression of somebody who was fascinated by what this woman was telling the interviewer. The cameraman looked up from his handheld minicam and winked at him. Danny nodded back, satisfied. He had been noticed.

The interviewer was a black woman with a carefully trained conk, and she was saying, "I guess you've heard the report that it might have been a Russian beam weapon that destroyed your spacecraft, Miz Keating. What do you think?"

Rainy Keating's smile sharpened a little, as though she didn't like the question. "We haven't been able to establish a definite cause," she conceded. "So it's hard to discount any theory, but I would say that was about the most improbable." The newsperson started to pull the microphone back for a follow-up, but the days since Arecibo had taught Rainy some media skills and she kept on talking. "We do know some things for sure. The Newton-8 overheated. It wasn't hit by a meteorite, because the particle counter was still functioning; it registered zero. It wasn't some sudden malfunction in the plutonium power source, because the telemetry would have gone out before we could read the change in temperature. It wasn't one of the tanks of propulsion fuel somehow exploding; pressure in the tanks was stable right up to the last."

The interviewer reclaimed the mike. "Sounds to me a lot like the way a laser weapon is supposed to work," she commented.

Rainy shook her head. "No, that makes no sense. Why would anyone attack a harmless old spacecraft like Newton? There are dozens right in Earth orbit, where they're a lot easier to get to."

The woman said, "Maybe they picked it *because* it was so far away—their killer spacecraft could observe it, while we wouldn't have a clue." Rainy was starting to shake her head, but the woman added, "Which we still don't. Thank you, Miz Keating. At the American Scientific Federation meeting in downtown Los Angeles, this is your reporter." And the cameraman swung the lens around the lobby of the hotel for a cutaway. "Thank you," Rainy Keating said dismally, but she was only talking to one person now, not the television audience, and that one person was looking around for the next interview subject. Danny Deere smiled and moved inconspicuously closer. He perceived he was just about in time, because others had noticed the television crew; Senator Pedigrue's kid brother was strolling casually in their direction, and several middle-aged men in business suits, surely scientists of some kind, were standing awkwardly around, indicating by their bearing that their reluctance to speak in public could be overcome.

But they were all out of luck. The noise level in the lobby suddenly increased. Half a dozen objects appeared in the air, fluttering down from the levels above.

Somebody was having a good time. Danny scowled as a squadron of hotel security men hurried past, heading toward the stairs to the upper levels. The number of floating papers increased. They were paper airplanes, swooping and swirling among the hanging blankets of Christmas-tree lights in the tall lobby, kamikaze-ing the sliding elevator cabs, bringing little shrieks from the crowd down on the lowest lobby floor as they were dive-bombed without warning.

Danny caught one of the paper planes as it dashed itself against his belly. It was a leaflet, crudely mimeographed on bright orange paper. It said:

Californians!
Wake Up!
The end is at hand! The city of Los Angeles is doomed! Scientists say the end of our world is just around the corner. Now we are going to be punished for our sins. The shameful abuse of Women, Blacks, Gays, the Free Irish and the Palestinians has brought upon us our

TOTAL DESTRUCTION!
* * *

Danny turned the paper over thoughtfully. There was nothing on the other side, but then there didn't need to be. He observed philosophically that the camera crew was scurrying to get this unexpected bonus on tape; there would be no quick interview with Danny Deere on the evening news this night. But what the hell, this was just about as good!

All over the Los Angeles basin the Santa Ana was searing the landscape like a blast from a hair blower. Up in the mountains, skiers lounged on the wide verandas of the lodges, looking mournfully up at the snow. It was pretty, and it was deep. It was also dangerous. Under the wind that curled up the slopes of the mountains the snow was softening. Every now and then an overhanging ledge slumped, cracked, broke loose and slid down a mountainside.

Tuesday, December 8th. 10:20 AM.

Dennis Siroca raced down the passage to the Arco Building bridge and collapsed on top of Saunders Robinson. They were both giggling. They clutched at each other, keeping an eye on the passage, and just as they were sobering up Robinson said, "Oh, *man!*" and they broke out again.

Thirty yards away, the noise from the hotel lobby was only a murmur. Nobody was following. They were both breathing heavily. Several flights of stairs, two or three bridges, a couple of laps around the circular balconies; it had been a pretty good workout for both of them. "Yeah," said Robinson, peering down the passage. "What's comin' down now, Denny? We goin' back in there?"

"Not right this minute," Dennis conceded. "I dunno." He fished a joint out of his breast pocket and lit it, passing it to Robinson while he thought. There had not been much of a plan past the distribution of the circulars, but that had been such a resounding success that he was

69

reluctant to let it stop there. The demonstration had been as much his idea as anybody else's, but that didn't give him any particular powers of leadership. The little event in Arecibo had been wholly unplanned; he was there because his old lady dealt a little drugs on the side and was scouting out East Coast supplies so she could pay her tuition when she went back to college next year. But the papers and the TV newscasts had used the pictures. Which suggested doing something like it again. Which had gone over big at the ashram. But none of them had thought much beyond the leaflets.

Robinson had moved cautiously down the corridor to see if anyone was coming their way. Returning, he reported, "Nothin' happening. Look, man. I ought to see how Afeefah's doin'."

"She's okay at the ashram, man."

"Yeah, well, you know, I got to get things goin', you understand what I'm saying?"

Dennis nodded and then remembered. He pulled a crumpled piece of paper out of his pocket. "Hey, this old dude gave me this telephone number. He said there'd be some bread in it."

"Yeah?" Robinson peered at the number, but it told him nothing. "For what, man?"

"He didn't say," Dennis confessed. "He was wearing a chauffeur's cap. Maybe some rich guy wants us for something?"

"For what?"

"Now, how the hell would I know? I'm just saying *he* said there was bread in it." Robinson looked irresolute, and Dennis pressed. "Let's give it a shot, okay?" Robinson shrugged. "Tell you what. Let's take a run around the hotel and see if any of the brothers and sisters are hanging around." He led the way out to the escalator, and Robinson followed. "If we did go back in," he schemed, "we better not try using those badges any more. They could bust us for that, maybe."

"Then we'll never get in!"

"Oh, yeah, we can. We can go down through the shopping center and cut in through the garage."

"Yeah? For what, man?"

"Well, we could—hey, hold it." There was a black and white at the Flower Street entrance to the hotel, with two city cops talking seriously to four young men and women. They glanced at Dennis and Robinson as they passed and then looked away, and Dennis and Robinson detoured around them. At the corner they paused and looked back. "They're not going to do anything," Dennis decided. "If it was a bust they'd be in the car by now."

"Hey, look." Robinson pointed to the parked cars down the block, where a couple of heads were sticking cautiously above the car hoods to keep an eye on what was going on.

"Yeah, there's at least a dozen of us that got out," Dennis agreed. "I think we ought to go in again."

"Oh, *man*." Robinson shook his head. "Hey, Dennis? You takin' this stuff *serious*?"

Dennis looked at him with astonishment. "What kind of a question is that? It's the end of the world, isn't it?"

"Well, now, man, the *book* say it is."

"All the books do!" Dennis shook his head. "No, it's for real, ol' buddy. We got four or five months, maybe, and then it's right down the toilet."

Robinson looked at him wonderingly. "Hey, I got to ask you something. You really believe that, why you here? Why din't you stay a thousand miles away?"

Dennis scratched his beard. Finally he said, "What would be the use? What would there be to stay alive for?"

Out in the direction of the constellation Virgo, but much farther away than the stars that composed it, a star ten times the mass of the sun had reached the end of its helium-burning period. Its core was poisoned with the iron it had manufactured, and it had no lighter elements left to fuse. The reactions slowed. The energy output of the core dropped. Radiation pressure no longer was enough to hold the immense mass of surrounding gases away, and they plummeted in. In less than half an hour the star collapsed on itself. The release of gravitational energy that resulted blew the star apart. It was a supernova, the most violent event any star can experience. In one burst of energy all the medium-weight elements in the core were hammered into all of the heavier elements, and the fierce plasma exploded into the galaxy.

Tuesday, December 8th. 10:35 AM.

With half an hour before her panel was to begin, Rainy realized she had forgotten to eat anything. The lobby coffee shop was, thankfully, uncrowded; she got a salad and a cup of tea, and was just finishing them when she realized somebody was standing next to her. "Miz Keating, what a pleasure!" he said. "May I join you?"

"Dr. Sonderman," she said. It wasn't either yes or no, but he took it for permission. He ordered coffee from the waitress and said politely, "Another interesting demonstration of stupidity just now, don't you agree?"

Actually she did; but there was something about the man that pushed her negative-reflex buttons. "I think they have a right to express their opinions," she said.

"There is no opinion involved, Miz Keating!"

"Really? But I understood there was a certain amount of evidence that the Jupiter effect might be real."

"Not in the least! As to the book, yes, perhaps; but these loonies are not scientists. . . . I think," he said gloomily, "that I am coming on too strongly again. It is a bad habit of mine. Please excuse it."

She looked at him with a little less hostility. "Are you on the program?" she asked politely.

"Oh, yes," he said vaguely, and then amplified. "It is always a good idea to be present at this sort of affair, of course." He shrugged as though the rest of the thought need not be said, and actually it needn't. Like everything in the world of practicing scientists, attending meetings like this was an investment. You interrupted your real work to fill out grant applications, and to sit in on faculty senate meetings, and to go to Arecibo to plead before a senatorial committee, and to come here to be seen. It was part of the job. Science was not just a matter of finding facts and assembling them into theories. It was big business. A single space shot cost as much as a hospital. A particle accelerator could use up as much tax money as a municipal library system. To both Tib Sonderman and Rainy Keating, as to almost all scientists, there was no question that the money for science needed to be spent. But the people who turned on the money spigots did not always agree. They always had decisions to make, this program or that, basic science or bigger welfare payments, a new astronomical observatory or a new bomber. Sonderman believed that if he could divert one major appropriation from, say, subsidizing sorghum farmers to geophysical research, he would have done as much for the systematic acquisition of knowledge as a Kepler or a Becquerel. . . . But of course, it was not for that sort of thing that you got your name in the textbooks. "And yourself?" he asked. "I have heard that your grant has been terminated?"

"The whole world's heard," she said bitterly.

"Please, don't worry. You'll connect. There must be two hundred Equal Opportunity Employers anxious to bring their statistics up to meet the guidelines. A female astronomer is a marketable commodity—of course, it would be better if you were black or Hispanic."

She swallowed the last of her coffee and called for the check. "You do have a charming way of putting things," she said.

He looked at her in astonishment. "Have I offended you again?"

"I've got to get to my panel. I'm a respondent, so I'd better hear what I'm responding to."

He sat back despondently. "I have offended you," he said.

"Oh, not unbearably," she conceded. "It's just that I've been Xeroxing my vita and sending out two or three hundred copies of it—and I guess I'm a little edgy."

"Very understandable!" He steered her to the cashier. "I hope you won't mind if I come to hear your panel?"

"It's not exactly your line, is it?"

"Oh, no, but I thought—" He stopped, then paid the

73

check and pulled her along by the elbow. "I must be truthful," he said. "I came here only because I wished to see you again. To apologize." It didn't come easy to him, Rainy saw; the expression on his face was more suited to a declaration of war than an apology. "Although," he added stubbornly, "speaking purely in general terms, I must say that I have not changed my opinion about the unequal treatment society gives men in certain sorts of relationships—"

She stopped and peered into his face. Finally she laughed. "You're a wonder, you know that? Listen, I accept your apology, so don't spoil it. Let's get to the meeting."

It was a dull panel, but a crowded one. The reason was obvious. The next program event in this room was to be a discussion of the so-called Jupiter Effect. Even though Tib and Rainy got there a minute or two before it was supposed to begin, all the good seats—the ones near the door, where you could get up and leave without any trouble if you didn't like what you were hearing—were already taken. Tib Sonderman followed Rainy down the center aisle. While she went on to the platform, he slid over to one of the few remaining empty seats, far to one side, in the second row.

According to the program, there were going to be six papers, all of them astronomical and none of them of the slightest interest to Tib Sonderman. He could not really see that they would be all that interesting to, for example, Lev Mihailovitch, the Russian cosmonaut who had apparently come to the meeting principally to be interviewed on American television. Like all cosmonauts, he was fairly short, not very young, but as polished in his public appearances as any NASA spaceman. And there were others whose specialties, he knew, were nowhere near X-ray sources in the Pleiades, or a possible new anomalous supernova. Tib knew why he was there. It was because he was enjoying the company of this attractive young woman who—at the moment, at least—appeared to enjoy his.

The longer the program went, the more crowded the room became. There was still a scattering of seats in the first row or two, but the reason was that the people coming into the room could not get to them. Capacity of the room was posted at 220 persons, but there were more than that standing at the back, sitting in the aisles, squeezed two to a chair near the doors. It was getting uncomfortably hot, and when the last speaker called for the lights to be turned out so he could show his slides, Sonderman was grateful that one heat source was extinguished.

It didn't help. Tib was sweating profusely, and wondering whether it was really worth staying in this tedious sauna. The speaker was feeling the strain too, because he was hurrying his presentation. His principal slide was a batch of black dots on a white background, and with his red laser pointer the speaker indicated one dot, tinier than the others. "This," he said, "is the anomalous object. It does not appear to be an artifact of photography—next slide—and in this other negative print, made with the multiple mirror telescope at Mount Hopkins, the same object appears. There." The laser pointed out another dot in a cloud of random dots. "We have no spectroscopy on this object. We have no other data of any kind. If it is in fact a nova, it is probably the shortest-lived ever observed. It does not appear on the plates we made the next night at UKIRT of the same section of the sky, nor in any plates made at any other reporting observatory. Except for one dubious short-exposure plate from Herstmonceux, and even electronic enhancement does not give a definite confirmation of that one. If it weren't for the Mount Hopkins confirmation I'd write it off. But there it is. Lights, please."

The projectionist turned off the slide machine and the room lights came back on. In just the five minutes of darkness the audience had added another thirty or forty people, and there was something about the look and bearing of most of them that did not say "scientist". They didn't act in the generally orderly, sometimes lethargic manner of scientists coming to a panel, either. A dozen of them were pushing determinedly along the sides of the room, and one, a bustly little man with a shock of close-cropped hair, pushed right through the row to the seat next to Tib. He was not evidently a part of the other group; who seemed younger and far worse dressed; in fact they looked like the paper-airplane pilots from the lobby. The speaker, drumming his fingers on the lectern, waited a moment for the noise to subside and then finished. "Now, what do we call it? A nova? Possibly a collision between a previously unidentified black hole and a small, dense gas cloud? A completely different event of some kind? I don't know. If anybody has a speculation to offer, I'd like to listen. And if there are any questions, I'll try to answer them."

The newcomer next to Tib Sonderman jumped to his feet, and in that moment Tib identified him. It was Danny Deere, the real-estate man, caught out of the corner of Tib's eye a dozen times a week in his TV commercials, while Tib was letting his subconscious worry at a problem as he played solitaire in front of the tube. "Sure, I have a question," Deere cried. "Is it true that the planet Jupiter is going to dump us all into the Pacific Ocean? And when does it happen?"

Alaska's Columbia glacier is the only one in North America that is not retreating, but it is about to do so. Because of its position on the shoreline it will not melt harmlessly. It will calve chunks of itself in the form of icebergs. Each berg will average about a fifth of a mile in diameter. About 100,000 of them will spill into the sea each summer, near the shipping lanes of the Alaskan oil tankers.

Tuesday, December 8th. 11:10 AM.

What a disaster! Tommy Pedigrue stood on tiptoes to try to see what was going on in the meeting room. He couldn't see. He could hear, though, and it sounded like a catfight instead of an orderly gathering of dispassionate scientists. Pure disaster. The worst part was that his father had told him to attend the Jupiter meeting. Well, he had tried! But there had been such a terrible crush. Tommy Pedigrue did not like being caught in masses of humanity—unless they were assembled to hear him, or his brother. He didn't like it all that much even then, but there was at least a profit to be gained from cases like that.

From this? He fidgeted back and forth, trying to make up his mind. According to the program, this panel was supposed to be on some rag-tags of astronomical stuff, of no interest at all, really; but cannily Tommy had schemed to sit in on this one to make sure of having a seat for the one that followed. That was the one on the Jupiter Effect, and that was the one that his father wanted him to cover. But he had not been the only person with that idea. The place was packed! Not just scientists, or anyway not just the kind of scientists that he was used to have coming to him and his brother with their begging bowls. The Russian cosmonaut was there, the governor's science advisor was there, there was even a young woman Tommy recognized as a talent scout for the Johnny Carson show there!

And most oddly of all, Danny Deere was there. Tommy had recognized him instantly, and wondered greatly that he was present. He got his answer when Danny stood up and started the riot, but it was an answer that raised new questions.

Then it became really disagreeable. As soon as Danny Deere got the words out, the mob at the back of the room took up the shout. Tommy hung around long enough to find out that the Jupiter meeting was canceled, and then headed for a quieter spot to think things over.

All those people! All that excitement! His hunch had been right. There were votes in there somewhere, he could smell them. Tommy had been in Chicago, building alliances for the upcoming convention year, when Mayor Bilandic failed to neaten up the streets after the 1978 snows. He had seen the election results a year later. He had heard John Lindsay's teeth-gritted self-abasement for the same fault in New York a few years earlier, when he was up for his second term—and those were only for *snow*. What would happen to his brother's career—not to mention his own hopes of following the senator right up the ladder—if, by any chance, all this was real and they let some part of California slide into the sea?

He made up his mind to report to the old man. He left

the hotel, cut through the parking lot of the public library, hurried across a couple of typical downtown Los Angeles streets—curb to curb with drivers who thought they were still on a freeway—and entered the grounds of the Pioneers Club.

When downtown Los Angeles *was* Los Angeles, and not just a place Los Angelenos boasted of never going near, the Pioneers Club was where millionaires kept their eyes on each other. For the old-timers at least, it hadn't changed.

As he expected, his father was still in the dining room, playing dominos with his secretary, Tim Paradine. The old man looked up briefly and nodded to a seat beside his wheelchair. "Gus'll bring you some coffee if you want it," he said, "or a drink, but let's finish this game before we talk."

Tommy sat down as bidden, as he always did when his father spoke, sulky with resentment, as he always was. T. Robert Pedigrue had given his sons everything, including the inside line to the levers of power in American society, but it was not to be forgotten that he was the Old Man. In 1940 the elder Pedigrue had been one of FDR's personal emissaries—to Latin America, to Madrid, at last to London in the middle of the Blitz. He got there in the middle of one of the worst West End raids, and when he left London his feet stayed behind. It wasn't a bomb. It was a bus. He stepped politely off the crowded sidewalk at Oxford Circus to let a gaggle of Wrens pass, forgetting that the traffic was coming the wrong way, and the Number 73 for Kensington High Street ground the lower ten inches of each leg to gritty suet. End of airborne diplomacy for T. Robert Pedigrue. It was almost the end of Pedigrue, too, but the surgeons at Guy's Hospital had had a lot of practice in carpentering mutilated limbs that year, and he lived. He even thrived. FDR remembered, and the week after Pearl Harbor Pedigrue got the job he asked for. He became the head of California's War Mobilization Board. When his wife asked what he would be in charge of, he said, "Everything." He still was. He was in charge of his sons, and before long one of them would sit in the chair where FDR had sat, warming it for the other one: there would be sixteen Pedigrue years in the White House, and by then everything would be shipshape.

T.R. fitted a double-six on a spur of the domino pattern and counted triumphantly. "Forty-one, fifty, double-nine is sixty-eight and the double-twelve is eighty, and I'm out." He flung himself back in the wheelchair like Dr. Gillespie and waited while his secretary, who doubled as his chauffeur, his bodyguard, and once in a while his procurer, added up the score. "That's forty dollars you owe me, Tim," the old man said. "You can wait outside until I'm finished with the boy, if you don't mind."

"I don't mind, Mr. Pedigrue," the secretary said, and he didn't. He didn't mind that the old man consistently won, either. T.R. was careful not to win more than half his salary back, and as Tim Paradine easily doubled his pay with the unbought gasoline allowance and the kickbacks from the gardener, the grocery store, the garage, and whatever contractors came along to make improvements or repairs on the house, it all evened out.

"More coffee, Gus," the old man called, and the waiter set down the plates he was about to bring to another table and hurried over with the pot. T.R. watched him carefully while the man filled the cup and added one ice cube out of the pitcher of water on the table to bring it to the temperature and tempered strength T. Robert preferred. It paid to be on the board of governors of the club. Apart from pepping up the service, it was a good way to keep the undesirables out of the club, the TV people who would turn it into a sales meeting and the land speculators who were chasing the crumbs that people like T.R. had left—and getting fatter on them than T.R. ever had, with the crazy way homes were going. Of course, you couldn't keep everybody out. There were six blacks, fifteen Jews, and a Mexican priest in the club. (But at least the priest was Episcopalian.) That was carefully planned. Some of the other undesirables were unplanned, like Sam Houston Bradison, but what could you do when he was on the board too? "All right, Tommy," he said, "what've you got for us?"

Tommy Pedigrue set his cup down fast and began his

report. "They never held the meeting," he said. "There was a goddam mob!" He told his father about the pickets, the paper-airplane leaflets, the scores of people who had shown up for the meeting that was never held.

The old man leaned back in his wheelchair. "Substantial people, any of them?"

Tommy reflected. "Yeah, sure. Some. And a lot of crazies, too. There was that stoned-out hippie from Puerto Rico and fifteen or twenty more like him."

"They're the ones we'll see on the six o'clock news," his father predicted.

"Just another bag of trash," Tommy said.

"There's votes in that trash, boy." The old man thought for a moment, while Tommy waited. He scowled and said, "I can't get a clear fix on this thing. I called up that old fart Sigismendt at the Foundation, and he wouldn't commit himself until he checked, and then he called back and said he didn't personally believe it was going to happen. But when you come to pin the son of a bitch down it's all, well, there *is* a possibility, of course, and, oh, the *theory* has some support. He says in six months we'll have evidence one way or the other."

"Bastard! He isn't earning his pay."

T.R. nodded, although in fact Dr. Sigismendt and everybody else at the Pedigrue Foundation earned their pay every day of their lives in tax credits, whether they worked or not. "All right," he said, "tell you what we're going to do. You're going to pick out a body of experts to look into this thing, and your brother's going to appoint them to the Senate committee."

"Not a chance, Dad! I can name six senators offhand that'll be making speeches about the Democrats wasting taxpayers' money again—"

"We won't pay them with taxpayers' money, boy," the old man said patiently. "We'll pay them out of Foundation money and donate them to the Senate as a public service. Sigismendt will okay it. About three scientists, a couple of assistants maybe, maybe a secretary or two. One month. And you can promise each one of them a Foundation grant for a year if they do a good job."

Tommy grunted rebelliously. "What can they do in one month?"

"You never know till you try, boy. Now, that's set. I don't want to use Foundation people, either. Sigismendt had some recommendations—don't follow them. Pick your own. Mix them up, make them look like an integrated group. You don't have to get top names. Get smarts. You can probably find everybody you want at that circus down the street. Got any idea who to pick?"

"Well—" Tommy snapped his fingers. "There's that woman who lost the spacecraft."

"Shit, boy! What do you want a dummy for?"

"She's going to come clear on that one, Dad. It wasn't her fault. And she's got a good TV presence." She also looked as though she might have a good bedroom presence. "She's an astronomer, and that's involved—"

The old man grunted. "I won't interfere," he said. "What about that geologist you were telling me about?"

As a matter of course, Tommy had informed the old man about the scene at Los Angeles International; he made it a rule never to keep anything from his father, unless he absolutely had to. "He's a pain in the ass, Dad!"

"He's a pain in the ass you owe, boy. Always pay your debts. And, hey, you probably need a weather expert, too. Try Meredith Bradison."

"Sam Houston's wife? Cripes, Dad! I thought you couldn't stand him."

The old man grinned fondly at his son. "Then we'll trade. You take one pain in your ass, and I'll take one in mine." There was also the consideration that if the investigating commission came out of this thing looking stupid, some of the embarrassment could be deflected onto the wife of Sam Houston Bradison. "I'll call your brother and fill him in," he promised.

"He's in Illinois, Dad."

"I know where he is." It was either the O'Hare Hilton or the Hyatt Regency, and that woman from Elgin would of course be there with him; Townsend Pedigrue did not keep many secrets from his father either. "Push me out to the door, will you?"

"Sure thing, Dad." After Tim Paradine had hurried over to take care of the task of shifting the old man from wheelchair to limousine, Tommy Pedigrue hesitated for a moment, then turned toward the hotel. There was a reception of some kind about due. Maybe he would find some of the people he was looking for there. Committee of three. Chosen freely by him, except that two of the names had been his father's.

But the good-looking one had been his own choice, and there ought to be some dividends from that. Tommy Pedigrue was not dissatisfied. In a horse trade you took what advantage you could get and you didn't worry if the other guy thought he got something too. That was the way he had been brought up, and it wasn't a bad way to run a life.

Every year on the continent of Asia twenty thousand square miles of forest are cut down, eight thousand square miles in Africa, and somewhere between twenty and forty thousand square miles in Latin America. Civilization, as Chateaubriand said in the eighteenth century, is preceded by forests and followed by deserts.

Tuesday, December 8th. 5:10 PM.

The ASF meeting had got itself back on track after the unfortunate episode of the crazies. It always did. The ASF was so ponderous an institution that its momentum would get it back on track no matter what the diversion. And the momentum of Rainy's life continued its track, too.

It was not a track she was enjoying. After the debacle on the panel meeting, the fire marshal had come in and cleared everybody out. Rainy's brilliant little talk was not heard; the panel on the Jupiter Effect that was to follow it had simply been canceled; the newspeople who had been tuning up for it began looking for other targets; and there Rainy was. Fat lot of brownie points she was going to get out of this day, she thought bitterly, as every conversation she struck up with some power in radio astronomy was interrupted by a reporter or a cameraman. When it was time for the six o'clock news she located a friend with a room and a TV set, and had the pleasure of watching herself once more, bracketed by the same familiar stories of the crazies raining paper airplanes on the scientists and the mobster hurrying out of the federal court building with his jacket over his face. She forced herself to go to the reception in the grand ballroom, but after half an hour of it she began to feel claustrophobia setting in. She thought longingly of those long, dull nights with Tinker, with her shoes off and reruns of Mary Tyler Moore or Kojak on the television. Dull? Oh, yes. Incredibly, incontestably, crashingly dull; but right at the moment a little dullness sounded extremely nice.

She looked around, speculating on whether there was any point in staying, and caught Tibor Sonderman staring at her across the room. She nodded, and the man took it for an invitation. He excused himself to the people he was talking to and came hurrying over to her. "I am sorry we became separated after the meeting," he said. "I looked for you, but there was such a crush— Can I get you a drink?"

"Actually, I was just thinking of leaving."

"I, too," he said promptly. "It is very hot in here." He took her arm and guided her through the press. "The fine thing about this hotel is that it has the little conversation nooks on the balconies—perhaps a quiet drink where we can sit down?"

"Well—" But he had already guided her to the elevator bank and pushed both buttons. There was a crowd there, too, but Tib was quick enough in some situations, and he managed to pull her through the first door that opened. Behind them a slim, dark man was hurrying to the same elevator. Rainy recognized him; the Soviet cosmonaut, hurling something over his shoulder to another Russian, who nodded and turned away.

Tib held the door for him and said politely, "*Pozhalsta, gospodin* Mihailovitch."

The Russian grinned broadly as the door closed behind him. "*Ponimaete pozrusski?*" he asked.

Tib grinned, shaking his head. "I learned to talk in Zagreb in 1947," he said in English, "so how could I not know a little Russian? But I've forgotten most of it."

"We're going up," Rainy said in dismay.

"What goes up must come down, so we'll go for a little extra ride. Oh. Miz Rainy Keating, this is Cosmonaut Lev Mihailovitch."

"Miz Keating, of course." The cosmonaut managed to turn around far enough to lift her hand and kiss it. "We were both becoming stars of television this afternoon, is that right? Yes. I hope the person who interviewed you was more sympathetic than mine—a dragon, I swear to you." He looked more carefully at Tib. "And we have met also."

"You have an excellent memory," Sonderman nodded.

"And in a moment I will recall the exact place," the Russian said, making room for a couple who wanted to get out and glancing up at the indicator. "The next floor is mine—I have a splendid idea! I have some excellent Armenian brandy in my room. If the two of you will care to join me for a drink . . .?"

Tib looked at Rainy. "Why, thank you."

"Excellent! It is just down the hall—room 1812, it is a number not difficult to remember, for a Russian."

Lev Mihailovitch was one of the mysterious early Russian cosmonauts who appeared in group photographs of cosmonaut trainees, was never identified by name, and was never seen taking part in an actual mission—for nearly twenty years. The assumption was that there was some sort of political trouble. Then, in the early 1970s, he turned up again, and this time in a full glare of publicity. He had occupied the Salyut space station for more than 80 days, setting a new record, if a short-lived one, for duration in orbit. Sonderman remembered that there had been a story about him in the morning's Los Angeles *Times* that said he had been carried out of the landing vessel on a stretcher. Bone calcium loss? A depletion of the blood corpuscles? Something of the sort; the Russians had never said exactly what. But he looked healthy enough as he scurried ahead of them to open the door.

He waved them to seats and began fishing things out of drawers. "What a crowd," he said over his shoulder, uncorking a slim green bottle. "I have not seen anything like that since G.U.M. had nylon panty-hose on sale. But I must say your police were more gentle than the ones who work for the department store—they have no patience at all!" He was opening jars and laying out little dishes in a typical Russian drinking buffet: smoked fish, pickled fish, dried fish—"And these," he said, holding up a packet of Fritos. "They are not very Russian, but I like them."

"Don't go to all that trouble," Tib began, while Rainy said, "Can I help?"

"It is not any trouble, and thank you, but it is all done." Mihailovitch surveyed the lineup on top of the television set, and then turned to look at them. "It was in Vienna in 1976 that we met, Dr. Sonderman."

"That's right, but my name's Tib."

"Yes. You gave a paper on tectonics in Yugoslavia, which I went to hear because I have always loved that part of the coast, near Dubrovnik and south. But it was quite technical." Something was troubling him, it was clear; he shook his head ruefully and said, "I hope we will all be friends, and one cannot begin a friendship on a false basis. I have not been entirely frank with you. It was not an accident that I saw you in the elevator, I was following you."

"Me?" Tib said, astonished.

"You? No! If it had been you I would have come up and slapped you on the back; after all this is California, not Moscow. I was following Miz Keating, because I wish to tell her something."

He was filling hotel tumblers and handing them out, and then he sat on a hassock before Rainy's chair and offered a toast. "To a beautiful woman for whom I feel much sympathy," he said.

"Thank you," Rainy said, gamely trying to swallow a significant fraction of the brandy. "But I'm a little puzzled."

The cosmonaut nodded seriously. "Dear lady," he said, "I am aware that you are in certain difficulties with your secret police."

She stiffened. "It's not exactly like that," she said defensively.

"No, not exactly." Mihailovitch tossed off his drink. "But in some respects, rather similar?"

Rainy said slowly, "I don't know how much of this I should be telling you."

"Nothing at all!" Mihailovitch cried. "Please, I did not bring you to my room to get you drunk so you would divulge the innermost secrets of NASA, such as what color the director's eyes are and why you should not order chili in the cafeteria. Not at all. But there is much that cannot be very secret, since I have seen it on your own television. First, you have no good explanation for why your spacecraft stopped transmitting. Second, there are some persons who think that it must have been the wicked Russians who did it—that is, of course, why everything bad has happened in your country, just as in my own— No matter. Third, there will surely have been many persons investigating, and quite a few will be rather quiet men in undistinguished clothes who want to know everything that can be known." He paused, looking at Rainy, who did not quite know what to say. "And all of this," he went on, "cannot have been very enjoyable for you, and I feel for you." He recharged all the glasses, frowning as he observed that Rainy and Tib had hardly dented theirs. "So what I wish to say, dear lady, is that it is nothing our people have done which has caused the loss of your spacecraft. We would never do such a thing to so sympathetic a lady. *Khorosho!*"

He downed his second tumbler of brandy and sat down, regarding them blandly. Sonderman stirred uncomfortably. There was something out of key here, and he couldn't quite put his finger on it. A cosmonaut was a mighty man in the U.S.S.R., likely to have his own apartment on Gorky Street, even his own sports car, even the freedom to attend international space and scientific conferences almost at will. But he was not likely to be volunteering information to near strangers, unless there was something else involved.

But what? To test the waters, Tib said, "Let me see if I

understand you. All these stories we hear about Russian anti-satellites, with laser weapons and proximity nuclear blasts—they're just the fascist cannibal propaganda of the American imperialists, right?"

The cosmonaut's eyes narrowed, and he took a moment before he spoke. But then he said, "My dear gospodin Sonderman! Our nations do many things. Not only mine, but yours as well—all nations do. We can have a discussion in these terms if you like, you say 'Afghanistan' and I say 'Vietnam', and you say 'Czechoslovakia' and I say 'Chile', and both of us then feel quite proud to have done our patriotic duty. Is that what you wish?"

"What I wish is a little less crap, okay? I want to know what you're telling us. Are you saying your boys don't have anything that could bust Rainy's spacecraft?"

"I said we had not done it," the Russian corrected, scowling. "And that is so!" Then his mood lightened. "If we did, do you think I could refrain from boasting of it to you? Or at least letting you worry, a little? No. We talk of other things, such as that mob scene we have just experienced downstairs. Is it your opinion, gospodin Tib, that there is a real danger of us all plunging into the ocean?"

"Not a bit of it. Or not because of the planet Jupiter, anyway," Tib amended. "But the point is that many people seem to believe in this, this *astrology*. I don't like to see science mixed up with it!"

The cosmonaut pursed his lips. "Another drink?" he asked. "Perhaps some music?" He gestured toward an instrument shaped like a lute; without waiting for a response he picked it up and strummed a sad chord. "Do you know your Ed Mitchell?" he asked abruptly.

"The astronaut? Yes. He is into some sort of psychic investigation now, isn't he?"

"Yes. He is a very sympathetic man. Very serious-minded. And I—I am not so sure. You see, my friends, I came very close to dying not long ago, and it caused me to think deeply. Astrology? No. I have no interest in astrology. But there are some questions for which I find no scientific solution, you see." He struck another chord. "It is very Russian," he apologized, grinning. "But Edgar Mitchell is not Russian, so perhaps it is not only Russians who think these things."

He got up to fix fresh drinks, putting the balalaika aside. Rainy, leaning against the edge of the hotel bed, felt moved toward the Russian, and not unmoved toward the man beside her. She could feel the warmth in her cheeks and knew that, if she stood up, she would experience the effects of the brandy; but meanwhile it was very pleasant in this room. And when there was a knock on the door she resented it.

"Is only my room-mate," Mihailovitch explained. But when he opened it it was Senator Pedigrue's kid brother, looking uncomfortable. "I'm sorry to interrupt," he said, staring past the cosmonaut at the couple on the floor. "Your friend told me I might find Dr. Sonderman and Miz Keating here."

"Yes, yes! Come in!" cried the cosmonaut hospitably, but Tommy Pedigrue shook his head.

"I hate to break up the party," he said, "but I'd like to see the two of you for a moment. I have an offer that I think might interest you."

The earth's north pole is not fixed; it shifts irregularly, usually within a small area. Sometimes the area is not small. About thirteen thousand years ago, in what is called the "Gothenburg excursion", it made a large-angle shift. At about the same time, the world's sea levels dropped significantly. At about the same time, the Nile flooded. At about the same time, the North American glaciers, which had been retreating, began to advance again. At about the same time, the Neanderthalers became extinct. A link between these events and the Gothenburg excursion of the magnetic field has been suggested, but not established.

Tuesday, December 8th. 5:30 PM.

In the computer files of the L.A.P.D., the F.B.I., and about sixteen other law-enforcement agencies around the West Coast he was listed as Melvin "Buster" Boyma, with a regrettable number of arrests and very few convictions. Boyma was an extraordinarily short man, not quite five feet tall. When he was young he was almost round, and the bulges were all muscle. The other hoodlums called him "Buster" because his bear-hug had broken at least three opponents' spines. On the grounds of his condominium no one called him Buster. They didn't call him Melvin, either; he was Mr. Boyma whenever any of the contractors had to talk to him, which they preferred to do seldom. He picked his way carefully around the raw red mud that one day would be plantings of lawn and shrubs, studying the steel skeleton that rose six stories into the sky, and sniffed the Chirstmas wreaths that hung around the sales office to make sure they were real. In spite of the heat, he was wearing a pearl gray jogging suit and pearl gray boots, custom made to fit his bulging calves. He lifted one boot and studied it fastidiously. "Jesus," he said, shaking his head, "you got six straight days of Santa Ana and everything in California burning up, and what do I get here?"

The sub-contractor said apologetically, "You always get some mud when you pour concrete, Mr. Boyma. There's always some spillage."

"Yeah," said Boyma. "You got spillage, and you got leakage, and what you mostly got is slippage. What kind of fairy tale you going to tell me today?"

The prime contractor coughed. "We haven't made up any of the slippage," he admitted.

"No? And maybe you slipped back a little more?"

"Well, there's the holidays coming up, Mr. Boyma, and it's hard to get full crews every day—"

"I want a date!" Boyma roared.

The prime contractor said hastily, "February first. You can start moving people in February first, I promise."

"February first. When we started selling, you know what we promised? We promised they could spend Christmas in their own home. You know how many units we sold last week? We sold one. And we got three cancellations. That means for the week we got two less sold than we started out with. Where's Fennerman?"

"He's waiting for you in the car, Mr. Boyma," said one

of the two young men who followed him wherever he went. He turned and picked his way delicately through the turned wet soil, pausing to glance out toward the Pacific. You couldn't see much from here, of course. Even less after the other buildings went in, which would not be until these first ones were fully sold. But from the penthouse apartment, complete with private elevator and private entrance to the private underground garage, you would see the Pacific, right over the buildings that would come in later. That was the one Boyma had reserved for himself—at least for the next couple of years, until he was ready to retire to that great mobster's heaven in Palm Springs, where you didn't have to worry about those unpleasant statistics of street crime and violence that were turning Los Angeles into another Detroit.

Melvin Boyma had come up the hard way, starting with a union local, expanding into women and drugs. As soon as he had a stake he put it into the growth industry of the time, which was porno films. Then the stake became really big and he didn't have to bother with that sort of thing any more. He was in investments. Some of the investments involved bookmaking. Some were called "shylocking" by the L.A.P.D. But his accountants had convinced him that, with the money market going crazy, it was almost as profitable to put his capital into legitimate business. Semilegit, anyway. He still kept a turf of his own in downtown L.A., but it had been a long time since he had taken care of any of that business in person. As an elder statesman of the underworld he didn't need to.

Of course, as an elder statesman of the underworld he was exposed to a certain amount of police harassment from time to time, like this grand jury indictment. But that did not weigh very heavily on him. That was what you paid lawyers for, and Boyma paid his very well.

The last few steps to the car were uphill, and Boyma was puffing as he squeezed into the car where his lawyer was sitting. "Cigarette," he said, and the lawyer held out a pack. The jogging suit had no pockets, because that was the way jogging suits were made, but Boyma never found that an inconvenience. He retained other people to be his pockets, not only for money and cigarettes but for whatever else one might have a sudden need for. "How come these people can get out of their contracts, Fennerman?" he demanded.

"State law, Mr. Boyma. Non-performance on our part."

Boyma grunted and leaned back against the cushions, unzipping his jacket. The tailored jogging suit fit him well, but not kindly. At best he looked like a well-designed pearl gray beachball, and when he sat down the barrel of fat that had once been muscle rearranged itself in ways no tailor could deal with. "You talk about non-performance," he said, "those turkeys I got working for me got a patent on it. Can I sue?"

"You can certainly sue, Mr. Boyma, but I wouldn't recommend it. It's very doubtful that you can recover damages unless you can show negligence on their part; that's state law, too." He cleared his throat. "What I wanted to talk to you about is the grand jury indictment. The D.A.'s moving for speedy trial."

"So? So stall it, Fennerman!"

The lawyer raised his eyes to heaven. "Sometimes I think you expect miracles from me."

Boyma didn't answer. It was, after all, true. Money could buy all kinds of miracles; it was what you acquired money for.

There is a valley in Iceland with shallow bluffs on either side. It is where two tectonic plates come together. The bluff on the west is the farthest extension of the North American plate, the bluff on the east, of the Eurasian. Iceland sits atop the Mid-Atlantic Ridge, where the sea floor is spreading. The island is slowly being torn apart.

Wednesday, December 9th. 11:00 AM.

Danny Deere's telephone room was the assembly line of his real-estate operation. It held eight steel desks, each of them surrounded on three sides by acoustic tile partitions.

All eight members of the phone squad lived with one eye over their shoulders, watching for Danny's inspection tours. Sometimes there was only one a day, sometimes six or seven. They never knew when he would materialize behind them, reaching over to thumb through the stacks of cards, calls made on one side, calls waiting on the other.

Today was a good day for the phone squad, because Danny was in a hurry. He walked quickly down one row and up the other, and spot-checked only one phone solicitor, the newest, hired because he spoke fluent Arabic. Unfortunately the son of a bitch didn't know anything about real estate. "Piss poor," Danny snarled, throwing the cards back on the desk. "I think I made a mistake with you, Mahmoud."

The man glowered sulkily at him out of eyes that, Danny was offended to see, had been enhanced with shadow. "These prices are so high, Mr. Deere!"

"No, they're not. They're investments for the future, and don't you fucking forget it. Whatever they pay, it'll be worth more in sixty days!" Or would be, anyway, unless Danny's plans worked out. But that had nothing to do with Mahmoud or the other soldiers of the phone squad. When it was time for the signals to change Danny would change them. He said severely, "You got a great list there, all sheiks and all. Fat and dumb, right off the plane; they don't know shit about values unless you tell them. You got one more week, Mahmoud. Keep an eye on him," he barked to the woman whose desk was at the end of the line and was nominally in charge of the others. Not that anyone was ever in charge of anything in Danny Deere Enterprises but Danny.

He left her to do the rest of the reaming out. That was what he paid for her, and besides he was running late. Not *late* late, because the appointment was one he intended to be late for in the first place, but late enough so that it was time to pay his other call first.

Deere House was a two-story frame building on Sunset Boulevard. To the right of the dividing stairwell was the storefront labeled *Danny Deere Estate Agent*, with its desks for the licensed brokers who worked for him, its walls of estate photographs and development plans. To the left was another storefront. This one was marked *Danny Deere Travel—Please Go Away*. Next to it was the smallest office, the one that held his shopping newspaper and what was left of his unsuccessful attempt at a public relations firm and talent agency.

The best things about the building were not visible on the outside. One of them was the offices on the floor above, where Danny did things that he did not want to do in public. The other was the private staircase on the outside, so he could get from any part of the building to any other without passing go. It meant going out of the air-conditioning, but the heat wasn't as bad as the last week, the Santa Ana was dying down, the weather report promised something in the Pacific bringing a change. All the same, Danny was glad to scuttle down the steps and into the blast of cold air in the newspaper office, where his secretary Anna-Livia was waiting for him. "I'm just writing it up, Danny," she said quickly, looking up from her typewriter. "I already interviewed them, and they're waiting outside your office."

"What 'them'? Dennis Siroca I was expecting, not some 'them'."

"He brought a black fellow named Saunders Robinson. He didn't say why, Danny. You want to hear what I got from them? There's more than two hundred people in the movement. They're going to open the new ashram next week."

"Say two thousand, and make sure you get the address of the what-do-you-call-it up big." He left by the front door, mostly so the people in the other offices would see him pass by the wide windows and know he was on the prowl.

Deere House had a book value of three-quarters of a million dollars, but didn't look it. It didn't reflect the magnitude of Danny Deere Enterprises, either. The real-estate firm alone had done sixty-two million dollars in business the previous year, for a gross commission of four million plus, a big chunk of that Danny's own. None of the other companies threw off that kind of profit. But they all paid their way, took little time or thought away from Danny's own personal schedule, and had occasional fringe benefits. When an airline or a hotel decided to compliment its travel agents with a free week in Moorea or Kenya, Danny and one of his girls was glad to accept. It gave him a feeling of pleasure to pass from the simple front door, up the winding but well carpeted steps, and into the little hall that led to his private office.

Two-twenty-five, and they had been waiting since two. Danny poured himself a drink and signaled Joel de Lawrence to bring them in. He didn't waste time with hellos. "Who's he?" he barked, staring at the young black man with Dennis Siroca. He let him stand there with his hand offered while Dennis explained that Robinson was an old buddy who had been through five or six street groups, and after all Danny had told him to hire an assistant.

"No. I told you to *find* one. *I* do the hiring. Tell me why I ought to hire you, Robinson."

The black man had a fluid poise that allowed him to draw his hand back without looking rejected. "Because I got background old Dennis don't, Mr. Deere," he said easily. "I been through black, I been through Hare Krishna, I been through Watts community drives."

"You been through jail, too?"

Robinson didn't even shrug. He simply said, "Yes, I been through jail, too."

"You owe any time?"

Robinson smiled gently. "If I did, would I tell you?"

"No," Danny said, "you wouldn't, but I'd find out. And then I'd burn your ass." He circled his desk and sat down. "See what the gentlemen'll drink," he ordered Joel de Lawrence, hovering in the door, and picked up his clipboard of notes. He didn't like Saunders Robinson. He felt strongly that the black man was likely to be treacherous, probably lazy, sure to fuck up if not watched every minute, and generally a troublemaker. There wasn't any bigotry in Danny's opinion. He didn't like most other people either, for the same reasons. Robinson, however, might work out. There was something about his eyes that made him stand out—soft, large, unwinking as they gazed at him. If Robinson had been a woman, or gay, Danny would have understood an invitation, but there was nothing sexual about it. He debated asking the black man what he had been in for, but discarded the thought; there was no point in it, and anyway, he could find out for himself. The first thing was to deliver his little set speech, and he got it over with fast:

"You probably got some questions, so I'll answer them first. One, why am I interested in your crappy little bunch? Because I'm worried about this Jupiter stuff. Two, why don't I go through official channels? Because those assholes can't make up their minds; one says it's going to happen, the other says it's a load of crap. Three, what can I do for you? I can put money in, and then I can show you how to get more. Any questions?"

Dennis Siroca opened his mild eyes wide and said, "I got no questions, Mr. Deere." Robinson didn't stir. Satisfied, Danny went on.

"So here's what you're going to do," he said. "You got to get your shit together. One thing. Jupiter. Nothing else. All that ERA and natural food stuff has to go. You just diffuse your impact."

"Well, Mr. Deere, some of our people feel that the preservatives in commercial food—"

"Kid," said Danny, "shut up." He waited for an argument, but Dennis only smiled sadly. "You stick to one thing, catastrophe. *Scare* them. That's all. No boycott the lettuce growers or down with the C.I.A. or save the whale, understand? Now, to get that across you got to have a slogan. Here it is." He paused for effect, and then chanted: "Let the world know—it's over!"

"Let the world know it's over?"

"Oh, Jesus, that's the words, but you don't get the music. '*Let* the world know—it's *o*-ver.' Get the rhythm. Dumpty-dum-dum, dee *dah*-dah."

Dennis repeated, "Dumpty-dum-dum—"

"Kid," Danny said dangerously, "when I say something you take it serious. Say it right."

"Let the world know . . . it's OHver."

"That's it. And that's all of it. No other words at all, not about anything. No one, two, three, four, we don't want your fucking war, no spur of the moment improvisations, no politics, no religion. Nothing but let the world know it's *over*. You just keep chanting that until it takes hold, and don't worry, it will. Next thing. You guys look like shit. You need some kind of special outfit, or way to look. I been thinking of shaving your heads—"

"Hey, no, man!"

"—but the Hare Krishnas have got that already. They've got a really good act, the yellow robes, the little dance step, the war paint on their faces. You can learn a lot from them."

Saunders Robinson said softly, "The guys might go for robes. Something silk or satin, maybe? With a bright red lining?"

"Oh, God, you know what silk robes would cost? I was thinking more something like paper bags over your heads, like the Iranian students used to."

The chauffeur stirred in the corner of the room. "Danny? Blacken their faces."

Danny glared, but de Lawrence persisted, "Blacken their faces. Danny. It's what the Indians used to do when they just gave up on the world. When things were so bad there wasn't any way out. And there's plenty of minstel-show makeup around."

Danny sank back, drumming his fingers on the desk top. At last he said, "Yeah, that could work. Find out what the makeup costs, how often you have to replace it, all that. All right. Next thing." He consulted his notes. "Right. When you're standing there on the street, don't just stand there. You want to do a little step, like the Hare Krishnas. I got one worked out. Let me show you."

He hopped up and moved before the desk, changing. "*Let* the world *know*—" step to the right, crossover, hands pressed together and pointing to the left—"it's over." Step back, crossover, hands pointed down. "Let the world know—" same step to the right—"it's over!" And back to the center. "Do it," he said, perching on the edge of the desk to watch. They both caught it quickly, but Danny rehearsed them like a director with a chorus line until he was satisfied.

"All right," he said at last. "Now, I want you people to be seen. Move around. I want everybody to see you. I want you in the Century City mall, and I want you along the Strip, and I want you in front of the hotels so the tourists can get a look, and in the Farmer's Market, and out at the Bowl and Dodger stadium whenever anything's happening there, and I want you along the freeways in drive time."

"The cops'll chase us, Mr. Deere," Dennis objected.

"Let them chase you. You don't have to stay any one place very long, and you don't have to have too many people. Four or five's plenty. Two will do. Make sure nobody goes out until you know what they're going to do, though, and make sure they do it the way I showed you. I think the best way is single file, and keep on walking. Joel? Pick up the glasses, will you?"

Dennis and Saunders Robinson started to get to their feet again, but Danny detained them. "There's a couple more things," he said. "Don't get discouraged if nothing happens for a while. I figure two weeks just to get you seen all over, so everybody's used to having you around. Then we start the push. I'll put up the front money, but we got to raise the real scratch from other sources, not me. Am I bothering you?"

Saunders Robinson was studying the wall of signed photographs of people like Van Heflin and Audrey Hepburn, souvenirs of a quarter-century ago. He turned to Danny with complete self-possession. "No, you're not bothering me, Mr. Deere."

"Well, that's good, because I hate to think my talking interferes with you having a good time."

"I do have a suggestion, Mr. Deere," the black man said. "I think the clothes we wear should reflect hot colors—fire, flames, volcano. Red and yellow and orange, I think."

Deere looked at him silently for a moment. "Yeah," he said at last. "All right. That's good. No blue jeans, no fatigues, no O.D.s All you people probably have something that will do, I don't care what—shorts, slacks, tank-tops, T-shirts, anything. Except the girls, anyway. You get some pretty little girls with nice builds, they can wear tight shorts, but those big fat mommas I saw at the hotel got to wear muumuus. You got that?"

"I have a suggestion too, Danny," the bearded one said. "Did I tell you about my grandmother?"

"What the hell do I want with your grandmother?"

"She's a professor at Caltech," Dennis said. "Senator Pedigrue's brother offered her a job to investigate the Jupiter Effect."

Danny scowled thoughtfully. "All by herself?"

"I don't know, Danny. I don't think so."

"Well, for God's sake, find out! And find out what she's going to say, and when she's going to say it! That could be kind of interesting, kid," he finished, more to himself than to Dennis Siroca.

He opened the door. "Let's see you do that shuffle out of here," he ordered. It was always useful to know just how far you could push a person; he expected an argument, if not outright refusal. He didn't get it. He got a quick look of anger, but from the white guy, not the nigger. Saunders Robinson did not even turn around; he just began the shuffle, whispering the chant to himself, as he moved down the hall toward the staircase. After a moment Dennis Siroca shrugged and followed him and, satisfied, Danny went into the pantry next to his office, where Joel de Lawrence was typing with two fingers. He interrupted himself to display the glasses Robinson and Siroca had used, lifting them by spreading his fingers inside. On the outside was a fine set of fingerprints, brought out by the garden-mister de Lawrence had sprayed them with. "I'm just making out the cards, Danny," he said. "You want me to run the prints through Lieutenant Pachman?"

"Nah, it isn't worth it—yet," Danny said. "Just keep them around. And don't get the labels mixed up."

In Siroca's VW beetle Robinson lit a joint and passed it to Dennis. "How much did you get?"

"Fifty dollars a day for you and me, twenty-five for the full-timers. Ten bucks each for anybody who goes out on the street."

"Shit, man, what can you do with ten bucks?"

"Well, I told him that, Saun. He told me forget it. He

told me he was giving us the ashram rent-free, and he was going to go for a five-thou investment, and that was all; after that we have to support ourselves."

"Figures, man. Did he say how?"

"I think he'll come up with something, Saun. Anyway, I've got an idea. Know where we can score some good dope?"

Robinson scowled at the joint. "What's wrong with this?"

"No, I mean at least a key. We can pay the troops off in dope instead of money."

Robinson took a long hit, considering. "Yeah, that's a good idea. I thought you were the pot expert?"

"I don't want to go back to my connections, Saun, they're pretty heavy now."

"All right, I guess I know who to talk to. You coming to see Feef? She's asking about you."

"Not today, Saun. I'm heading out for the Valley. Any place you want me to drop you?" He passed the joint back to Robinson, who took a roach clip out of the glove compartment; they finished the joint, and then Robinson got out at a shopping center and Dennis Siroca turned toward one of the ravine roads. As he stopped for a light a couple of bikers roared up behind and yelled something at him. He didn't look around, just turned enough so they could see his beard. Dennis was slim and fair, and when he wore his sulfur-yellow hair pulled back in a leather thong studs were always hitting on him from behind. So at twenty he had tried cutting that down by growing the beard, and then the situation had reduced itself to an amusement.

In his twenty-some years Dennis had had time for three years of college—well, call it two years, one semester and a couple of incompletes. When he went he did well, even stoned, even tripping through classes for a week at a time. He couldn't see a point in going, though, except to please his grandparents. At twenty-two he stopped going at all. A little bit, it was money. The scholarships stopped coming when he stopped attending regularly, and he had objections to taking money from his grandfather. Then, after the second winter up among the redwoods, he had plenty of money—more than eighty thousand dollars in twenty- and fifty-dollar bills in a safe-deposit box in Pasadena. But he couldn't see the point of that, either.

Dennis had never taken a drug arrest, much less a conviction, but they'd had him for shoplifting in Medford, Oregon, and Minneapolis, Minnesota, and he was still on probation for resisting arrest in Dallas. He hadn't resisted. He just hadn't got out of the way fast enough when a gay-rights demonstration he was watching from the sidelines got maumaued by some up-tight citizens and the police moved in. Dennis had nothing against the police. They did their job. He didn't want the job himself, and didn't blame the people who did want it for being the kind of people who would. Dennis was religiously non-violent. That was why he'd given up the profitable, socially admirable and ecologically sound profession of marijuana farming up among the big trees in Humboldt County. The hijackers were not at all non-violent. When one of his neighbors bought an AK-47 and Dennis heard it being fired, he harvested his crop, drove it to Eureka, made a left turn and kept on going. In Los Angeles he took the first offer for the load and retired from the business.

Dennis disliked freeways, and so his trip over the mountains and through the developments to grandmother's house took nearly an hour. As he got to the intersection where the road his grandparents lived on began to wind down from the hillside, he stopped the car and closed his eyes. Twenty minutes of meditation was always useful. Dennis had done a lot of exploring in his fairly short lifetime. In between schooling and dealing and wandering, he had had a relationship with the Hare Krishnas, and a flirtation with the Moonies, two months of Scientology, and a sort of step-sister course in est—his old lady spent three hundred dollars for the weekend, and came home to give it to him second-hand for free. Of them all, the only one he still had any confidence in was Transcendental Meditation—not counting, of course, the Jupiter Terror. And that he had all too much confidence in. He had no doubt at all. No doubt that it would happen, and no doubt that it was well deserved by a human race that had forgotten how to be gentle.

When the twenty minutes were up Dennis Siroca squirted his mouth with Binaca, smoothed back his hair, buttoned his leather jacket and put the Volkswagen in gear to descend to his grandmother's house.

When Meredith Bradison heard her grandson's VW turning into the driveway she was making up the bed she and her husband shared in the large, light room that overlooked the road. She peered through the louvered shades to make sure, then tugged the corners of the coverlet approximately straight and left it. It was good enough. It had been made once already that day, anyway, by the mornings-only maid, and still showed traces of order. She took time to run a brush through her hair, studied her reflection in the bathroom mirror for a moment and then shrugged and went down to admit her grandson.

Meredith Bradison was sixty-six years old, her husband sixty-five, and they still made love with a frequency about two-point-five times the twenty-five-year-old normal, in the afternoons when the maid was out of the house, in hotel rooms between her convention sessions or his politicking, in the back of their camper, parked beside a lake or in a national forest, wherever. When the grandchildren began to be old enough to come for visits, any of the five sets of grandchildren, it cramped their style very little. The grandchildren learned that when Grandma said she was going to catch forty winks with Grandpa in the middle of the day, the kids were not invited. At night for a tuck-in story, yes. In the morning, when they woke up early and climbed in with the old folks, sure. But not always. And the way Emily or Dennis or Junior or Merry could tell the difference was by whether or not the door was locked.

There were times when the way Meredith felt about her husband embarrassed her, or at least made her wonder why her contributions to conversations with her contemporaries were so unlike theirs. Those times rarely lasted more than a minute. The rest of the time she knew a good thing when she had it, and she had Sam Houston Bradison. When they got married, him still in his junior year at Stanford and herself a dropout he was encouraging to return to school, it hadn't looked all that promising. Her mother wouldn't even come west from Lehigh County,

Pennsylvania, for the wedding. But it worked out pretty well, at that.

Sam Houston Bradison had been mentioned as a dark-horse candidate for governor more than once. One time he had even made his run for Congress. But he was before his time. That was in the Franklin D. Roosevelt years, when he was a young man, when California was profoundly New Deal when it wasn't Ham and Eggs or Thirty Dollars Every Thursday. Or worse. On the Republican ticket Sam got creamed. After he got his doctorate he stuck to teaching political science instead of practicing it. At least, openly. But the inner circles of the California Republican Party were open to him at all times. He was an academic, and the husband of a woman who was becoming a famous scientist, and the bearer of a proud name. He spent weekends with John Wayne on the actor's converted landing-craft yacht. He was one of the strongest supporters of Dick Nixon, and bled with him in the hotel room in 1962 as the bad news about the governorship race was coming in, just before the "you won't have Nixon to kick around any more" outburst. Later, Ronald Reagan phoned him at least every other week to ask his opinion before doing as he pleased. It was queer of Professor Bradison that he had never supported the war in Vietnam and, even in the 1950's, spoke out against academic blacklists. But what would you expect of a professor?

In any event and whatever the cause, Meredith was there with him. After the New Deal fervor that had brought her out to join a boy-friend in the CCC and, briefly, share the life of the migrant workers John Steinbeck was writing about, she cleaved to Sam Houston Bradison as to a rock. She made her decision early. Birthing five children was a full-time job. Adding a scientific career on top of that made a double load. She handled both easily and well, but add in her forty-five-year love affair with her husband, and there simply were not hours enough for getting involved in politics, or women's groups, or even in shopping, cooking or fashion. Meredith Bradison was widely known as the worst cook west of Texas, and she cheerfully identified herself as a frump. It didn't matter whether her clothes were color-matched or her hair coiffed. At sixty-six she still had a graceful, slim, boy's body, and whatever she wore she improved.

She stood at the open door, waiting for her grandson. "What's holding you up now, Dennis? Brushing your teeth so I won't smell beer on your breath?"

Dennis looked up, startled. Actually he had been making sure the stash that had been in the glove compartment was now securely out of sight under the floor mat, but she was close enough to what he had been doing earlier to disconcert him. "You just missed your grandfather," she said, tilting her cheek to be kissed. "He has a late independent-study group tonight. My God, it's nice to see you!"

Dennis put his arms around his grandmother without squeezing, as though she were a porcelain shepherdess, and let her lead him into the living room. He noticed the bowls of Fritos and salted peanuts on the coffee table and his eyes widened. "Am I interrupting something?" he asked.

"No, dear. I have some people coming over in half an hour or so, but you're welcome to stay. I know you're interested in the subject, since you're in that bunch that was at the ASF meeting."

Dennis shrugged politely; he had half expected to see his grandmother there herself, was not surprised that one of her friends had recognized him and passed the word on. "That's the only way I knew you were back in California," she went on, sitting down across from him to study him better. "Is Zee with you?"

"No, Gram. She's got a business deal in P.R."

Meredith sighed. "She's always got a business deal," she said. "I guess that's one of the reasons I liked her so much. You're not eating enough, Dennis." She had nine grandchildren, but he was the one who worried her the most. To Meredith's knowledge he had been arrested five times (the actual count was nine). The only conviction she knew of was for shoplifting, but it was Meredith's opinion that he had been guilty as hell of all of them, and probably a lot more. Not out of evil. Not even out of any need. Dennis was just willful, and had been ever since he had run off to join Reverend Moon—and been ejected unceremoniously when they discovered he was only twelve years old at the time. Her daughter, Amy, had simply given up. When Dennis returned to his family, it was his grandparents he returned to. Sam Bradison yelled at him, half an hour at a time. For a marvel, the boy listened. But he did not change. Meredith didn't yell. She took him out to McDonald's and filled him full of cheeseburgers and shakes, and slipped him pocket money.

When he was little she had given him cookies and milk. The cookies came out of a supermarket box; it was the best meal that any of the grandchildren usually could expect at grandmother's house. Now that he was one of those curious people with placards and beards, her resources seemed inadequate. He didn't want anything to eat, although he accepted a can of beer and a handful of Fritos out of politeness. "Gram?"

She straightened up from the floor of the closet, where she was looking for the attachment to the vacuum-cleaner hose. "Yes, dear?"

"Who are these people?"

She frowned thoughtfully, one hand on the closet doorknob. "Dr. Tibor Sonderman's in earth sciences. I believe he used to be with Scripps. Georgia Keating doesn't have her doctorate, but then she's quite young. She has a JPL grant, but I believe it's running out. I've never met her—haven't met either of them, really, although I think Dr. Sonderman and I were at the governor's conference together, two years ago—oh, thank you, dear! Let me take that." While she was talking Dennis had walked to the closet, picked up the cleaner part she was looking for and fitted it onto the hose.

He stroked her shoulder and grinned. "What do you want cleaned, just the carpet here?"

"I think so," she said, glancing around at the room as though it were his. "Let's see, what else do I need to do?"

"You need to sit down while I do this for you," her grandson said. "You can go on telling me about these two people?"

Obediently Meredith sat on a hassock, watching him

expertly slide the vacuum over the rug. "Well," she said, "this is just a sort of get-acquainted meeting. I haven't actually accepted the job, although I suppose— Good heavens!"

The glasses on the sideboard tinkled together, and she felt a sort of vibration through the house, as though a very heavy truck were rumbling by. But there were no trucks on Mountain Laurel Drive. It lasted only a moment. But the effect on her grandson lasted longer than that. He was transfixed, and the look on his face was very much like terror.

Tibor Sonderman was stopped for a light on Ventura Boulevard when he felt the tremor. A man making his way across the street in front of him with a four-legged crutch stopped, scowling angrily at the world. Hanging ferns outside a florist's shop at the corner swayed briefly. Tib switched on the radio and began to hunt across the dial.

All the stations were blandly continuing with whatever they had been doing, rock, folk, soul, sports, or talk. By the time he reached Meredith Bradison's house he had made his own assessment: no more than 3.5 on the Richter, or there would have been something said about it; no less than 3.0, or he wouldn't have felt it at all. Just another of the several hundred shocks that hit Southern California every year.

Rainy Keating's car was tucked into the little drive space ahead of him. Tib eased his little Horizon into the space between it and somebody's old Volkswagen beetle, and was admitted by a handsome, tiny, elderly woman. "Dr. Bradison?" he asked.

"Please call me Meredith," she said, letting him in through a sort of greenhouse of a foyer. From the look of the entrance Tib expected something Hollywoodian for a living room, if not a salon, but what he saw was a quite plain room furnished in clutter. On what was obviously a retired sofa bed Rainy Keating was listening to her telephone messages. "I think you two know each other?" Meredith said, and Rainy looked up with the phone to her ear to acknowledge Tib's presence.

"I'm sorry," she said after a moment, hanging up the

phone as a tall, fair-bearded young man came in with a tray of glasses. "I was just checking to see—hey! I know you."

Dennis Siroca said apologetically, "I guess you do, Miz Keating. I'm the one that broke your what's-it."

"My orrery."

Meredith Bradison said, "Well, I didn't know you two knew each other, either."

"Just a little bit," Tib said, grinning. "It is probably your grandson's fault that we are all here now, Meredith. He put on a little exhibition for us in Arecibo."

"Oh, Dennis! Were you that one?" He shrugged, not really embarrassed, and offered drinks around. "Well, you're full of surprises," she told him; and to the others, "I'm really grateful you came here today. I thought it was a good idea for us to know each other a little better before we got into any formal activities."

"It was a fine idea, Meredith," Rainy assured her. "Have you read the book?"

"Oh, yes. It's out of my field, of course, or most of it is. I can testify that the expansion of the atmosphere does take place under the appropriate conditions, of course— that's what brought Skylab down a few years ago. And there does seem to be a connection between large air mass activity and the glitches in the earth's rotation. After that I'm lost."

Rainy said, "We really need more experts. Maybe a nuclear physicist, a planetary astronomer, somebody with special training in the reactions between the solar wind and the atmosphere—no?" she added, looking at Tib.

He was shaking his head. "No, I think not. That's a herd, and we'd never get anywhere. You're all we need for the astronomical parts, Rainy."

"I don't know diddly-squat about the interior of the sun!"

"You know who to ask, though. And anyway, we're not going to worry about the interior of the sun. As I see it, that's the weakest link in the argument. Point two at the most, I'd even say point one."

Dennis, sitting on a footstool behind the couch and nominally out of range, asked, "What's point two mean, Mr. Sonderman?"

Tib glanced at Meredith, then, politely, to her grandson, "The probability of that happening, I would say, is only two chances out of ten." He held up his hand as the boy started to speak. "How do I arrive at that figure, you are going to ask? I don't. I guess. Or, you could say, if I asked ten experts if it is so that the configuration of the planets could affect nuclear reactions in the core of the Sun, eight of them would say it was, excuse me, a load of bull. In fact, I think that is the weakest link in the argument." He was fumbling in his pocket as he spoke and paused to ask Meredith, "Shall I?" She nodded and he pulled out a pencil. "There are eight parts to the argument," he said. "One, the configuration of the planets, all on the same side of the sun—that we can take to be certain, probability one point oh. The effect of their gravity on the nuclear reactions I have already mentioned—does anyone want to suggest another value?"

No one did, and the three others watched silently as he talked and wrote down a little table:

Alignment of planets	1.0
Effect on core reaction	0.2
Consequent increase in flares	0.9
Consequent expansion of atmosphere	0.9
Consequent glitch	0.5
Consequent strain on tectonic faults	0.2
Consequent major earthquakes	0.5
Net probability of Jupiter Effect	?

Dennis, who had risen to look over his shoulder, exclaimed, "So you think it's about fifty-fifty?"

Sonderman looked up wryly at the boy. "You're averaging the chances, aren't you? No. That's not how you do it. You must multiply them—like so." He pulled out a pocket calculator and began to punch figures. After a second the little red digits displayed a figure: 0.0081. "Eight chances in a thousand," he said. "A little worse than a hundred to one, and I would say that is generous."

Meredith looked at him wonderingly. "Then what are we all doing here?" she asked.

Tib shrugged. "Add to that the fact that one of the

co-authors has already recanted, and I ask myself this question too."

He paused, and Meredith looked at him quizzically. "And what do you answer?"

"That if I don't do this someone else will," he said.

Meredith got up thoughtfully and handed around a bowl of peanuts. Then she said, "I have a different reason, Tib. If there's even a hundred-to-one chance that this is going to happen—"

"Not that much!" Tib protested.

"Even a *million*-to-one chance, then I think it ought to be investigated. There are ten million people along the San Andreas fault, or at risk from broken dams, or in trouble any way at all. If it happens, I don't want it on my conscience that I could have warned them and didn't."

"Meredith," Tib said courteously, "have you thought about all of the implications of this?"

"Certainly I have," she bristled. "Or—well, I don't know. Are there some implications I haven't thought of?"

Tib picked up a couple of peanuts and rolled them between his fingers. "Let me tell you about the barrier islands in the Atlantic," he said slowly. "Ten years ago or so—no, not that long ago; it was in 1976—there was a hurricane watch along the Atlantic. It was August, the middle of the summer season. All the beaches were full of people—"

She interrupted. "That's my specialty you're talking about," she reminded him gently. "I know, and I think I know what you're going to say. Someone in the national bureau had to make a decision. Should he warn the people on the islands to leave? Or should he not? If he failed to warn them and the hurricane veered a few miles closer to the shore, every one of those islands would be drowned out by the winds and the tides—hundreds of thousands of people. If he did warn them, and they left, and the hurricane stayed offshore, he would have cost the beach merchants millions and millions of dollars. They have to make their year's income in two months. They'd go broke by the thousands."

"Yes," Tib nodded, "that is what I would have said, but there's more. Suppose he did warn them. Along New

Jersey's shore, for instance, there is a whole series of barrier islands, just shifting sands that people have built jetties and dikes and retaining walls for, to try to keep them where they are. And there are only so many bridges. As I understand it, the warning could only be highly probable if it were given no more than a few hours before the hurricane struck?"

Meredith nodded. "In 1976, yes—no more than six hours, really."

"And in six hours there was not time to get everyone across those few bridges, isn't that right? So there would have been total catastrophe. Every bridge blocked. Cars smashing each other out of the way. So even with the warning, many, many people would have died."

Meredith sighed. "What you're saying is that even if we found proof somehow that Los Angeles was going to be destroyed, we couldn't get the people out in time?"

Tib shrugged and didn't answer. From his chair on the sidelines Dennis Siroca spoke up. "It is going to happen, Gram."

In 1976 the core of a burned-out comet, identified by astronomers as Asteroid 1976 UA, came within not much more than half a million miles of the earth. It was a close miss. At Earth's orbital velocity of more than sixty thousand miles an hour, it missed by less than eight hours.

Friday, December 18th. 9:15 AM.

In the week before Christmas both *Time* and *Newsweek* carried stories on the latest outbreak of California crazies. All three networks had film clips for the evening news, and the *Today* show sent Jane Pauley to talk to the group petitioning the mayor of Los Angeles for immediate release of all drug-related prisoners. "It's cruel and unusual punishment, Jane," Saunders Robinson explained to the camera. "They're gonna *die*, you know? There's no *way* they'll get out of those cells in time when the earthquakes hit!"

Outside of California, most of the world paid little enough attention. But there were exceptions. Pickets began to appear in front of the White House, most days, except when the weather was too bad, and their placards urged a day of national penitence before Jupiter struck. A farm wife from Wisconsin announced that she had always had a talent for sensing earthquakes before they happened, and agreed to let ABC know when Los Angeles was going to get it. And a man named Jeremy Lautermilch canceled his plans for a week-long psychic seminar in Austin, Texas. There had not been all that much response to the ads, anyway. He made a few long-distance calls to Los Angeles and got on a plane.

Jeremy Lautermilch had learned a number of survival skills that were of benefit in his profession. He was a highly trained person. With three degrees from good universities, he had not expected to need such tricks. But the kinds of careers the degrees opened to him had turned out not to be very interesting. He could have taught in some other fairly good university, or done research for some fairly uninteresting employer like the United States government. He had higher ambitions.

The degrees were not wasted. They were cosmetically wonderful. They became a major part of the "publisher's press release" that Lautermilch himself carefully prepared and updated and made available to everyone who would look at it. The degrees helped. They didn't keep newspaper reporters from calling him a crackpot or a fraud. They only kept them from doing it in public.

One of Lautermilch's survival tricks was being unfailingly polite to everyone in related professions, and so when he arrived in Los Angeles International he made the rounds of colleagues. He had prepared a map showing the locations of six persons with whom he had had previous contact: a phrenologist in Hawthorne, two palmists in Beverly Hills, a couple of astrologers and, of course, the ashram of the True Believers in Jupiter Fulgaris. In his first four hours in California he had secured the expressed good will of his acquaintances and two firm offers of a place to stay. He turned down the ashram. He chose to accept one of the astrologers. She was not only well off, with a good address and a handsome home, she was herself handsome in a dark, dramatic way. When he moved his bags in from the trunk of his rental car he discovered she was also married, but you couldn't have everything.

The second survival trick he had learned was how to get a turnout for a press conference. It involved the long-distance telephone. No matter who you were, if you called a managing editor from a distant city to announce that you would be available the next day, he would seldom turn you down. So when, that afternoon, he drove up the hill to the Griffith Observatory he was gladdened to see a newspaper panel truck parked in the lot, and four people waiting for him on the terrace above the museum. He had timed it very well. The interest in the future of Southern California was climbing every day. His lecture was going to be a winner.

Since the park was public, there was no problem about getting permission to use it. He placed himself with the observatory domes behind him and began to talk. "Thanks for coming," he said, smiling genially as he handed out his press releases. "Shall I get right into it? All right. I am in Los Angeles to give a public lecture—the place and time are in the material you have—about the situation that confronts Los Angeles. The basic outlines have been known for a long time. According to Edgar Cayce, for example, by the year 2100 AD Los Angeles will no longer exist, because it will be at the bottom of the Pacific Ocean. It will be a long way from land, too. Cayce states that Nebraska will then be a seacoast state on the Pacific. If you will look at the little map on page three of the release, you'll see what that means. Utah and Nevada will be gone completely, along with most of California, Arizona, New Mexico, Colorado, and Oregon. What I am in Los Angeles to discuss is in what way the present predictions relate to this ultimate catastrophe."

One of the reporters looked up in perplexity. "According to this, Dr. Lautermilch, you have a degree in physics and a doctorate in mechanical engineering. I thought you were some kind of psychic?"

Lautermilch smiled gently. "I am both, you see. I am a psychic scientist. That's why the orthodox scientists can't stand me, the same as with Velikovsky. The degrees are genuine. And so am I."

Ash from violent volcanic eruptions is hurled into the upper air, where it lingers and, it is thought, reflects back some of the heat of the sun. In the year 1815 the volcano Tambora had such an eruption. In the following year, crops failed to ripen in much of Western Europe, and in the United States the summer was so cold that the year was called Eighteen-Hundred-and-Froze-to-Death.

Monday, December 21st. 2:15 PM.

Danny Deere leaned forward and banged on the window. "Roll it down, Joel! Roll the goddam window down!"

The driver nodded to show he had understood, and reached back to press the partition button. "Yes, Danny?"

"Keep your eyes open now!"

Joel grinned patiently. "I don't have to, Danny," he said. "I can hear 'em."

Danny spluttered in indignation that his driver could hear something he could not hear, and then pressed his own button to roll down all the car's outside windows at once. It was true. It was only a confused shouting at first, but the rhythm was unmistakable, and as the car slowed for a light on Wilshire Boulevard the words came clear: "Let the world know—IT'S OVER!" In a moment Danny could see them, at least thirty people in a double row in front of the Los Angeles County Art Museum, their shirts bright red or orange, their faces black, doing the side-to-side shuffle exactly as he had rehearsed them.

He regarded them silently as they waited for the light to change, and then conceded, "Not too bad. Joel! Up on the corner, see her?"

"I see her, Danny." Opposite the May Company store there was a tall, fair-haired girl in camouflage-streaked orange denims, moving from car to car among the traffic waiting on the cross street. Her face was made up jet black, lips and all. Joel de Lawrence eased the limo to the curb just past the intersection. The girl saw Danny and came gravely over, pausing to do the shuffle on the way. She handed in the collection can and received an empty one from Danny in return. He grunted acknowledgement to her, and as the car moved off toward the next solicitor he held the can to his ear and shook it gently. "Not too bad," he said again; by the weight it was more than half full, and the muted sound of the money inside suggested that there were bills to cushion the silver. There were three of the collectors stationed along the block across from the museum, and Danny gave each of them a fresh collection can in exchange for a partly filled one. "Make a U-turn, Joel," he ordered.

"Danny, if there's a cop anywhere around—"

"Make a U-turn, Joel!" He watched out the window as Joel obeyed. No cops. They made the U-turn successfully, but as they glided to a stop before the plump young man in blackface at the park entrance Danny saw that his hands were empty.

"It isn't my fault, Danny," he began at once. "Some guys ripped me off."

Danny regarded him with distaste, then opened the door. "Get in," he barked. "Joel, get on over to the ashram."

"They were heavy guys, Danny," the young man said apprehensively. "I think they had a gun."

"You think? You didn't see it?"

"I didn't argue with them, Danny! 'Hand it over,' they said, so I did. I didn't sign up for any shit like this."

"Shut up," Danny said, staring out the window as Joel made a right turn, heading for Melrose. "What's your name?"

"Buck. Buck Swayne. Listen, there wasn't much in the can anyway. Nobody goes into the park from there, and if they do they don't see the main bunch first. If I had a corner with a light and a lot of traffic—"

"Will you shut up?" Danny screamed. "I want to think."

113

It was the first time any of the collectors had had his money taken away from him, and it was not a precedent Danny Deere wanted to see followed. Buck was able to give a pretty good description of the two men—youngish but not really young; dangerous-looking. It didn't sound like kids, dopers, or drifters. It didn't sound good at all. It didn't even sound sensible, and Danny sat glowering to himself, not speaking, all the way down Wilshire Boulevard to the side street with the ashram.

The ashram had been dressed up considerably since he had seen it last. It was a narrow storefront, between a massage parlor and a plumbing supply wholesaler, but it stood out even against the psychedelic paint of the massage parlor. The windows were painted black, with scarlet and gold lettering:

The True Believers of
JUPITER FULGARIS

A small loudspeaker played wailing sitar music from the record player inside. Danny appraised it swiftly as he got out of the car, nodded at the fund collector to follow and charged into the store. "Where's Siroca?" he demanded of that black fellow, Robinson.

"He ain't here right now, Mr. Deere."

"Then where the hell is he?"

Robinson folded his hands on his belly and rocked back. "Well, Mr. Deere, he's been trying to score some, uh, some tradin' goods for the troops."

"Trading goods? What's trading goods?"

"The good mellow stuff, Mr. Deere. *Smokin'* weed."

"Oh, for God's sake," Danny said, but it was not an objection. Or not exactly. He was calculating in his mind the risk involved in steering Robinson to his caretakers, who certainly had plenty to sell. It was not something Danny Deere was anxious to do; he had stayed completely away from drug dealing. "Where's he gone for it?" he asked.

"Well, Mr. Deere," said Robinson, "see, I don't exactly know. He called his lady in Puerto Rico to see did she score, but she didn't. He was talking about goin' with her when she comes back west. Supposed to be some great stuff on the islands."

"Islands?" Danny exploded. "Jesus, you guys take the cake! Well, listen, when he gets back, you tell him I want this guy fired. Right now!"

"Buck? Buck's one of our best men, Danny," Robinson said mildly. "I don't think we ought to fire him."

"Then stick him in with the main bunch. He ain't fit to be trusted with the money. Get one of the big guys out with the cans."

Robinson shook his head slowly. "I don't think that would work out real well, Danny," he observed. "The little girls and the, uh, the inoffensive kind of looking guys like Buck here, they're the ones that bring in the money."

Danny stared at him, frustrated. Then he stared around the room. "Just get him off the collections," he grumbled. "What's that stuff?" He was looking at the black drapes that draped the entire room that comprised the front half of the store. A plywood partition divided it from the private section in back, where the money was counted and the actual members of the group gathered for assignments.

"That's muslin," Robinson said comfortably. "We got it for a dollar and a quarter a yard and my daughter dyed it with Tintex."

Danny nodded. "All right, but you don't want all black. Get some bright red in there, and what the fuck is that?" He was scowling at a stand with a huge Chinese vase on it, draped in what looked like a white bedsheet.

"Dennis found the vase. It's got a big crack in it, is why we got the sheet around it. It's for like love offerings. We been getting fifteen, twenty dollars a—a week."

Danny looked at him suspiciously, then looked around the room. "I got some stuff for you. Joel! Go get the stuff out of the trunk. Over there," he decided, pointing at a space on the rear partition next to the overlapping section of drapery that hid the door to the rear room. "I want you to hang one of these posters Joel's bringing in. It's actually from a movie, shows Los Angeles falling down, and I want you to keep a big candle burning in front of it all the time. No, wait. A little candle, and I want you to have a lot of

115

little candles that people can buy and light up. And I've got a whole bunch of posters, so you can sell them to anybody wants to buy one. Five dollars apiece. Maybe ten. And we've got some books about disasters, and I want you to sell them, too. I got the prices all covered up with stickers, and we'll sell them at a special price. You got a lot of people coming in?"

"It's a little slow, Danny. No parking space, you know." Danny knew; that was why the store was such a bitch to rent. But he said:

"How many?"

"Well, we had about fifteen last night. Not all at once, of course."

"Christ!"

"Well, but we're going to do it a different way now. Dennis and I worked it out that we're going to get some of the people in regular clothes, they're going to follow the group here from wherever they're on the street, and they'll get converted and come up and get some of the black stuff for their faces—"

"Hey, that's okay," Danny said, pleased for the first time. "Only use different ones each night." He sat down on a low, black-draped bench with a table at one end, off someone's pile of discards for the trashman in Beverly Hills. "I expect it to go slow at first," he conceded. "I'm worried about the people getting ripped off, though."

Robinson said, "I tell you what we could do, Danny. We could sort of double up the people with the cans, so they could watch each other."

"Yeah," Danny said, brightening. "That's a good idea. And don't use the old buddy system, either, because the other thing they can do is watch each other to see if anybody's dumping money out of the cans before they turn them in." He got up, cheered. "It's gonna work out fine, Robinson," he said. "The way I see it, we got to build slow, say another two weeks to get the image across. There's not going to be much action right at first. Then we pick up the tempo. I'll get you some name people to come in here every night. We'll give away prizes. Maybe a group to play a little. Yeah," he said, getting up to leave, "you're doing a piss-poor job, all right, but that's about all I thought you'd do right now. Hey, Joel! Get the hell out of the beer and drive me home!"

Before you got to Danny's house there was a sharp dip in the road, with a sign that said:

RUNAWAY VEHICLES
Emergency Deceleration Strip
600 Feet Right

Danny was fond of that sign. He owed his house to it. Once, in a moment of weakness, he had showed the house to a retired printing broker from Montclair, New Jersey, and it was all "go" until the client saw the sign. "I don't like the looks of *that*," he declared, and Danny had risen to the cue.

"First big snow," he gagged, "and you'll wind up in Brentwood." And then, when the client didn't call back, he realized that a printing broker from Montclair might not know snow was a joke in Beverly Hills. It worked out just great; Danny had turned down two million dollars for what he'd offered the printing broker for six hundred thousand. But after that he never joked about snow.

But the house became His Place.

Before that fact became clear to him, Danny had lived in eighteen or nineteen houses in half a dozen years, one fixer-upper after another. Each one might have been the right one. Some he thought really were, especially at first; the split-level in Malibu, the old ranch house in Pacific Palisades. When he bought them he meant to live in them. Forever? Perhaps not forever, but indefinitely. And so he neglected some simple little tricks his accountant taught him later on, and when it became clear to him that none of them was actually the place for Danny Deere he had tax problems. The capital gains were there for any auditor to find, with only the most marginal off-the-books profit to show for his work and time.

That was no good, so Danny spent a week with his accountant and at the end of that time he understood what he had to do.

From then on his life style became more lavish and more mercurial. He didn't buy single old houses to fix up. He bought two at a time. He specialized in properties that had been farms, or family compounds, or whatever eccentric or practical thing would produce two livable structures on a single piece of land. When he found one such he bought it. He moved into the better of the two structures while the other was being rehabbed; then into the second while the first was done; then separated the two by ivy, a trellis, a wall, a hedge—whatever. And he sold two properties for more each than the two together had cost.

The prices went steadily up. There were only 156,361 square miles of land in California, far the bulk of it desert, mountain, buried by freeway or out in the boonies, and for the pitiful few million desirable acres there were ten million people anxious to own a piece of it. Danny's prices went up faster than his competition's, because he was smarter. Every client he showed a house to taught him what clients looked for. A swimming pool. The stranger the shape the better, and, really, it cost very little more to pump concrete into the shape of the state of California, or of Texas, than to make it square. Tennis courts. Even for the people who were obviously decades past the playing of tennis. Privacy. There never was any, really, for most of them, but if you planted enough hedges and put up enough slat fences you could produce the illusion. It all paid off. An acre and a half he bought in January for eighty or ninety thousand dollars, plus the fifty or sixty thousand in real money that he paid for cement and paint and plaster and plantings, plus the wages of the people who put them in, sold in two sections in October for a hundred and fifty thousand each. The big problem became what to do with all his money, but the course in accountancy helped with that, and Danny was growing rich. Of course, he lived free for all that time, in one fixer-upper or another, but that was only the least part of the profits.

And he fell in love—not with a woman (he gave that up after his third wife), but a house.

It was more than a house, it was an avocado plantation, and there were thirty acres of it.

Growing avocados had not been a very good idea, because they didn't grow well in California outside of one little belt far south of Los Angeles. But they didn't grow badly, either. Marginal. That was the word for the avocado farm. It was also, unfortunately, the word for the house that was on it, because it was falling apart. The whole thing had belonged to some movie star of a day even before Danny's own. She had been a smart enough movie star to buy land when she had the money. And when she stopped having the money she began selling the land as she needed to replenish the bank accounts, and this last parcel was all that remained free of the developers. It had been her home, although she hadn't lived in it for twenty years. No one had, and the place was a disaster.

But to Danny it was a *beautiful* ruin, a Coliseum among ruins, the wreckage of a Chartres. Its architecture was silent-movie-star hacienda. It was peeling pink stucco and crumbling wide, tall arches over a veranda of grass uncut between the flagstones. It looked like hell. But it was built for the ages, and under the rot it was sound. It had two swimming pools, not one—an oval jobber just outside the house, with a diving board on the sleeping porch outside the master bedroom for mornings when it was just too much trouble to walk downstairs for a dip, and a deep rubbly one in a fern grotto fifty yards away. Neither had water in them, only tree branches, dried mud and broken bottles. Neither would hold water as they stood. One was cracked, and the other seemed to have been bulldozed open, perhaps to avoid breeding mosquitos.

When Danny first saw it he was alone. The movie star's lawyers had given him the key and instructions to sell, and he had taken the first look by himself. He spent an hour outside, visualizing what the place must have looked like, what it could look like again, before he went in the house; and then he knew it was his own.

The master bath was as big as the bedroom. It had no fixtures on the marble tub—perhaps they had been gold and long since pulled out and sold? But the bath had a long clerestory window, and sitting on the pot you could look out at the tops of the avocado trees and a distant smudge that might have been the Pacific. It had a "rumpus room"—the lawyers' letter actually called it that—in the basement. The billiard table smelled discouragingly of mildew, but the cabinetry was sound. It had a private projection room, of course, and a wine cellar, of course, and a wing for the servants, of course; and it also had a gatehouse, and a rusted but solid wall around the central core of the property, topped with ornamental steel daggers. You could not see the house from the road. Two hours of driving around the area convinced Danny of that; the house could not be seen at all, from anywhere, unless you got past the gatehouse. And that you would not do without getting past the Mexicans who lived there.

There were supposed to be four resident aliens in the family, a momma and a poppa and two kids old enough to help out in the avocado grove. When Danny walked in on them the first time without warning, the new padrone inspecting his tenants, there were three battered vehicles in the gravel space behind the gatehouse, and beds in every room.

The census was right: two adults, exclaiming with pleasure at the sight of him; a boy and a girl, sitting on either end of the home-built seesaw in the yard, not moving the whole time he was there. He was not surprised at the discrepancy between vehicles and human beings. They had opened the gate for him, and that left plenty of time for a dozen others to make themselves invisible in the avocado grove. Danny sat down on the steps of the gatehouse and regarded them seriously. "*Ese,*" he said, "you hear me? If I buy, I will keep you on, perhaps. If I keep you on, I will never enter your house—unless it is to throw you out for not doing the work you are paid to do. Or because you make too much noise, or become in trouble with the law. Perhaps you will have some, ah, friends visiting you. If so, there may be odd jobs for them sometimes, to be paid in cash, so there is no nuisance with the authorities."

Manuel looked at Elisaveta and then back at Danny, and said prayerfully, "We hope very much you will buy the ranch, *señor.*"

And so he had. Not easily. Thirty prime acres came to a lot more money than he could put his hands on at that stage of his life. It took every penny he had, even the bearer bonds in the safe deposit boxes, even the petty cash out of the office till. It was fifteen years back, but even at 1967 prices thirty acres of Los Angeles real estate—however dilapidated, however much on the wrong side of Sunset Boulevard, however anything—meant serious money. He put up the down payment, with the rest on a suicide note. If he didn't make the payments on schedule he lost it all. And then he scurried, selling hard. Six acres to this one, five and a half to this other; the eleven-acre strip along the boulevard to his worst enemy, who happened to think that shopping centers were the big new place to put your money. They all knew he was wriggling on the hook. They priced their offers accordingly. But he knew what he had to have, and he knew what the land was worth. He did not sleep for ninety-six hours, but at the end of that time he had sold twenty-five acres for what the entire parcel had cost him. He didn't make a profit in cash on that deal. His profit was the house.

Danny had ways of making that profit really handsome. He found contractors, good ones, who had their own reasons for preferring to get paid in cash, off the books. For six years every house he fixed up paid a tithe to Rancho Deere. For plastering and painting, for landscape gardening and carpentry, out of every dollar's worth he spent, a nickel or a dime went into his own home. It helped with the taxes on the other houses, no small item, because the profits were getting serious. When you came right down to it, Danny realized with some embarrassment, he could have made a hell of a lot of money even if he'd been strictly honest. Everybody else was. California real estate was generating more millionaires than oil. It didn't even take capital. There were people he knew who had run up a couple thousand dollars on the tables in Vegas and parlayed it into millions; all you had to do was buy, hold for a little while and sell, because the prices were always insanely leaping up. And they didn't have the problem he had, of what to do with the profits he didn't want to display.

On the other hand, they probably hadn't found as intelligent a way of dealing with them as he had.

Nobody pushed the button that raised the gate as Joel turned into the little drive. He turned to frown at Danny, shrugged and blew the horn. "I guess they're out," he said, opening the door.

"You guess they're out. You got a brain I can't believe," Danny snarled. "Come on, get a move on."

Joel ducked his head and hurried to unlock the gate. He jumped back in, pulled the car past it, and then ran back to lower and lock it again while Danny scowled at the house. There should always be someone there; what the hell did they think he kept them around for? But the house was silent. Joel trotted back in and eased the limousine around the gentle curve that led to the house itself.

There was a car in front of it.

There was *never* a car in front of Danny Deere's house unless he specifically invited someone, and that not often, and certainly not when he wasn't home! He began to sputter with anger. Then, as they drew closer, he saw that the car was not empty.

Four men were sitting in it, all looking directly at him with empty, uncaring eyes.

"Oh, my Jesus," Danny said. "Joel, let's get the hell out of here—"

But someone had thought of that. Without seeming to look at what he was doing, the driver of the car backed it around in a gentle curve, blocking the driveway. There was no way past it, and the door nearest the limousine opened and one of the men got out.

Danny rolled up his window and shrank back into the seat. "Joel! See what they want."

The man opened the door and leaned in. "What we want, Mr. Deere," he said, "is to talk to you a little bit. Why don't we go in your house?"

Danny stared at him while his mind ticked through possible alternatives. None appeared. "Say," he said genially, "why don't we all go in my house?" Cracking wise could be a mistake, he thought.

How big a mistake he only realized when the limo's rear door opened and the oldest and ugliest of the men hopped out. He was wearing a pale green outfit that looked like a jogging suit, and made him look like a watermelon. The face was tantalizingly, then frighteningly familiar. Danny knew it well, though he had never seen it except on TV . . . and had had no intention of coming anywhere near it in the flesh.

Buster Boyma.

The mobster stood rocking on the toes of his pale green boots, studying Danny's home as though he owned it and was thinking of selling. Or owned the world. "Oh, God," said Danny, but only under his breath. He scurried to the door and held it, quaking.

Danny had lived close enough to the edge of the law long enough to know what trouble he could be in with the people who had passed the edge. "Sit down, fellows," he said, as forthcomingly as he could manage, but swallowing hard. "Joel! Get these gentlemen something to drink."

Boyma hopped onto the lowest couch and moved the corners of his lips a fraction of an inch—it might almost have been the intention, at least, of a smile. "We don't want anything to drink out of those glasses of yours, Deere," he said, "we only want to talk to you a little bit."

Danny swallowed. "Have I got a problem with you?"

"I don't think you do, Deere. Although you never can tell." He glanced at his nearest colleague, who opened a dispatch case. "You can have this back," he said, as the man handed Danny the collection can that had been taken away from his Hancock Park hustler. It was empty, but the man reached in his pocket and counted out two dollars and forty-five cents in coins and stacked them on the marble coffee table in front of him.

"There wasn't much in it," Boyma said, "but we figure your boy had a bad spot. What do you take in, two or three hundred a day?"

"About that," Danny agreed. "I mean, some days. But it's not really my money—"

The mobster shook his head. "I'm not looking for a partnership right now," he explained, "although you never can tell about that either, when somebody gets some action going in my territory. Actually, I've got other business interests involved here. What I want to know is, is there any chance this is on the level?"

The scales fell from Danny's eyes. "Oh," he said. "Oh! I see what you mean. Well, see, here's the thing. I don't know anything about science, but I felt that the people of Los Angeles had a right— I mean," he amended, as the lip-corners moved minutely down, "I mean, I don't really know. But there's some scientists that probably do, or will, anyway, because they're about to start a whole shmaffis to investigate it, and I have a line into them. One of my associates. Young fellow named Dennis Siroca. Joel! Get Dennis's address for these gentlemen."

Boyma shook his head. "No," he said, "the way we're going to do it is you're going to find out and let us know."

"Oh," Danny said, nodding his head. "Right."

"And you're going to do it pretty fast, Deere, because there's some important interests involved here, isn't that right? You're a pretty interesting fellow. We've been keeping a sort of eye on you for a long time, and I have a lot of confidence that you'll get what we want to know."

"Thanks," Danny said glumly. Then he brightened a little. Twenty years of dealing with construction people had given him a small, private list of useful names for an emergency. "Say, I bet we have a lot of friends in common, now that I think of it. You know Angie Collucci? He's from San Pedro, and Angie and I—"

"Deere," the man said, getting up—as soon as he started to move all three of the others were up ahead of him— "from now on, I'm your friend, isn't that right?"

"Oh, sure!"

Boyma nodded. "You only need one friend," he said wisely. "Of course, you got to make sure he stays friendly. We'll keep in touch."

Danny jumped to the window and watched them get in the car. He pushed the remote button that opened the gate for them, and when they disappeared around the bend in the driveway and the light indicated they had passed the gate he discovered he was sweating. "You want me to get you a Seven-Up or something, Danny?" Joel asked.

"No! Go put the car away. And tell the Mexes they can come out of the bushes now," he added, heading for the bathroom. He had never needed to go so badly.

The invasion of the gangsters into his private home had bothered Danny more than he could handle. It was an act of rape. It was entering into his most private parts. Plenty of tough people came around the office on Sunset Boulevard, some through the front door, most up the back stairs; and all that was the normal course of doing business and Danny Deere dealt with them head to head and never raised a sweat.

But this was his home. It was private. It was *safe*. He didn't even get mail here!

It was not just the property itself that had charmed Danny Deere. It was the marvelous isolation, and the way it was situated. Danny had a lifetime's experience of Los Angeles, with its mud slides and brush fires. The place was exempt from both. The county had taken a slice through one edge of the property, after he subdivided it, for a cemented spillway. If there was flooding above, it would come down the spillway, not down Danny's avocado grove. Behind and above the house was a forty-foot rise, a hummock on the side of the hills; but if there was a mud slide higher it would stop on the far side of that hill, and the hill itself would not slide as long as the avocado grove tied it down with its roots. Fire was always a problem. But there were irrigation sprays for the avocados, and that upper swimming pool was now repaired and always full of water. Power? After his accountant explained the tax advantages of solar, Danny invested in ten thousand square feet of photovoltaics on the roof. There would be power for the pumps.

And all that was part of the total security, the womblike environment, that was Danny's home, that had now been breached.

It was not all psychological. There were very good reasons why Danny wanted the safest, securest, privatest place in the world, and they had to do with money.

When the profits began to get embarrassing Danny had to figure out what to do with them. He could put just so much into the house itself. By the time you had two Jacuzzis you didn't really want a third. He missed the boat on gold and was afraid to take a chance on diamonds. Silver was too bulky. Bearer bonds paid off not much more than inflation, so your money wasn't working for you. Swiss bank accounts paid nominal interest or none at all.

Then he discovered art.

The house had come with a huge wine cellar, a lot bigger than Danny ever needed for wine. But he enlarged it and walled it off with concrete; and there, under his house, air-conditioned and humidity controlled, row on row, there were ashcan moderns and smuggled Russian ikons, kinetic light sculptures by somebody in Ohio, and crude wood carvings from some somebodies in Africa. Danny bought with a lavish hand, and always for cash. At first he hired a UCLA graduate student for expert advice, but she didn't seem to pay off, in more than one way she refused to pay off, and expert advice didn't seem necessary. The art was all getting more valuable anyway. The graduate student had left a legacy of subscriptions to art magazines and, month by month, Danny delighted to see the auction prices going up.

It was a hundred per cent guaranteed investment. The Feds didn't know it existed. No one did. When he decided to sell, he could sell the same way he bought. For cash. Off the books, no records. Until then there was very little that could go wrong. If the artists lived and continued to produce, they often continued to get recognition, and the prices went up. If they died it was even better. Every time an artist died Danny felt a tingle of pleasure: there would be no more works to dilute the value of his holdings. The house could burn to the ground without warming the inside of that concrete vault. Burglars would never find their way in—and anyway, Manuel's relatives were always on patrol among the avocados.

Or almost always. . . . But if anyone less heavy and

well connected than the day's visitors tried anything, the Mexicans would have the sense to call the police, and the black-and-whites would be there before the burglars got past the TV sets and the Tiffany lamps.

There really was only one thing that Danny could imagine damaging his collection, and that was if California really and truly should actually slide to the bottom of the sea.

Well, two things. The other was if he made some really bad enemies.

The tens of thousands of volcanos in the world are classified in three categories: active, dormant, and extinct. It is not clear how real the distinctions are. Mt. St. Helens was a "dormant" volcano until the spring of 1980. Even "extinct" volcanos hold surprises. In Papua, Mt. Lamington was classified as extinct until 1956. Then it erupted and killed three thousand people.

Wednesday, December 23d. 8:00 PM.

Because he still had a job to do, Tib had to fly up to Marin County for two days with the mobile seismological stations monitoring the Hayward and San Andreas faults; it was not a special trip, it was one of his functions to keep them in line. Because it was two days before Christmas, he had to go directly from the airport to the lecture by this "Doctor" Lautermilch. Rainy had some sort of relative in town; Meredith Bradison simply refused to get involved in anything that was not family; Tib was the only one left, if anyone was to hear this probable quack.

The lecture was in an old church not far from Pershing Square, and to Tib's horror it was packed. This madness was spreading! He sat at the back of the room, hoping no one would recognize him. The church hall was incongruously decorated, a great green tree in one corner and flights of gold paper angels across the windows, but there was nothing Christmasy about Dr. Lautermilch's message. He drew on every "psychic" and "seer" from Nostradamus

127

to himself—no, even before Nostradamus, because he actually pulled out a set of measurements of the Great Pyramid at Gizeh to prove that Western civilization was on its last legs.

Duty or no duty, it was more than Tib Sonderman could stand. He left long before Lautermilch was finished and took a taxi to his home. Everyone had gone insane! The Jupes were all over the airport, more of them than of Santa Clauses and a dozen times as visible. In the plane he had been forced to endure fifty minutes' conversation with a young high-school teacher from Oakland, on her way to spend Christmas with her parents in Van Nuys. As soon as she found out he was a geologist, she wanted to be reassured that Los Angeles would last at least until the first of the year, when she would be flying back. And she was a teacher! Presumably an educated woman! Presumably sane!

Tib's mood was not Christmasy as he paid off the cab at the street entrance to his house, and started up the steps to the front door he almost never used.

The lights were on inside the house. Something was wrong.

As soon as he let himself in he was certain. Someone had been there. Bare stretches appeared in the living room bookshelves, where once they had been tightly packed; someone had removed about a quarter of the books. The coffee table with the Moorea shells under its glass top was gone, and two paintings were missing from the walls. Tib didn't think of burglars. His first thought was "ex-wife", and when he entered the kitchen he was not surprised to find the row of copper-bottomed skillets gone from the rack on the wall. He heard voices outside, and knew before he turned to the window what he would see. Wendy was there, Wendy and her new husband, or next husband, or let's-try-it-on lover, or whatever he was at the moment; he could see the shape of his pale green VW van, and then he saw them at the door.

His former wife stopped cold at the door. "Oh, my God, Tib, you scared me. I thought you were off in Puerto Rico or Iceland or something."

"Just San Jose, Wendy. Hello, Don." The young pale man who Wendy had preferred to him was carrying empty cardboard cartons, looking as though he wished he could make them disappear. "I didn't expect to see you here, is all."

Wendy grinned. "Thought we were three thousand safe miles away? Sorry, Tibber. We got to missing California, so we just hopped in the van. We've got a little place in Venice—my God, what they want for rent—but there's nothing in it. So we're just taking some of the stuff I left . . . ?"

"Yes, of course, fine," said Tib, glowering. It was not in any way fine.

Wendy's pale young man cleared his throat. "I hope we're not making a mistake," he offered.

"What kind of mistake?"

"Well, all those Jupiter people in the shopping centers, you know." Wendy was looking at him with bright interest, waiting for academic authority to settle the matter.

Oh, God, Tib thought, you too! He said shortly, "I do not think there is anything specific to fear." And then, driven to be polite, "Please, go right on, I'll stay out of your way. Would you like some coffee?"

Wendy glanced humorously at her young man. "Not your tap-water special, Tibber, but thanks. I've been keeping a list for you of everything we take."

"That's all right. Uh, I didn't know you still had a key—"

"I'll leave it for you when we go. I think this'll be about the last load. We took all the heavy stuff yesterday."

"Fine," he said, although he didn't really think it was fine. When Wendy had taken off for Soho she had left a note saying she didn't want any of her possessions, and over the three years since the end of their marriage Tib had got used to thinking of the coffee table as his own. Not to mention the books. Not to mention— "Yes, that's fine," he said heartily. "Look, I'm going to make some real coffee, so why don't you have a cup?"

He got out of their way and carefully did not watch over his shoulder to see what else was going. They had been divorced for a year and three months now, and separated

129

for nearly two years before that; he had almost forgotten what she looked like, he thought. But not really. He had just forgotten what the two of them looked like as a portrait pair, Tib and Wendy, Wendy and Tib. She was wearing her hair in some way different now, smoother and more severe. The bangs were gone, and it was all pulled back. She had put on some weight, too, he noticed. And wondered what she was noticing about him—pulling in his gut, standing up a little straighter over the stove.

Wendy was twenty-eight years old, nine years less than Tib; perhaps it had been a mistake for him to marry one of his graduate students. Anyway, she seemed to be going in the other direction now. This Don person was surely younger than she. As near as Tib knew, Don Fingle was a wholesale druggist, or pharmaceutical salesman, or something of the sort. Wendy had been a little evasive about that part of it, when she first appeared with Don in tow—when, out of burning curiosity disguised as polite conversation, Tib had asked. But what Don did for a living he did in one place. Wendy had made it clear that that was important. He was not going to be off to Tokyo or Tierra del Fuego to measure earth movements for weeks at a time, leaving her to sit at home.

"Coffee's ready," he called, pulling cups out of the cabinet and discovering that the company set of china was gone. Don and Wendy politely washed their hands after they had moved the last load into the van, and all three sat down for a polite ordeal. It was not easy for any of them, and for Tib, suddenly conscious of the way Wendy smelled, it was more than disconcerting. The scent was arousing. Wendy had always poured on the cologne with a liberal hand, and he had established that as the modality for all women. They covered the weather, agreeing that it was fine that the Santa Ana had stopped; the old mutual acquaintances Tib and Wendy had run into recently; what Tib was doing with the Jupiter Effect; and they managed to deal with them all, as well as finish their coffee, in well under ten minutes.

And then they were out the door. Tib turned away from the door and picked up the cups to put them in the sink, just as Wendy poked her head back in the door. "Oh, Tibber? Somebody put this under our windshield wiper. Thought you might be interested. And Merry Christmas!" She handed him a sheet of pink, printed paper, kissed him quickly and was gone again.

Tib sat down, very conscious of the aura of cologne that hung on his cheek and opened the paper. Its headline was:

SCIENTIFIC PROOF!
Scientists now agree ancient laws of astrology ARE FACT!

At the bottom was the address of a storefront "reader" in Malibu. So the astrologers were getting into the act! It was only what one could have expected, but it did not decrease Tib's growing mood of depression. He crumpled up Madame Lucy's flyer and threw it into the kitchen wastebasket—or threw it in that direction, but tardily discovered the wastebasket was gone, so it landed on the floor next to the sink.

He swore and got up. Might as well see what the looters had carried away! He prowled the upper floor of the house, a task which took very few minutes because there was so little of it. But there was even less than there had been. The bedroom looked quite bare without Wendy's family hand-down dresser and vanity. The soft, fluffy mats were gone from the bathroom floor. The record shelves were nearly empty. All of the schmaltzy nineteenth-century romantics that Wendy doted on were gone, along with the rock albums and the little bit of dance music they had bought for parties they never gave. All that was left was his own few records of Vivaldi and Correlli and Bach, and some of the twentieth century electronic stuff he had tried to interest himself in. But, he saw, it didn't matter much, because the stereo was gone too.

In the middle of their large double bed (count your blessings, he thought—that was a present from her mother; she could have taken the bed, too) was a neatly hand-printed list of the items she and Don had removed, and on it the keys to the door.

And that was all that was left of Wendy Sonderman.

Tib went back to the kitchen and looked at the refrigerator without opening it. It had been his intention to take something out of the freezer for dinner, but he discovered that his appetite was gone—his appetite for eating alone, at least. It was getting late, too. He shrugged and went down to the lower level.

He did not bother to take a census of what was gone. Nearly everything in the basement was unarguably his own, anyway, and if Wendy had found a few pieces to remove their absence was not at once evident. He entered his private room and sat down in front of the computer; might as well do some work.

But that wasn't going to be easy. For some reason the nets were busy and he had to wait for computer time. Twice a minute the little golfball zipped across the page to say LOGON PROCEEDING, but after fifteen minutes of sitting there he had not yet been able to log on, much less get anything done.

And it was getting less interesting all the time.

He wondered what Rainy Keating was doing. Probably there had been some developments in their committee while he was away. He really ought to call her. He picked up the phone and dialed her number, and got a busy signal. He tried again, rehearsing the things he would say to her—"Hello, Rainy, listen, I've been thinking we ought to get together" or, "Hey, Rainy, is anything new?" Or just, "Hello," and see where the conversation led from there.

But an hour later—it was past ten o'clock and the little golfball was still zipping out a LOGON PROCEEDING every thirty seconds—her telephone at last did ring and she was on the phone; and what he said was, "I'm lonesome."

In a typical year the United States eases its balance of payment by exporting about one hundred million tons of grain, for which it receives tens of billions of dollars. It is its largest export item in dollars, though not in volume.

For each ton of grain it exports it also exports two or three tons of topsoil, through erosion, to the Gulf of Mexico.

Wednesday, December 23d. 6:05 PM.

When the door closed behind the latest pair of Feds, Rainy looked at her watch and moaned softly. Where had the day gone? For two weeks her time had been fully taken. If it wasn't interviews for jobs that she was not going to get it was interviews with these opaque-faced people from various branches of government whom she didn't want to see in the first place. And still, now and then, news reporters. Those she could shut off, sometimes, but the Feds were not under her control. What the Russian cosmonaut had said had come up close enough to true. Perhaps you could not call these men in gray suits with American-flag pins in their lapels "secret police", but they were as close as she wanted to come to the real thing. CIA, F.B.I., Military Intelligence, ONI—she had seen them all. It was getting so she hated to answer the telephone, and for Rainy Keating that was nearly a terminal condition. The questions became more sophisticated as the agents grew more practiced. Still, they always came to the same thing: What had she done wrong? And she had no answer!

And, between times, there was the work of the commission.

It had seemed simple enough when she took it on. A few meetings. The development of a protocol. A literature search, and then a simple program to map correlations: under similar conditions in the past: had the predicted events actually occurred? That was the sort of thing you could turn over to a computer, or at least to an assistant.

Well, that hadn't worked out; Tommy Pedigrue had proved surprisingly stubborn about assistants. It was a matter of budgets, he explained. Her honorarium, like Tib's and Meredith Bradison's, was paid out of the private Pedigrue Foundation's money, and there was just so much of that. Computer time, on the other hand, could be run up against the limitless credit of his brother's United States Senate committee. Computer, *si*; payroll, *no*.

No matter, the job still had seemed easy enough. But it refused to get done! Too late she realized they were up against one of the fundamental axioms of the scientific methodology. *It is impossible to prove a negative.* It was not hard to prove that the predicted events *hadn't* happened under similar conjunctions of the planets in the past. But they could find no way to prove that, this time, they *wouldn't*.

And, every day, the pressure was growing to provide an answer. The Jupes were everywhere, with their blacked-out faces and flame-red clothes, and even sensible people were beginning to ask questions. Especially when every crackpot in the western world seemed to be descending on Los Angeles to capitalize on the panic.

"Panic" was perhaps a little too strong a word, Rainy conceded to herself. There was still a lot of skepticism, and plenty of jokes—Johnny Carson's monologue had a dozen new ones every night. But underneath the jokes there was worry.

It was like breaking a mirror. Rational people did not believe in bad luck. But even rational people were more careful with mirrors than with other kinds of glass.

There was another consideration, and a scary one. Rainy herself was beginning to worry.

It had not occurred to her that she was becoming a convert, but that kook, Meredith Bradison's grandson, had noticed it in her before she had seen it in herself. The man seemed always to be hanging around, watching and asking questions, and when he told her he thought she was beginning to take the danger seriously Rainy snapped at him. "I do *not* believe in your Nostradamus, or your Jupiter Effect, or your Edgar Cayce, or the tooth fairy!" Then honesty had made her add, "But I admit I'm beginning to think about what might happen. A lot." It was true. She looked at the foundations of buildings now before she entered them. Like everyone in Los Angeles, Rainy knew perfectly well that the danger of earthquakes existed. Everyone knew that death existed, too. With practice, you learned not to remember that.

But you could not not remember earthquakes when you were spending ten and twenty hours a week with a man who knew every subterranean crack in California by name. The tectonic plates came alive in her mind. Great stiff slabs of grease, floating on cold soup. When they touched, the edges crumpled and crumbled. As she drove around the city she looked up at the hills and imagined them thrust high and toppling, the buildings shaking themselves to rubble. . . .

It was, after all, certain to happen—some day.

Part of Rainy's job was to counteract the cries of wolf from the lunatic fringe. That meant she had to talk to the news media—i.e., to seek out people she was anxious to avoid—and then to try so to steer the discussions that they did not ask her again about her satellite, while trying at the same time not to reveal her own growing disquiet. She left public relations as much as possible to Tib and Meredith Bradison—even better, to Tommy Pedigrue, who blossomed under press attention at any time. But when Tommy was in Washington, and Tib and Meredith were busy at something else, it was up to her. So she had spent all the afternoon explaining simple planetary ballistics to two feature writers. Then the gray men from the federal government had dropped in—"Just one or two questions, Mrs. Keating, to fill in the picture"—and the moment when one of them stopped at the door to wish her a Merry Christmas was the moment when it first became clear to her that the next day was Christmas Eve.

Christmas Eve! And her shopping not done!

So there had been one more bad day for Rainy Keating, out of a long series of bad days. As late as Arecibo she had been right on top of the world, and now she was under all 6595×10^{18} tons of it. She had never felt less Christmasy.

It had been her intention to get rid of the Feds, work out for an hour at the apartment health club, do her hair, go to bed early. That was all out now. She went Christmas shopping instead. It was not arduous; she had only three gifts to buy. A pipe and a bottle of perfume to take to San

Diego for her parents, and one other; and as soon as she had found a nice-looking wallet and glove set and had it gift-wrapped, she got in her Volkswagen and drove to deliver it, in the home that had once been her own and now belonged to her ex-, or anyway almost ex-, husband.

Why the hell am I doing this? she asked herself, reaching out to perform the unfamiliar act of ringing her own front doorbell. She knew the answer. It was better to do this than to do the alternative. She could not forget Tinker for Christmas, because he wouldn't let her forget; if she didn't come here, he would go to her apartment. She had gone to a lot of trouble to prevent that—including bribing the doorman to keep him out, or, more accurately, rebribing the doorman after Tinker's own bribe to let him in. And if she went to him she had the option to leave. "Rainy, love!" he cried at the door, throwing his arms around her and kissing her on the lips. "Merry Christmas! It's marvelous to see you! I wasn't sure you'd come."

She shrugged herself free. "I promised," she said.

"Yes, you did." He closed the door behind her and had the coat off her back before she could say she couldn't stay. "I know I can trust your promise. Money in the bank. You'd never break a—"

"Tinker, God damn it!"

He paused at the hall closet, her trench coat in his hand. His expression went down through the spectrum, from the welcoming joy through apology to self-loathing. "Oh, Rainy," he said humbly. "I'm sorry, but I can't help feeling physically jealous."

"Oh, God, Tinker." But she wasn't really upset. Not any more; the nerve had worn out. "I'm keeping my promise about other men. Just as agreed." Then, quickly, "Listen, I can only stay a moment. I've got to get home and pack—"

"You're going to see your parents? Wonderful. They're such great people, and I've got something for you to take them for me, if you wouldn't mind." He was fluttering around the room as he talked, winding up at the sideboard. "Of course, you'll have some eggnog," he said, setting out the crystal cups. "It won't take a minute, I've just got to get it out of the fridge."

136

She sat down, looking around the room to see what had been changed. Very little had. This exact corner of the couch was exactly where she had sat, night after night, to watch PBS television with Tinker by her side, with the same pillow that fit just properly into the curve of her back and the same remote control for the TV just at her left hand. From the kitchen he called, "I was talking about you in group today. Were your ears burning?"

Oh, God. "How's it going?" she asked out loud.

"Oh," he said, carrying in the crystal punch bowl, "you know. Slow. But there's real progress." He was still a good-looking man, she thought—balding a little, a little too plump, but with a face that had to be called "nice". That was a good word for all of Will Keating. It was strange that she hadn't been able to stand such a nice man. The mannerisms that were objectively most attractive were the ones that got under her skin. That soft, gentle voice—how marvelously, paternally reassuring it had seemed when they were dating. The soft, caring way he looked at her and touched her, how much more adult and suave than the clutching of her age-mates in Griffith Park.

And the things that she had found strange and repellent no longer seemed serious. Tinker Keating was a psychotherapy junkie. Encounter group, bioenergetics, Primal Scream, Rolfing, Transcendental Meditation, orgone energy—all of them; first she had been startled, then it had seemed funny, finally pathetic. He was telling her now about the afternoon's session with his new group. She had turned her ears off, but the reproach in his voice seeped in: the pain he was trying to get rid of was pain that only she could heal. She stood up. "That's marvelous, Tink, but I really have to fly."

He dropped the story in mid-sentence. "But surely you're going to open your present?"

"Not until Christmas, Tink. Santa Claus would be mad."

"At least another cup of eggnog? It's early. . . ."

She couldn't avoid the second cup of eggnog, but she left as soon as she possibly could, his lovingly wrapped gift in her purse. She could feel that it was jewelry, and was glad she had avoided having his eyes on her when she discovered what tenderly thoughtful, madly extravagant bribe he had selected for her this time.

He had selected the furniture for their home, too. Oh, not as a matter of seniority. He had consistently asked her opinions at every step, and listened to what she said. But they both knew his opinions were better. She parked in the lot at her apartment, entered her home and looked it over appraisingly.

After an hour surrounded by Tinker's good taste the furniture she had bought with such pleasure for herself now looked tacky. It was not as good as the pieces she and Tinker had so carefully collected—not counting that it wasn't paid for.

At least there were messages on the answering machine. Three, of course, were from Tinker, all received while she was shopping for his Christmas present. One was from her instrument technician, Margie Bewdren; but when she called back Margie's number didn't answer. That was disturbing, because Margie had never called her at home before. What a drag! Plus the other drags, which was to say the fact that three times the answering machine had given her beeps but no message, which meant that, three times, someone had called but had hung up without speaking. She hated that. She tried to imagine who, or what three whos, it might have been while, every few minutes, while trying to catch up on all the other things she should be doing, she kept trying Margie's number.

Finally the technician answered. Her voice sounded remote and a little vague. "Oh, Rainy. Hi. Listen."

"I'm listening." What was wrong with the woman?

"I hate to bother you, but—well, have you been getting a lot of pressure from the F.B.I.?"

"Have I! You mean they're after you, too?"

"You bet your ass, hon. More all the time. I thought after the first time they'd just file their reports and go away but, jeez, Rainy, they just won't believe I'm giving them all the data. You think they suspect me of something?"

"I guess they suspect both of us, hon. Or maybe what they suspect is the Russians did it and we're too dumb to know it."

"Well, whatever it is, they've been bothering me at work. And I was supposed to go to the Cape for a Skylab payload job and that's been called off—I think they asked my boss to keep me here."

"Tell me all about it," Rainy ordered. "Let's see if they're asking us both the same questions."

It took forty-five minutes of comparing notes to be sure that the pattern was identical. Half the agencies of the federal government had taken an interest in the fate of Newton-8, but after the first few days it had settled down to the pair from the F.B.I. And they were not satisfied. Every interview with Rainy had provided questions to ask Marge; every answer from Marge had sparked a new question for Rainy. By the time Rainy said good-bye to her technician she was no longer scared. She was furious. And the phone rang again almost immediately and it was Tib Sonderman, looking for company at this irregular hour of the night. Rainy told him to come on over before she realized what she was saying; it wasn't so much that she wanted to see him as that she wanted to get him off the line so she could think about this harassment. But by then it was too late. Resentfully she went back to her thoughts and her chores; and then the phone rang again and, of course, it was Tinker. "Did I wake you up, dear?"

"No, Tink but—damn it, it's late!"

"Well, I knew you were awake, because I've been getting a busy signal for the last hour. I just wanted to thank you for this evening—"

"You're welcome, Tinker. Good night, Tinker. Merry Christmas." Civility to an ex-mate could make excessive demands on a person, she thought, and then remembered that she had started to touch up her hair and hadn't finished. She fled to the bathroom. By the time she had dealt with the emergency it was the doorman on the house phone, announcing her guest Tib Sonderman. "Oh, God," she said, "send the son of a bitch up."

Rainy lived in an immense apartment complex, eleven hundred units altogether, perched on the side of a hill. It would have had a fine view of the valley at night if it weren't for the smog, and also if it weren't for the fact that most of the units looked directly into the windows of the units across the court. Tib parked his car in the wrong lot and took a while to find the right building, and then the doorman kept him waiting while he checked with Rainy Keating. Maybe this was a bad idea, he thought; but then the doorman waved him in and he was committed.

As Tib navigated his way to Level B, Apartment Eight, he smelled a dozen varieties of recent cooking in the halls, heard all seven audio channels of TV and a selection of pop, rock, classical and all-news radio stations and got invited to two Christmas parties. The second one, which had spilled over into the hall, was only a few doors from Rainy's apartment. For a moment Tib thought some of the guests were about to follow him in.

So did Rainy, as she opened the door and looked over his shoulder. She let him in quickly and closed the door behind him. "This wasn't such a good idea, Tib," she said, obviously making an effort to be polite. "If I'd been thinking I would have asked for a rain check."

"Have you been having a bad day?"

"Christ! You don't know. Listen, come in and sit down." She pointed to a chair and took one herself, across the room. "I've been having more trouble with the Feds," she said, and told him about the phone conversation with Margie Bewdren.

"That's partly why I wanted to see you—no," he corrected himself, "there is no reason to lie to you. I wanted to see you because, as I said, I was lonesome. But as I was leaving I remembered." He pulled a sheaf of offprints out of his pocket and handed them to her. "My friend Wes Grierson thought you would find these interesting." He hesitated, and then shrugged. "He thought that two weeks ago. But I forgot."

She took the papers from him, glanced at them absently, and then frowned. "Did you look at these things?" she asked.

"Yes, of course. It is not my field. They seem to be about gravitational focusing of starlight by the sun."

"Did you look at the date?"

She was holding the first of the Xeroxes out to him; before the date he noticed the name signed to it—Albert Einstein! And the year was 1936!

It was not like Grierson to play practical jokes, but Tib said uncomfortably, "I apologize if I am wasting your time—"

"Oh, hell, Tib. Sit down. Make us both a drink, will you? Canadian whiskey and ginger ale for me—not too strong." She was speaking absently, her attention on the papers. Sonderman took off his coat, found ice in the freezer, made Rainy a mild highball and himself a plain ginger ale and sat down on the couch, looking around her apartment. Apartment was too strong a word. It was one room, really, and he had a conviction that the couch he was sitting on opened out to become her bed. But it was comfortable looking. Almost all new. At least she had not looted her ex-husband's home!

"Hey, Tib," she said at last, pushing her glasses up over her hair. "I think I know what your friend was talking about. Not the Einstein paper itself; that's pretty out of date, but the later papers—especially the one by this fellow named Von Eshleman at Stanford. What do you know about relativistic physics?"

"Zero," Tib said honestly. "Near enough, anyway. Say zero."

"Well—" she fished in a drawer of the desk for a pencil—"here's the thing. Einstein said that light had mass, you know that much, right? That's the famous experiment of 1919 that confirmed relativity, when the eclipse expedition found that starlight coming around the sun was bent—focused, like a lens—just as he predicted."

"That was a lot earlier than 1936," Tib objected.

"Right, and then Einstein had some afterthoughts. If you're looking past the sun at another star—assuming there's an eclipse or something so the sunlight doesn't drown it all out—then the light gets deflected all around it. The gravitational field of the sun becomes a sort of spherical lens—a telescope. This is the Eshleman formula."

Tib moved to the arm of her chair to peer down at what she was scribbling:

$$I = \tfrac{1}{2} \left[\frac{x^2 + 2}{x \cdot (x^2 + 4)^{1/2}} \pm 1 \right]$$

"I'll take your word for it," he said. "Unless you want to tell me what the Xs and Is are."

Rainy grinned. "I'm taking his word for it, or at least I am until I get back to JPL. But what it comes down to is that the sun focuses millimeter radiation to a point. Radiation from another star—wait a minute." She sketched rapidly again:

"There's your distant star, there's the sun, and there's my poor old Newton! Right at the focal point, in syzygy with the other two bodies!"

"What's 'syzygy'? And which star are you talking about?"

She put down the Flair and stared thoughtfully at the diagram. "Syzygy just means they're in line, and I don't know which star—that's easy enough to check, though. I think it would have to be a fairly bright one, maybe an A- or an F-type star at least. And not too far away. A hundred light-years or so? There aren't really bright ones much closer than that. . . ." She shook her head. "Anyway, at that point in the diagram the radiation is so focused that it's like holding a piece of paper under a magnifying glass. My poor little spaceship would suddenly be right in the middle of a heat ray! Except for one thing, it fits the facts just fine. The shorter the wavelength, the better the focusing. Right under the millimeter microwave is infra-red—heat! So we got some sort of squeal on the radio receiver at the one-millimeter length, and then the heat began to build up and burned out the spaceship! It wouldn't really have to burn. It had those photovoltaic sails—the way it generated part of its energy, from sunlight. A sudden

142

concentrated burst of heat would overload them; they weren't built for it. Only . . ."

She fell silent, staring at the paper.

"Only what?" Tib prompted.

"Only it's in the wrong place! According to Eshleman, the nearest focal point is 550 A.U. out—five hundred and fifty times the distance of the earth from the sun. Way outside the orbit of Pluto. And Newton wasn't anywhere near that far." She brightened. "But, what the hell, maybe Eshleman made a mistake in his arithmetic! Or even if he didn't—"

"He didn't," Tib said. "The offprint's from *Science*. It's been refereed."

"I know that! But even if he didn't, it's at least something to show the Feds. Get them off my back. Maybe get the idea that the Russians did it out of their heads. Tib! This calls for another drink!"

Since Tib was not really sure of his motives in visiting Rainy, it was confusing to him that he felt somehow frustrated. She was friendly enough. But her mind was on her satellite, and she excused herself to spend some time at her desk. Tib turned on the television and browsed through her slim library. Either she was not a reader or she hadn't acquired many books since the separation from her husband. It was not clear in Tib's mind just how recent that event was. Or, for that matter, how real. Half the couples he knew spent half their lives moving out on each other; he and Wendy had been a curiosity in their social circle for having had only one definitive split.

"What's this thing?" he asked, twirling a sort of mobile that stood by the window. It seemed to represent the planets.

"What? Oh, that's a funny thing, Tib. It's an orrery, and it came for me yesterday. I think it's from Meredith Bradison's grandson—anyway, he broke one in Puerto Rico, and I can't think who else would do it. There wasn't any name."

"I wouldn't have thought he had the price of something like this," Tib commented, pushing Jupiter around and watching the other planets spin to keep up.

"Me, too—it's all hand-made. Listen, I'm being a lousy hostess, I know, but this Eshleman thing—".

"That's all right." He was not unhappy that she was concentrating on something other than himself, but he was restless. His wanderings took him into the kitchen. The doors of the cupboard over the sink were ajar; he pulled them a little more so and found what he had expected, a jar of instant coffee. He made the decision that it was less impolite to go ahead and make it than to interrupt her to ask if he might. While the water was boiling he realized what it was that pleased him so about Rainy's apartment. It smelled feminine. It was a scent that Wendy's visit had reminded him to miss.

He brought the coffee to where Rainy was sitting over her desk, cheek on the hand that was supported by the desk, scratching absent-mindedly behind her ear and scribbling slowly.

"Coffee? Hey, what a good idea." she said, coming back to the planet she was on. "This isn't working anyway. The damn satellite has a tangential velocity of about six miles a second, and according to Eshleman the spot of focus is only tens of meters across. So I have to know the exact time when it began to screw-up—not when we received the signals in Arecibo, but when it happened, out there past Saturn—before I can locate the position of the probe precisely enough to take the reciprocal coordinates and identify the star—if there really was a star—if I had a good enough star catalogue, which I don't have here anyway. I thought I could do it on my calculator, but it only goes to eight places—eleven if you coax it, but then I always forget what the first few significant figures were—"

"I'm not understanding a hell of a lot of this," Tib objected mildly.

She grinned, took off her glasses, put down her pencil and turned to face him. "You understand that I'm stuck, right? That's what it comes to. Tomorrow I'll go up to JPL and let the big machines work it all out. And then—wow! Wait'll I tell the Feds!"

Tib leaned toward her, putting his hand on her shoulder. "Why?" he asked.

"Why what?"

"Why should you wait? These agents work around the clock to defend our freedom and complete their paperwork. Why don't you call them and tell them the good news now?"

She looked perplexed for a moment, then sunny. "You have real good ideas sometimes, you know that?" She jumped up, put her glasses back on, and began to rummage through the drawer in the telephone table. Feeling pleased with himself, Tib stood up and stretched. He had been so taken up with the tensions of, what did they call it? dating?, that he had not really looked at her apartment. It was obviously new to her; the furniture all new, the floors skimpily covered with throw rugs, also new. She had impressed her own personality only in patches. Over the couch was a huge, framed monochrome of herself. The slit-bamboo roller curtains were an obvious temporary expedient before investing in drapes, but she had tacked up a variety of badges and buttons on one of them. Keepsakes and souvenirs: he recognized her I.D. badge from the Arecibo meeting, along with one from the ASF, in among political badges and jokes: "We're All from an Unratified Country— ERA" next to "If You Can Read This You're Too Close".

She found what she was looking for and punched out a number. "This is Georgia Raines Keating," she said into the phone, "calling Burnett Harscore. I'm sorry it's so late, but I've just received some important information."

She was evidently enjoying herself. She held her glasses in her hand, gesturing with them to make her points, and her face was far more relaxed and, yes, sexually attractive than he had seen it for some time. "He's not there? Then write down this message. Have you got a pencil? —Oh, silly me, of course, you're taping the whole thing. Well, I believe I have an explanation for the event he has been discussing with me. I'll give you the literature citations; he can look them up and then, if he needs further information, he can call me." She rattled off the Einstein and Eshleman citations from *Science*, and finished, "Of course, I am not sure that the phenomenon described is what actually happened, just that it's a lot more likely than either that I screwed it up or the Russians did. What? Yes, you're welcome. And Merry Christmas."

She hung up and turned, grinning, to Tib. "I didn't even promise to keep it quiet. Maybe I can get a paper out of it!"

She looked so pleased that he put his arms around her and kissed her to celebrate. She kissed him back and then freed herself. "Hey, Tib? I don't want to go to bed with you."

He stroked her hair. "Yes, many women have that attitude," he agreed.

"No, really. I don't mean I don't like you. Listen, I don't want you going bananas like in Arecibo—"

Tib bristled. "I did not go 'bananas'."

"Yes, you did, so let's leave it there, all right? Anyway, it isn't you, honestly, Tib. You're a pretty attractive man, not counting going bananas every now and then. It's Tinker."

"Tinker?"

"My ex-husband," she explained.

He said seriously, "No good person has ever been named Tinker."

Rainy laughed and reached for the coffee cups. "Would you like some more? Come on in the kitchen." As she was heating the water she added reflectively, "It's actually worse than just 'Tinker'. It's from when he was a baby. His mother used to call him 'Little Stinker', and when he got bigger they just cleaned it up a little. But he's really a good person, Tib."

"Yes?"

Her expression was getting stubborn. "I made him this promise," she said, paused, and then shrugged. "He's sort of a sad person sometimes. Very jealous. I don't want to hurt him. So I, uh, I promised him I wouldn't get involved with anybody else here in L.A. Conventions and trips and so on, that's something else, I didn't make any promise about that."

Tib threw his head back and laughed. "That's, excuse me, the stupidest thing I ever heard of."

"Stick it up your nose!" she flared.

"No, let me understand," he persisted. "I had my opportunity in Arecibo, then, and missed it?"

"You had no chance in Arecibo, buster!"

"I mean in a theoretical sense. I am simply trying to understand the rules. That would have been okay, correct? Or also at the ASF, because that was a convention?"

"Now, look! Don't push too hard on this. We didn't sign a treaty, it was simply a kindness for someone I don't want to hurt."

"Yes, of course, but you have interested me in this. I believe I understand the terms of reference now." He thought for a moment, then nodded. "Excuse me," he said, turning back into the living room. She followed him to the archway, staring as he considered the array of badges on the bamboo blind.

"Tib?"

He nodded and selected two. "Yes, these will do," he said. "Here, one badge for you, one for me. The name is wrong on mine, but I will change that." He took a pen from his pocket and crossed her name out, substituting his own. "Fine. Now we are at a convention, all right? We have had a scientific session about your spacecraft, you have delivered your report, and now we are at a room party."

She glared at him, outraged, and then her expression began to clear. "I have to say you've got some cute aspects, Tib Sonderman."

"Oh, yes, sometimes cute," he agreed, "but I am not making you an appeal from cuteness. This is only to comply with the technical requirements of this technical undertaking you have made, and now we can consider this situation on its merits."

"Oh, can we?"

"Yes. And as someone said to me, I believe in Arecibo, though perhaps in different words, if one is through with a marriage one should be through with it."

She looked at him for a moment, shaking her head ruefully. "You strange man, the water's boiling. You're going to make me ruin my teapot."

"I will be glad to turn it off for you, but that is not the point, as I see it. That point is that what I would really like now is not coffee but to make love to you. Please excuse my nervousness. It is because of that that, I know, I am talking too much."

She sighed. "Much too much," she agreed. "Why don't you go turn off the coffee?"

They were both eager; they were both clumsy, and forgiving of each other's clumsiness. Tib Sonderman was not inexperienced with women, but he had run up no Leporello lists; after Wendy left he counted on his fingers all the women he had ever made love to and discovered, to his chagrin, that all ten fingers were not needed.

Nevertheless he had learned a great deal in his sexual experiences. The most interesting discovery was that women were individuals. They were not all the same. They did not say the same things. They did not feel the same or taste the same, and the terrain of each woman's erogenous zones was different from every other; the road maps in the textbooks could not be trusted.

It was astonishing, and greatly pleasurable, and he was eager to learn more. So while he and this newest of his—could the word still be "conquests"? (And "Number seventeen!" crowed the calculator in the back of his mind) —while he and Rainy Keating, that was to say, were making love, Tib was storing data in his retrieval system. This seemed to please her. This other did not. There was never a time when Tib Sonderman's conscious mind was not observing, recording, and analyzing.

Nevertheless they spent themselves gloriously and rolled only inches apart when they were through, their fingers still interlocked. It was not surprising that it had gone so well. Both had been for some time deprived. And as soon as Tib had caught his breath, he propped himself on an elbow and said seriously, "I think it will get better as we go along, my dear Rainy."

She said, "Oh, my God." She freed her hands and reached out to the night table for her glasses in order to inspect this person. "Tib, honey," she said, "look. I just as soon not have the instant analysis, all right?"

"It was all right, then?" he asked.

"It was at least all right," she agreed, peering at him

with warmth and amusement. She stroked his cheek with her finger and touched his shoulder. Her eyes were big and unfocused behind the glasses. "What's that?" she asked.

He shrugged away from her touch and sat up. "Look at the window!" he said. "It's getting light!"

Rainy glanced uninterestedly at the gray, dismal morning. "We got a late start," she said, and sat up beside him. "Are you going to tell me what it is?"

Tib glanced down at the tattoo on his upper arm, just about where most people his age had a vaccination. "The guards at the concentration camp put it there," he said reluctantly.

"Oh, Tib!"

He said slowly, "That is where I was born. In the camp. My father was a Yugoslav partisan, and the Nazis took my mother hostage to force him to surrender. He did not surrender. He was killed in battle. Of course, since my mother was pregnant with me at the time, I also became a hostage."

"Oh, Tib," she said again; there was nothing else she could think of to say.

But his face was relaxed. "It is not that terrible, you know. At least it was not for me. What did I understand of what went on? By the time I was a year old and able to understand, to begin to understand, the war was over. We were at home in Zagreb, with my mother's family. This has been troubling me, Rainy," he added, "that we know so little about each other."

She stretched and yawned, and reached for a robe. "There's time for that, Tib. I have to go to my parents' for Christmas, but when I come back you can take me out somewhere for a taco and you can tell me all about Bulgaria—"

"Yugoslavia!"

"—about Yugoslavia, and I'll tell you about Lehigh County, Pennsylvania."

"You have to drive to San Diego? And I have been keeping you awake all night!"

She grinned. "I should certainly think so, and, listen, don't start apologizing, you hear? You've got some strange ways, dear Tib."

"Yes, so you have told me," he said stiffly.

"Well, you do. And I do have to get dressed. And I suppose you have something you have to do—or had you planned to stay here all through Christmas?"

"Not at all!"

"Aw, come on, Tib, that was a joke."

He said seriously, "I know you joke with me a lot, and I am not always sure when it is at my expense." He hesitated, and then confessed, "I am not at ease with women. I do not know why, but every relationship I enter leaves me with guilt feelings at the end. As early as seventeen, in London, I must tell you—"

"No, you mustn't," she said fondly. "Go home, Tib. *Dear* Tib. But go home."

The supernova in Virgo had completed its contraction and explosion, and by now it was radiating one billion times as much energy as the sun. It was far the brightest object in our galaxy, in itself, but so far away that gas clouds and distance would keep its light ever from reaching the earth. Such events are not rare. On an astronomical scale, even supernovae near the earth are not specially rare; one occurs every one or two hundred million years, on average. They are dangerous. The cosmic rays from the supernova damage the earth's ozone layers. The ozone layers can no longer filter out the destructive ultraviolet from sunlight. All exposed organisms suffer extreme sunburn, cancer, often death. In the last six hundred million years there have been perhaps eight such nearby supernovas. There have also been about eight episodes in which all life on Earth was decimated.

Thursday, December 24th. 10:45 AM.

In the suite of offices belonging to the Pedigrue Foundation, which was in the Pedigrue Tower, located in Pedigrue Center, Tommy Pedigrue had the third best private room. It was not a corner office. It did not have a wet bar, like his father's, or a complete taping and sound system, like his brother's. But it had two windows and a couch, and a door that locked even against his family. It was all right. When the time was ripe he would move to his brother's office, and no doubt his brother's seat in the Senate—whenever his brother made the move to those larger offices on Pennsylvania Avenue in Washington.

He sat at ease behind his desk, and Myrna Licht looked in on him as he was dialing his telephone. "Tib Sonderman isn't answering, Tommy," she reported. "Do you want me to leave a message on his machine?"

"Oh, hell," he said in annoyance and frowned, considering. "Yeah. Tell him to call me—no, wait. Tell him he's booked to appear on the Sunland Saturday television show, and I want him down here two hours before the show for briefings—you know what to tell him," he added quickly, as the phone in his hand came alive. He waved to Myrna and addressed the phone. "Walt? Merry Christmas! This is Tommy Pedigrue, calling for Townsend and my father and all of us. Townie's stuck in Washington, otherwise he'd be calling you himself. . . . No, he won't be able to take part in the tree-lighting ceremony tonight. My father's going to do it for him. But we're hoping we'll all be together tomorrow for Christmas dinner. . . . Thank you, Walt. And the same to you and—" he ran his finger down the list of names—"to Mary Ellen and the boys." He hung up, checked off name number fifteen on his list and put another card into the automatic dialer. As he leaned back he could see the great dark tree at the enter of Pedigrue Plaza. Tonight it would be his father who would make the little speech and press the button that would light it up, but sooner or later. . . . "Hello? Rachel? Yes, this is Tommy Pedigrue," he said, "and we wanted to wish all of you the best of the season—"

It was astonishing how important these little things were. Tommy did them very well. He had begun when he was five. Now he had thirty-five heavyweights on his list for personal greetings. Of course, his brother had fifty, the even heavier political people around the state that he would call from Washington on his WATS line, and, even more of course, his father would be the one to call the dozen and a half big money contributors and old family friends. It was a nice personal touch. Christmas cards were computerized, gifts could be left to Myrna and the girls. But Christmas calls had to come from a member of the family.

It did not, however, require a functioning brain to make them. All the time he was working down the list of VIPs, or Fairly IPs, his eyes were on the couch that he and Myrna had found so many good uses for, and his thoughts were on the evening. Not the early evening—that was compulsory attendance at the tree-lighting. Not the late evening, that was Christmas Eve church services with his family. But the three hours between six and nine, when he would stop by Myrna's flat and give her her Christmas gift, and she would give him her very special gifts in return. She was a good person, Myrna, Tommy thought indulgently. The best thing about her was that she really, seriously did not expect, or even want, to think about marriage.

He finished the list of calls and took a moment to review the other list he kept with him all the time, on paper or in his head. The political list. The bills to be interested in, the constituents to placate, the alliances his brother wanted to make. The performance of every member of their staff— every member of all their various staffs, really. They had half a dozen: personal-political; personal-domestic; Senate committee; Foundation; ad hoc groups. Because the holy tide of Christmas all other did deface today's list was short. There was no sense worrying about political moves just now, because every other senator was making good-fellowship Christmas moves, just like he, and his brother, and all their merry elves.

Time to report. He patted Myrna's bottom as she bent over the paper shredder, whispered a reminder of their date for that night and headed for his father's office.

When he got to the corner suite his father did not acknowledge his presence at first. He was glowering at the newspaper spread out on his desk. The headline said:

PRIME RATE, QUAKE FEAR
DEFLATE L.A. HOME BOOM

"I already read it, Dad," Tommy reported efficiently.

"I read it too, and then I called up the fellow who wrote it," said his father, "and he got it backward. It isn't the interest rate. It's this Jupiter stuff."

"Right, Dad! We're on top of it. I've been kicking ass with those scientists, and we're going to book one of them on the Sunland Saturday program to talk about it."

"Which one? Sonderman? Some radio personality! He talks like a gravedigger."

"He sounds like a scientist, and anyway I'm going to tell him what to say ahead of time."

"Get Townsend on it too," his father ordered, and spun his chair moodily to gaze out the window. It had begun to rain again, but nevertheless there were Jupes at the traffic lights, running out to solicit the drivers of stopped cars. "When I came in this morning," he said, "I took one look at Dave, the elevator starter, and what do you think I saw? He had a streak of black on his forehead. Just like it was Ash Wednesday, for Christ's sake."

"*Dave*? He's been working for us for twenty years!"

"And I told him if he wanted to stay to collect his pension he'd get his face cleaned up. And he's not the only one." He turned to stare at his younger son. "Tommy, you want to lead the people, you've got to stay in front of them. Not much in front. But in front; and, the way it looks to me, on this one the voters are getting away from us."

Earthquakes can sometimes be predicted by measuring sight lines with surveying instruments. It doesn't always work. On October 10, 1980, a geodetic survey team made a morning's worth of measurements near El Asnam, Algeria, and went back to their hotel for a well earned lunch. While they were eating an earthquake measuring 7.2 on the Richter scale shook the building down on them and killed them.

Thursday, December 24th. 4:15 PM.

Dennis Siroca paid his Christmas call on his grandparents, and got what he expected. Two cups of mulled wine, a storebought cashmere scarf for his neck, all the storebought Christmas cookies he could eat, and no information. Meredith Bradison was sweet about it. "You take everything I tell you and use it for those hippies of yours, Dennis, and so I just don't want to tell you anything more."

"I don't use it for anything bad, Grandmerry," he said, nibbling another cookie.

"No, but you use it. No offense. We're going to make a public statement sometime soon, and then I'll tell you anything you want to know. Would you like some more wine?"

His grandfather reached encouragingly for his cup, but Dennis shook his head and got ready to leave. It was time to go—not only because Saunders Robinson was waiting in the car, but because his grandfather's hand was more and more frequently pressing his grandmother's knee. Dennis knew that what they really wanted was to be alone.

"Nothing," he reported to Robinson as he put the car in gear. Robinson shrugged and passed over a joint.

"Long's you're the one that has to tell Danny-boy," he said. It had been at least a week since their pipeline to the Pedigrue committee had produced any results. "You gonna be there for the Christmas party tonight?"

"Might as well. My old lady's still in Florida. I got no other place to go." He took a hit on a fresh cigarette and leaned back, resigning himself to the traffic. Santa Monica Boulevard was bumper to bumper, in spite of the fact that it was raining again. He peered into the cab of a pickup truck next to them at a light, and nudged Robinson. "Hey, see that guy?" The driver was a young man in jeans, and his forehead bore a black smudge. "We're sure getting a lot of people scared," he said.

"Yeah."

Robinson's tone caused Dennis to look at him. "What's the matter, Robby? This is all for real, you know."

"I guess."

"No, really! Never mind this scientific crap. It's in the Zend Avesta and all, and even old Immanuel Velikovsky says the old Greeks knew about it. Like Heraclitus. He told us the earth gets destroyed every ten thousand eight hundred years."

"Not like ten thousand *nine* hundred?"

"What's the matter with you, Robby? I didn't make all this up. In the Patagonian peat bogs there's all this volcanic debris that comes from 9,000 B.C. If you add nine thousand to 1981, what do you get? Close enough, right?"

Robinson didn't answer. After a moment he peered out at the Pedigrue Center Mall, where the great Christmas tree was standing. "Hey, they didn't light it yet. Step on it, will you? Maybe I can take Feef over to see them light the tree."

Dennis swung over to Wilshire, which was almost as bad, then down to the crummier, more dilapidated avenues to the south. Even so, it was slow going. He parked in front of the ashram. Robinson jumped out, collected Afeefah from her chore of stringing popcorn for the tree in the anteroom, and was gone.

There were only a couple of people in the ashram. Most of the troops were ordered to stay out in the malls and shopping centers until the stores closed in the last-minute rush. Two of the shyer, and fatter, girls were in the back room cutting out cardboard models for the parade on New Year's Day, and Buck was dispiritedly hanging ornaments on the tree, getting ready for the children's party that night. The plump little man had been scared out of his mind by the encounter with Boyma's hoods. The next day he turned up with a bulge in his waistband that Robinson diagnosed at once as a .32 automatic. To protect himself if it ever happened again, he insisted; but they had banished him from the ashram for three days, until he promised to leave it at home. "Danny Deere's guy called," he reported. "They'll be here any minute. Didn't say what they wanted."

"Fine," said Dennis heartily, reaching for ornaments. Probably Buck's main trouble was that nobody paid enough attention to him, he thought. Basically he was a good man. "It's going to be a nice party," he predicted. That had been Robinson's idea, to have a party for the kids of the ashram's workers, and it was surprising how many of those youths and young women had a kid, or a niece or nephew, somewhere around. There would be at least a dozen children there. Buck nodded without answering, so Dennis tried a different tack. "Going to be a great parade, too. You got the hearses lined up?"

"I rented six, Dennis. All I could get this far ahead. But they all have those glass sides, like you wanted." The plan was to fill each of the hearses with a model of some celebrated Los Angeles landmark—the Century Plaza, the space ride at Disneyland, the Arco Tower—and drive them through Pasadena on New Year's Day. The mobs for the Tournament of Roses parade would be the best audience they could have, although of course the cops wouldn't give them a permit. Didn't matter. They'd go up the hill to Jet Propulsion Lab or somewhere, and then they'd get into the traffic on the way home.

Buck twisted the wire from the ruby-red glass sphere to the end of a branch and stood back. "You been to see that grandmother of yours?" he asked.

Dennis looked at him more closely. The little man was in a surly mood tonight. He'd been running three days scared and three days angry ever since Boyma's people shook him up, and he seemed to be starting an angry phase again. "You got something against my grandmother?" he asked.

"I'm not talking against your family, but she's a scientist, isn't she? She don't believe in the pralaya."

It was Christmas Eve, after all; might as well be placatory. Especially to Buck, who had been part of the ashram group, not only before it became the property of Jupiter Fulgaris, not only when it was a semi-Zen temple, but when it had been a martial-arts school with overtones of

Tai Chi. He came with the lease. "See," Dennis said reasonably, "scientists aren't the enemy. They just try to find out things. What do they know? The Pedigrue family hire her to dig up all the stuff they can on Jupiter and stuff, and she does it."

"Then what?"

"Well, I guess that's up to the Pedigrues, you know?" The little man looked sullen and unconvinced. Dennis changed the subject. "Did you get soda and candy and all for the party?"

"All I could. Robinson said to wait till the collection cans come in and take the money out of that."

"No, we can't do that; anyway we need it before that."

"Then you'll have to give me some plastic."

Dennis hesitated. He carried as many credit cards as the average jet-setter; they were his lifeline, wherever he might be, because he kept the charges paid. The trouble was, his droogs did not share his responsible attitudes toward credit. To them the cards were wishing lamps, or a painless substitute for shoplifting. He shrugged and took one out of his wallet—one that had a $300 credit limit.

"Okay, be right back," said Buck, and then hesitated at the door. "Dennis? I didn't mean anything against your family."

"That's all right, Buck."

"The fucking politicians like the Pedigrues, they're the real enemy, right?"

"Right, Buck. Buck? You better get along before the stores close."

"Right, Dennis." He moved aside to let Joel de Lawrence in, then scurried off to the deli at the corner.

"Merry Chirstmas, Dennis! Danny's around the corner in the car, and he'd like to see you."

"I don't like to leave the ashram alone—"

"That's all right. I'll keep an eye on things till you get back. He's not in a good mood, Dennis, I wouldn't keep him waiting."

The fact was that, actually, Danny Deere was in as good a mood as he ever got. To start off it was Christmas, and Danny dreaded every Christmas with its bonuses and presents and Christmas parties, all of which he had to pay for; but this year was no worse than any other, and the rest of his life was going nicely. The year-end figures on his real-estate business looked like they were going to be better than ever, even without the Jupiter coup, and that was going fine. True, no one had yet signed one of the yellow-dog sales agreements at fire-sale prices that his lawyer had drawn up. But a couple were coming close, and the scare was growing. He could feel it. He didn't need the occasional hints in newspaper stories to tell him, he could see the signs, in the people wearing smudges of black on their foreheads and the jokes the night-club comics made. It was peaking faster than he had expected. Maybe the time had come to turn the heat up a little? A little more pressure? He had plans made— Inside he was smiling; but of course it didn't pay to let the people who worked for you know it. So when Dennis came slouching around the corner to the darkened limo (why attract attention in this crummy neighborhood by having the lights on?) Danny snapped, "So where're the fucking collection cans?"

Dennis let himself in before he answered. "They're not back yet, Danny. Big night. I'm keeping them out as long as I can."

"Oh, shit, you expect me to make an extra trip? Never mind. I'll send Joel back for them. So what's the score?"

"Well, Danny," Dennis said, settling himself comfortably, "things are going pretty good. We've got hearses for that parade, and the models are almost done. The Christmas party's all set up—"

"I don't give duck shit for your Christmas party! Jesus! I got a Christmas party of my own to go to, everybody's hand out! I can't wait for the whole fucking thing to be over."

"Yeah, well, that's about it. One little problem. Two of the sisters got busted for possession of a controlled substance, and they're in Sybil Brand."

"Tough shit. Merry Christmas to them both."

"Yeah, well, it's only a hundred dollars bail each. That's only ten bucks if we send somebody up there to spring them, so if you don't mind—"

"Hold it, Dennis. Maybe I do mind." Danny sat drumming his fingers, staring off into space, then nodded. "Yeah. They're more good to us in than out, don't you see that? Besides, I wouldn't want them to miss those good jailhouse Christmas dinners."

"I don't actually see why, Danny."

"You don't use your head, that's why. Look. We'll get a protest march going! Let's see." He paused, visualizing the East Los Angeles area where the Sybil Brand Institute for Women stood. "Yeah. We'll start from the freeway exit at Eastern Avenue and march right up the hill. Tomorrow. Right at dark, with candles!"

"I don't know if I can get the people out on Christmas day, Danny."

"You can if you kick ass."

"Yeah, but that's sheriff's country up there. It'll be our asses that get busted."

"So then it's a civil rights thing, all the better! That's county property and us taxpayers own it."

"But the rain'll put the candles out—"

"So light them again. Jesus! Quit making objections, you hear? Now listen, two things. First, I've got you booked on a radio show Saturday afternoon, so you want to get all the people out then, too. My PR woman'll tell you what to do."

"Television? I don't know if I want to be on television."

"You got no choice if you want to stay with me," Danny said reasonably, "so quit bitching. Second thing. You know that big new condo that's going up, Pacific Overview Estates? I want you to keep that on the list every day. At least a couple people there in front of the sales office, handing out leaflets and all that, you got it?"

"Well, sure. If you want. But why there, Danny? It's way out at the end of nowhere—"

"Because I said so. Now," said Danny, "get Joel's ass back here so I can get home. I got another bunch of loafers to hand out Christmas presents to."

Some volcanos erupt with violence. Some merely squeeze out a flow of lava, ash, mud, or gas. Each activity has its own perils. Curiously, the flows of lava are the least likely to kill human beings, although they can cause immense property loss. A lava flow is generally quite slow. It can be diverted by bombing, even by chilling parts of it with firehoses if there is plenty of water. It was possible to walk without harm on the congealed surface of a still-moving lava flow. Ash and mud flows can smother or drown. Gas flows sometimes kill by collecting in caves or cellars.

The eruptions, too, come in several varieties. A pyroclastic fall of ash or tephra is only dangerous to life if there is so much of it that the victims are buried alive. A Plinian eruption is a heavier and much more dangerous pyroclastic fall, sometimes with large boulders hurtling through the air. The most spectacular sort of eruption is the nuee ardente, in which an avalanche of glowing gases and ash rolls down the mountains at hurricane speed. Anyone in the way dies instantly of cadaveric spasm. Even the bodies are boiled away.

Friday, December 25th. Christmas Day. 4:00 PM.

Going to her parents' home for Christmas was good, leaving again was even better. Rainy drove up the freeway feeling as though she had just completed a recurring, weighty task, like cleaning an oven. Christmas was a glitch. The world stopped spinning for a moment—well, for twenty-four hours. But it was a time outside of time, and Rainy was glad the steady roll of the clock had resumed.

She had salvaged something from the long morning. First was the tradition of opening of the Christmas presents. Then the tradition of helping her mother get the turkey into the roaster. Then the tradition of everyone going back to bed for another hour's nap—but that tradition she had skipped in order to work on her report for the Pedigrues; and that had been her excuse for leaving almost as soon as the leftovers were put away and the dishes were in the washer. So she was ready to turn her paper over to Meredith Bradison, and as she turned into the hardstand by the Bradison house she was singing carols to herself. For everybody else Christmas was over. Rainy was just beginning to enjoy it.

Sam Houston Bradison let her in, wished her Merry Christmas and offered her a drink. He was pink and moist, as though he had just shaved. "Merry'll be out in a minute," he said. "Did you have a good Christmas?"

"Yes, fine." He was wearing what Rainy had often heard of but never seen on a live human being: a velvet smoking jacket. Obviously new. Obviously a present. It suited him. He smelled of shaving cologne and toothpaste, a sanitary old gentleman in a good mood. When she refused the drink he made her coffee and brought it to her in Meredith's tiny office, overlooking the beautiful garden and the Christmas tree with its white lights already blinking. He entertained her with scurrilous anecdotes about the Pedigrues until Meredith showed up, apologizing. "You caught me in the shower. Is that your preliminary report? All right, let's trade."

She sat down on a small settee and tucked her feet under her. For the next twenty minutes both were silent as they read each other's study papers. Rainy finished first, and silently got up and went to the kitchen for a refill on the coffee. Meredith's report ran fifteen closely reasoned pages, all neatly supported with citations and footnotes, but there was something troubling about it. When Meredith was ready to talk, Rainy asked, "Why are we interested in all these data from around Korea?"

"Weather comes from the west. I've gone back fifty years, as you can see, with the standard reports, and I've included all the unusual reports I could find since 1510— mostly from whalers and naval ships. Maybe a few pirates." She took off her glasses and gazed at the pile of charts, with their gentle curves and tiny symbols. "Actually it was kind of fun. The last time I paid this kind of attention to the Western Pacific was at the Ninth Pacific Science Congress in Bangkok—and that was a long time ago." A quarter of a century by normal human standards. A full generation. But, for the science of meteorology, back to the Stone Age: before weather satellites, before facsimile, before any of the sophisticated aids that were now the basic tools of every forecaster. Especially before the big number-crunching computers that could take a pilot's report from south of Tahiti and a ground station's synoptic from Truk and deduce a low cell in the very act of being born. At Bangkok two of the meteorologists had been insufferably vain of their acquisition of the first real weather radars. "I was looking for two things," she told Rainy. "One was historical records of exceptional weather to match against earthquakes and volcanic eruptions; there's no real correlation there. The other was the same exceptional weather mapped against planetary positions. I couldn't see anything there either. These mean isopleths here, for instance—"

"You say there's no real correlation?" Rainy interrupted.

"Not that I can find. I draw a blank."

The thing that was troubling Rainy loomed suddenly clear. "And yet," she said, "reading your report, I kind of get the feeling that you're really worried that all this might happen."

Meredith sat back. "It shows, huh?"

"*Are* you?"

The older woman said slowly, "I don't know if I am or not, Rainy. You know, we don't have enough talent for this job. We could use about a dozen more experts; there's all those magnetometer readings from all over the earth's surface. Can you interpret them? I can't. But that geomagnetism surely reflects changes in the ionosphere and magnetosphere—doesn't it? And those are definitely linked with the solar wind, which is to say with the amount of energy the earth receives from the sun. And what about carbon-14 production? Shouldn't we have one of those tree specialists, dendrochronologists, to check that out? And what about—"

"We aren't going to get any of those people, Meredith."

"That's my trouble, Rainy. I can go just so far with my own area of specialization. I can't say any more than that."

She hesitated, sipping her cold coffee. "It's the rabies syndrome," she said.

"Rabies syndrome?"

"A long time ago," Meredith said, "just after Dennis was born, his grandfather and I were hiking in the redwood country, and Sam went off to answer a call of nature. He came running back, with the back of his hand all blood. A squirrel had bitten and scratched him—and there had just been a scare about rabid squirrels. So I washed it out and put a bandage on it, and then we sat down and talked it out. What should we do? We could go right back to Eureka and see a doctor and start the rabies vaccine series—there were a lot of them in those days, very painful and sometimes people died of the vaccine. Or we could do nothing. It all depended on whether the squirrel was rabid. If it was, then there was no choice—Sam had to have the shots, because otherwise he would certainly die within a few weeks, in great pain. But if it wasn't, then obviously we should avoid the shots, because they were also very painful, and might be fatal. It's the same way with Los Angeles, Rainy. Do you have the courage to tell them there's nothing to worry about? I don't."

At the door Meredith peered at the rain. "I think we're getting a Fujiwara effect," she said. "Remember that mess up in the North Pacific on the maps? The Siberian high and the Aleutian low are both unusually deep, and there are two smaller lows circling around and peeling off pieces of themselves—I think we'll be getting these storms for most of a week yet. Give my regards to Tib."

Rainy was halfway to the freeway entrance before she realized what Meredith had said. Actually, Rainy could have sworn she hadn't mentioned Tib's name the whole time she was there! But perhaps that was the giveaway. Rainy didn't mind. Little secrets of that kind were no good if no one could guess them, and the best person in the world to guess them was someone who wouldn't ask questions. Rainy wasn't ready for questions. She hadn't worked out any answer. Of course, Tib was not to be taken seriously—assuming that the word "serious" equated with the word "marriage." Rainy had no intention of taking anyone "seriously" for a good long time yet. Least of all Tib Sonderman. Still, while it lasted—

She grinned to herself and switched the radio on. The Jupes were at it again—some kind of demonstration at the women's jail. She caught a familiar name, and learned that her cosmonaut friend was making quite a hit in Mexico City, finishing up his grand goodwill tour of the Western Hemisphere. There was a rehash of the grand jury investigation of some mobster, and an unusual number of traffic warnings. It looked like Meredith was right about the rain. It was going to go on for a while, and there were reports of creek floodings.

She carried her Christmas gifts up to her apartment and dropped them in a chair while she went to see what the telephone answering machine had for her. Nothing from Tib—well, he hadn't expected that she'd be back so early. Two Merry Christmas wishes from Tinker—of course. And, among the others, a husky, fast-talking voice she did not at first recognize. "Hello, I'm Danny Deere and I want to talk to you. There might be a little something under my Christmas tree if you come over as soon as you get back. Give a call. I'll send my car."

A dirty snowball of frozen gases, a few miles across, crossed the orbit of Neptune. It had begun its fall toward the sun eighty thousand years before. As it grew nearer it picked up speed; when it came a little closer the gases would evaporate, sunlight would reflect from them and it would be visible as a comet. The people who would observe it when it reached the orbit of Earth were already born. By comparison with the mass of a planet, a comet is not very large; the astonomer Babinet called comets "visible nothings". But they are not trivial. A much tinier comet, in Tunguska, Siberia, in 1908, had leveled thousands of square miles of forest. This one would come very close to the earth. How close would depend on the alterations in its orbit imposed by the large planets it would come near, but, for millions of the earth's people, it would be either the most spectacular sight they would ever see, or the last.

Friday, December 25th. Christmas Day. 8:50 PM.

The boss did not like having Manuel and his sons work for the new condominium down the hill, but the boss did not know everything. Today the condo had phoned for help, and so he and Onorio, and Jose, Tomas, and Rafael, had spent two or three profitable hours spreading huge sheets of plastic over the bare ground that would some day be landscaping. It was wet work, in slickers and boots, and Manuel tired of it. When he was out of sight of the maintenance engineer he called his eldest son aside. "You will sign me in when you leave," he ordered, and slogged up the hill, admiring his new boots.

As soon as he was at his door his wife was opening it, her face worried. "The Deere has called for you! I told him you were in the orchards, inspecting for damage from the rain, but he has called three times!"

"I will deal with it," he growled, but he picked up the house phone without waiting to take off his drenched poncho, and Danny Deere came on at once.

"Now, where the fuck you been, Manuel? I got a fucking roof leak! I got water coming in my greenhouse, and what am I supposed to do, climb up there myself?"

"I will attend to it at once, *Señor* Danny."

"You goddam better! Right away at once! And, listen, I got company coming, has Joel showed up at the gate yet?"

"Not yet, *Señor* Danny. I will watch for him."

"You will get your ass up here and get my roof fixed!"

"Of course, *Señor* Danny." Manuel hung up gently and beckoned to his woman, silently waiting. "Run to the condo and tell Tomas to come at once," he ordered. "He must put tar on the roof of the big house."

"He will be very tired, hombre," she ventured.

165

"I, too, am very tired! Run! You may take my poncho," he added generously, slipping it over his head and handing it to her. For a moment he debated going up to the house himself. To work at the condominium was very good business. Not only did they pay in dollar bills, with no Social Security numbers attached, but one could sometimes keep a pair of boots or a few tools. But Danny Deere had made his feelings clear, and it was important to Manuel that his boss be happy with him. He had come to the United States four times to get there once. He did not want, ever again, to have to make that trip. The long walk to the bus, the long bus ride to Sonoita, the ride huddled under tarpaulins in the back of the pickup truck, the crawl through the gap in the barbed wire and the last long hike to Pia Oik—success!—and then, at once, failure! In Phoenix the agents of the Border Patrol ambushed them, and then there was another bus ride back to Nogales and it all to do over again.

It was only on the fourth try that he comprehended that he must not trust his guides and smugglers any further. He jumped off the truck outside the town and, miraculously, managed to hitch a ride to California and a job.

Even to remember it frightened him. Those night walks! Two of the youngest men always patrolled ahead with great sticks, for the purpose of killing the rattlesnakes that came out to forage in the cool desert night. And the money! At every point, every person's hand was out. The truck drivers. The guides. The farmhands who hid them overnight. The vendors of sandwiches and tacos and Cokes who fed them along the way—at five times the prices in the stores they did not dare enter. But there was no choice, for there were no jobs in the Sierra Madre. You either gave your hoarded pesos to some black-jacketed wise fellow from Sinaloa, or you starved.

But, once you had a job picking in the citrus groves, what wealth you could send back to Aguatarde! Enough to bring a wife, and then the children. Enough to bring in a couple of nephews and a cousin or two, to pay you back with great interest for the favor. Enough, finally, to make your way to Los Angeles itself.

And then to fall in with such a man as Danny Deere—what fortune!

Of course, the Deere was not a good man. What boss was? But Danny Deere's kind of badness exactly fit the needs of Manuel and his brood. So when his nephew Tomas came trotting up to learn what he must do Manuel dispatched him immediately with a bucket of tar to the roof of the big house; and when the limo came up the drive Manuel did not trust to electric controls. He himself rushed out into the rain to open the gate. He bowed, but not so low that he did not catch a glimpse of the young woman in the back seat, looking about her in wonder and pleasure. Manuel shrugged and returned to the house. It had not been a bad *Navidad* for himself; why should *Señor* Danny not enjoy his holiday as well?

Rainy had never been poor, but she had never before been in a car that had a private stereo, a private television set, a chauffeur who looked like John Houseman—and, she discovered when the chauffeur invited her to make herself a drink, a private bar stocked with fresh ice cubes. She leaned back with a Seven-Up she didn't really want, staring out the window at the rain as though she lived this way all the time. She was sure she was fooling no one, but there was no one to see.

If the car was grand, the house was awesome. Danny Deere must have been warned from the gatehouse, because he was out under the pillared porch roof waiting for her when the car arrived, and came bareheaded out into the rain to open the door for her. "Thank you for coming out on Christmas," he said, taking her elbow. She could not reconcile this person with the bumptious clown who had trampled past her at the ASF meeting. "I bet you score a lot of women this way," she said.

He grinned. "All I ever want, doll." And then to the chauffeur, "All right, Joel, now get lost."

That was more like it. "I bet you lose a lot *that* way," she said as she let him help her off with her raincoat.

"What way is that, doll?"

"Talking to that nice old man like that."

"Who, *Joel*?" He stopped and stared at her for a moment, as though she had said something so inane and inappropriate that he was embarrassed for her. Then he shook his head and pointed to the couch. "He's got no bitch," Danny said reasonably, moving to the bar. "He used to be my producer, you know that? And what you don't know is, I'm paying him more now than he made then."

"Really?"

"Yes, *really*. Scotch or bourbon?"

"Nothing. Maybe a bourbon and ginger, but weak. Of course," she said, "there's been a lot of inflation since then."

Danny grinned. "Work on it a while, doll," he invited. "You're sure to come up with a reason why I'm screwing him by paying him forty-five thousand a year." He mixed the drinks triumphantly. There was no reason to spoil the story by mentioning what happened to the money after Joel got it. Nearly seventeen thousand went to the IRS; three hundred dollars a week, in cash, came kicked back to Danny Deere personally. But that still left the old man with almost fifteen thousand a year to put in the bank, because what did he have to spend money on here? And a title as vice president and marketing consultant, so it could all be deducted from the business expense. With his back between Rainy and the bar, Danny Deere put a double shot in her drink and carried it over to her. "I didn't bring you here to talk about his troubles anyway," he said. "I got a problem."

She tasted the drink and shuddered. "You know, I suspected that."

"And you're just the doll that can solve it for me. It makes a difference to me what you people are going to decide."

He sat down, oppressively close to her on the big couch. "What people is 'you people', Mr. Deere?"

"You know goddam well. You and old lady Bradison and the hunkie and Townie Pedigrue's kid brother."

She reached to set the drink down, edging away in the process. It was really a very seductive couch, in a most handsome room. She was itching to get up and look at the paintings on the walls and see the view in the courtyard— no, not a courtyard! It was all glassed in! "Well," she said,

"I guess everybody's worried about earthquakes around here."

"No, doll," he said patiently, "I don't mean whether L.A.'s going to go down with the turds, I mean whether you people are going to *say* it will. That's what matters to me."

"I'm sorry, Mr. Deere, but I really can't release information before—"

"Fine, 'cause that's not what I want. I don't just want to know what you're going to say, I want to tell you what it is. I want you to say it's practically going to be the end of the fucking world, and I want you to say it so it's *scary*."

He moved closer to her and she flared, "Back away, friend! My God! Do you know what you're asking?"

He shrugged and withdrew the hand that was touching her thigh. "Don't bullshit me, doll," he said mildly. "You're not some kind of priest. You got no holy duty involved here."

"No, but I've got a *job*. And that job is to find out the truth, as well as I can, and report it. This committee isn't some Academy Awards jury you can rig, it's a determination of fact."

"So's a court trial, doll," he observed.

She was caught off stride. "What?"

"So's a court trial, and that don't stop the lawyers from trying to bend the facts their way. Holy shit, doll, the reason you're doing this is you people all disagree on the facts, right? So are you telling me there's no room for arguing? Specially if I, like, retain you?"

"What?" She was repeating herself and knew it.

"I said, if I retain you. Like five thousand dollars. Cash."

She stared at him, and then got up and headed for the wet bar. It was the first time she had ever been offered a bribe. She tipped half the whiskey into the sink and replaced it with tap water, but even after taking a sip her reflexes failed her. She didn't know how to react. Indignation sounded appropriate; but she didn't feel indignant, only stunned.

"I'll give you five thousand dollars," Danny repeated from the couch. "Come on back and sit down, doll, while I explain it to you. I want you to tell the world the big Q is coming to come, and it's easy for you. You got the swing vote. The hunkie's going to vote no, and old lady Bradison's going to vote yes."

She was shaken. "How do you know that?"

"I know," he said patiently. "So you swing it. If it really bothers your conscience you can wait a while—sixty days anyway; no less than that. Then you can say, oh, wow, you just turned up this new evidence and you're changing your mind. And you come out with this." He pulled an envelope out of the pocket of his leisure suit and pushed it across the coffee table to her. "Off the books. You don't declare it. Just have a good time with it, and Merry Christmas."

He stood up and took the drink from her hand. "Don't make up your mind right now," he said genially. "And while you're thinking it over, let me show you my house."

The big question in Rainy Keating's mind was, Why was she doing this? Why was she letting this man offer her a *bribe*, and then give her the two-dollar tour of his *house*, for God's sake, like some rich uncle from Waukegan? Not to mention his hands, because every time she went through a door, or turned to look at a painting, he was helpfully touching her. She didn't even like him. He was shorter than she, though Rainy was not a tall woman. He was by no means a nice man or a kind one. Not to mention the fact that at the moment her big interest was seeing just where this thing with Tib Sonderman was going to go.

Still, the tour was interesting—no, fascinating! She had never been in a home like this. The paintings were on every wall, and they were every style and school she had ever heard of. The silver service on the dining room sideboard was lustrous sterling. The pool table in the game room, the one-armed bandits that stood along the wall, each with a fire-bucket of quarters next to it; the stereo speakers in every room, the deep-pile rugs, the sculpted plaster ceilings—it was what she had imagined Hugh Hefner's pad to be like. Or Louis the Fourteenth's. Danny saved the best for the last, of course, and of course that was his bedroom. It did not have its own bathroom. It had its own bath *suite*, three connecting rooms: one with toilet and washstand, one with a vast shower and a marble tub, one with a ten-foot Jacuzzi. The bedroom itself was almost bare—he demonstrated the concealed closets and dressing tables in the walls—with the bed, circular, to be sure, on a pedestal in the middle of the room. She resolutely stayed in the doorway. "How come no mirrors on the ceiling?" she asked.

"That would be gauche, doll. Nobody ever said Danny Deere was gauche. Of course," he added, taking her shoulder to guide her to the French doors, "if you don't like it inside, we could always go out on the nice soft grass outside."

"It's raining outside."

"It never rains on my outside, doll." He pressed a switch, and the same enclosed atrium she had seen from the living room was visible again. As promised, the glass roof kept it dry; but Danny gave a sudden shout of rage. "Son of a bitch, you get your kicks peeping into my bedroom? Get out of there! Vamoose!" The man of the roof, who had been gazing at them in open-mouthed fascination, almost dropped his bucket of tar as he scrambled down.

"Sorry about that, doll," said Danny. "Well? What about it?"

Rainy laughed out loud. For the first time since she entered on Danny Deere's turf, she felt in command of the situation. "What about which?" she asked.

"Either way, doll. I give you my word. Either way, you truly will not regret it."

She shook her head ruefully. "I guess I'll never know," she said. "It's time for me to go home now."

Danny saw her off, the envelope still in his hand—you never could tell, sometimes they changed their mind at the last minute. Not this time. He watched the limo snake down the road, glowered at the skeleton of the condo outlined against Los Angeles's red sky glow and then, for perhaps the three thousandth time in his life, closed the door, made himself a drink and turned the stereo on loud to put some life into his empty house.

With Dizzy Gillespie blowing from all four corners of

the room, Danny pushed aside the big Emshwiller and spun the combination on the safe behind it. He riffled through the banded twenty-dollar bills, dropped the envelope on top of several others and picked up the three-by-five index card on the bottom shelf. It bore cryptic rows of letters, as though someone had been playing write-it-down Scrabble; Danny wrote the letters TSSS under the last line and added the total in his mind.

That was one of the ways in which Danny amused himself when no one was around: by keeping his records in code. He had two codes, each based on a ten-letter phrase, one for the office and one for no one but himself. He had begun the system when a bright secretary had taught it to him, years ago. You selected a ten-letter word or phrase—Danny had picked out "FILM STAR, HE"—and assigned a digit to each letter:

$$
\begin{array}{cc}
F & 1 \\
I & 2 \\
L & 3 \\
M & 4 \\
S & 5 \\
T & 6 \\
A & 7 \\
R & 8 \\
H & 9 \\
E & 0 \\
\end{array}
$$

Then it was simple to record all your private notes on asking prices and real prices and rock-bottom prices in code. So every associate on his staff could write that a house whose asking price was $850,000 but whose owners needed the sale badly enough to let it go for $615,000 in a pinch was an RSE/TFS—you didn't have to write down the final thousands—and no customer would be able to peek over anyone's shoulder.

But Danny also had a private code that no one else knew, not even Joel, for the "off the books" money in the safe and the safe-deposit boxes and what looked like an unopened box of Kleenex in his private bathroom. The code phrase for that was "FUCK THE IRS". According to the card, the living room safe at the moment held IERTS in cash, which was to say $87,950.

Which was not enough. Or too much. Not enough to cover his ass if some of the buy offers he was making got taken up; too much to be sitting there idle and eroding every day with inflation. Of course, there was more in all the other places, and even in the legitimate accounts of Danny Deere Enterprises, Inc.; but all of it was not enough.

Danny roamed restlessly into his playroom and switched on the projection TV without looking at it. There were too many problems. He had not expected money to be one of them. Not with all his assets! But when you came right down to it, what good did they do him right now? He could sell some stock; but he had gone to a lot of trouble to conceal ownership of most of his securities. He could mortgage his house—there was a million dollars there, easily enough—but that meant declaring its real value. Another trail blazed for the IRS. Besides, there was a softness in the mortgage market right now. Maybe it was his own doing; maybe he had scared off some investors.

There remained the contents of the wine cellar in the basement, none of which were wine.

Danny switched off the television and went down the stairs. The gentle purr of the air conditioning greeted him as he opened the door. He switched on the daylight fluorescents that were the closest thing you could ever get to actual sunlight indoors.

This was the treasure room. This was where the real stuff was. He ran his fingers over the canvas-covered stretchers in their racks and lifted the little labels on a couple of the paintings. USS. FTTS. There was even one at KERSS, nearly fifty thousand dollars. He had paid out in actual cash nearly two million dollars over the years, and they were easily worth twice that now. Probably much more, if he sold them carefully, in the right places, a few at a time.

But if he had to get cash in a hurry, he might not have time. He especially might not have time to cover his traces well enough to keep the tax snoops at bay.

He sat down in a red leather Barcalounger at the end of

173

the main aisle, gazing unseeingly at the line of racks.

There was one place where, Danny was sure, he could always get money. As much as he needed. The interest would be ridiculous, and the penalties for slow payment severe.

But maybe. . . .

Tidal waves have nothing to do with tides, for which reason they are properly called "tsunamis". Perhaps the tallest tsunami ever reported (although somewhat ambiguously) by an eyewitness took place in Alaska when it was still a Russian colony, on August 7th, 1788. According to I. Veniaminov it was a wall of water three hundred feet high. Much higher ones have been inferred from wave and water marks on cliffs and mountains, particularly in the western Mediterranean, where one apparently reached a fifth of a mile.

Saturday, December 26th. 11:00 AM.

The quadrille of the elements had begun a new figure. Fire gave place to Water, while Earth and Air responded. There were no more brush fires, but there had been warnings of mud slides. No more gasping for breath in the Santa Ana, but a dank chill that even Tib's car windows did not keep out. And none of this affected Tib Sonderman's spirits in the least, because he was thinking about Rainy Keating. It was pleasurable thinking. It made him feel impatient with the car and careless of the rain; it made him want to get out and walk or run or, actually, he admitted to himself, to make love.

Over the years Tib had had a fair number of lovers. Nothing at all, really, compared to the scores some of the twenty-year-olds on his surveying teams bragged about. But still, not a few. Rainy was something special. She was a lot younger, relative to Tib, than any woman before her. She was also the only one who happened to be a scientist. Tib had had chances with female scientists, and some of them very attractive. But on all those field trips he had stayed away from his colleagues. It was only common sense. You did not invite that sort of trouble. But it was also true that Tib had a romantic view of marriage. He was never untrue to Wendy when she couldn't possibly catch him at it.

So any new woman was a major event in Tib's life, Rainy more than any recent other. New airs and graces, unfamiliar tastes and textures. And a trained mind! Pillow talk with Rainy Keating added a whole unexperienced dimension.

There was also the fact that his loins ached to invade her again.

It was only the vibration of the car, he told himself severely, and leaned forward to thrust a cassette into his tape deck. It was not music; it was a recording of a recent session at the New York Academy of Sciences. He had not been able to attend, and it would be many months before the papers appeared anywhere. By the time he reached the neighborhood of Pedigrue Center he had absorbed three reports on theories of earthquake prediction, ranging from measurements of radon gas emission to the behavior of barnyard animals. But out of it he had learned nothing new, only something quite old: there were no reliable ways to predict earthquakes.

They were at it again. The young people in flame-red shirts and blackened faces crossed Santa Monica Boulevard at the traffic light, their faces streaked from the rain and the makeup smudging their collars. There were more than there had been at the ASF meeting, and better organized by far. They had become a whole hell of a lot more professional. No one in the cars stopped at the light, no pedestrian, no person at the windows of the buildings nearby missed them. *LET the world know . . . it's OVER*. The chant was backed by sticks on a drum-rim, with a double boom on "over". Shaking his head, Tib pulled into the down-ramp for the underground garage, surrendered the car to an attendant, and entered the Pedigrue Mall.

Los Angeles, which could not manage to build a subway

in its silty soil, had nevertheless found ways to put up fifty-story skyscrapers and dig catacombs beneath them. The Pedigrue Mall did not look like a catacomb. It looked like the corridors of some very large hotel, lined with shops and restaurants. It seemed to go on forever, on three underground levels. Tib had been in the mall before, but not often enough to help him find his way. It took twenty minutes of turning corners and taking escalators, past the smells of Mexican food and Chinese food and frying eggs and pizzas, to find the radio station. He identified it at last by the rows of benches in front of its plate-glass window. What was being broadcast at the moment seemed to be a cooking demonstration, but there were still nearly ninety minutes to go before air time; and, satisfied, Tib took the elevator to the offices of the Pedigrue Foundation. Most of the desks were empty—Christmas weekend, after all. But Tib had no trouble finding the conference room where the briefing was to take place. He simply followed the shrill sound of Tommy Pedigrue's voice.

He was surprised to see how many people were present. The first one he noticed was Rainy Keating, her expression troubled but managing a wink to Tib as he entered; but Meredith was there, and the senator and the old man Pedigrue in his wheelchair, Tommy, of course, bullying Rainy Keating about something, Myrna Licht dutifully taking notes at the foot of the oval table. Tommy glanced up at Tib without interrupting what he was saying. "You should have reported it at *once*. Not the next morning. Right away!"

Rainy shrugged. "I didn't know what to think. I thought of calling you. Then I thought of calling Tib, but he wasn't home. So this morning I went over to see Meredith, and we talked it over and came down here."

"Excuse me," said Tib, taking his seat, "but what are we talking about?"

"A bribe attempt!" said Tommy angrily. "Tell him, Rainy."

"Well," she said, "last night I got a call from Danny Deere—" She reported it like a paper at a scientific congress. Tommy listened to the repetition with a scowl on

176

his face, drumming his fingers on the conference table. He didn't give Tib a chance to comment.

"So what I've been saying," he took up, "is that Rainy shouldn't have waited—"

His father looked up from the sheaf of papers in his hand. "We know what you've been saying, Tommy," he said. "That's not what we're here for, though."

"But, Dad—"

"This Danny Deere needs looking over, that's agreed. Townie? What about the Senate Banking and Finance Committee?"

The senator stirred. "Maybe so, Dad. I'll give Harris a call and see if they want to look into it. And I'll check it out with the state attorney general, too."

"That's fine," said his father. "Now let's get back to business. We've got a show to do, and I have to tell you I'm not satisfied with these preliminary reports of yours I've been reading. They're all yes and no and on the other hand maybe, and there's not a statement in them a man can get his teeth into. I see by the account books that the foundation has laid out fifty-three thousand dollars so far, and that's not a lot to get for fifty-three thousand dollars."

"That's the way science is, Mr. Pedigrue," said Meredith Bradison.

"Yes, Mrs. Bradison, that's right, but as you know that's not the way politics is. So we're going to make a little change in this show today. I'm going to ask my son Thompson to sit in along with you, Dr. Sonderman. You're free to say anything you like about science, of course, but I'm going to ask that my son give any concluding remarks. Especially about recommendations for action."

Tommy scowled. "I don't know about that, Dad. Is the station going to let me just walk in on their program like that?"

"That station is our tenant for the next nine years, Tommy, so don't worry about what they'll let us do. Dr. Bradison, I've been informed that your grandson is also going to be on the program. Do you want to join us?"

"Heavens, no!" said Meredith. "It sounds like there's going to be a whole circus parade there anyway. I don't want to make it worse."

"Then, with your permission, let's go over what we're going to say. I see in your report some remarks about a 'Palmdale bulge', Dr. Sonderman. Would you mind telling me what that is, exactly?"

An astronomy major at UCLA was studying in a text on cosmology. The prevailing theory, she discovered, was that all the elements heavier than helium were formed in supernova explosions. When her date came for her she was preoccupied with a nagging thought that took several hours to come to the surface. They were eating Big Macs when it came clear. She put down the french fries and stared around her. The aluminum and steel in the table, the carbon and nitrogen in the hamburger meat, the calcium and phosphorus in her body, the silicon in the rock of the earth itself—they had all come from the same place. Except for the hydrogen that made up the water in her tissues, every atom of her body had once dwelt in the core of an immense exploding star.

Saturday, December 26th. 1:40 PM.

Being in the studio was like being in an aquarium. There were five of them scattered around the doughnut-shaped table, fish circling a vacuum, while outside the tourists gaped. Dennis Siroca took his seat between the host and somebody named Jeremy Lautermilch and gazed around with interest. He had never been in a broadcasting studio before. He examined everything: the microphones at each place, the complicated button board at the place of honor where Stephen Talltree flipped irritably through his notes on commercials and promos, the two engineers balancing coffee mugs on their control boards behind the double glass windows. Counting off from Talltree, the host, at the twelve o'clock position, there was himself; then Lautermilch, then Thompson Pedigrue, then the geophysicist Tibor Sonderman, then an empty seat, and finally a black woman in a lavender sari and turban. Her name was Mrs. Rugby, and before sitting down she had left her business card at every place:

Mrs. Rugby
World Renowned Psychic
Reader & Advisor
This religious holy woman can with the help of God
remove bad influences and guide you through peril.
Located in a refined neighborhood.

The card was not going over very well with Tib Sonderman. He was glancing incredulously from it to the woman, who had folded her hands on her forty-four inch bosom and had closed her eyes in meditation. Dennis grinned to himself. It was a good thing there was an empty seat between them.

Outside, on the audience benches, there were no empty seats. After they had circled Pedigrue Center twice the Jupes had marched solemnly down through the mall to the studio, and occupied every vacant seat. Before long the seats that hadn't been vacant were mostly vacated; civilians did not like sitting next to a young man or woman with charcoal smeared on his face. They liked even less the smell of wet sheep that the Jupes were giving out, because every one of them had been drenched on the way in. So had Dennis, of course, and of course the studio was air-conditioned down to the misery level. He shivered and looked invitingly at the coffee of the engineers. He decided he was wrong; being here wasn't like being inside an aquarium, it was like being inside the frozen-food cases at a supermarket.

Stephen Talltree picked up his phone and whispered into it, scowled, snarled something, hung up, thumbed through his papers, whispered once more into the phone and then raised his hands, eyes on the engineer. When the engineer pointed a finger at him, Talltree began speaking at once. There was no trace of the frantic irritation of a moment before as he said, "Good afternoon, friends of the Southland. This is Stephen Talltree with you again, and today we've got with us some very interesting friends from the Southland who are going to tell us about the World's First Myst-O-Rama, which is coming up next week, and then we've got a couple of other guests who are going to explain what's going to happen to Los Angeles when all the planets come into conjunction—right after these messages."

After the first twenty minutes Dennis was no longer aware of being cold and damp, but he was not in any sense comfortable. The whole thing was a bummer! These people were not interested in acquiring wisdom, they were each one of them trying to promote some buck-hustle or defend some establishment position. The overall vibrations were terrible. During the first commercial break Tib Sonderman was whispering fiercely to the Pedigrue person, and as soon as they were on the air he spoke up. "I was not aware that this discussion would include so-called psychics and astrologers," he declared stiffly. "I would like to make it clear that I am a scientist, not a mystic or a faith healer, and I can see no mutual ground for discussion with these people."

And then, of course, it all hit the fan. Sonderman could've thought a long time without thinking of anything to say that would unify the table against him as well as that. The lady tarot reader opened her eyes and fixed them on him with the look of a basilisk. The host was steaming; not because of what Sonderman had said, who cared what any of the dummies he had for guests ever said? But because he had spoken out of turn. Tommy Pedigrue was furious because he had the political sense to see that Sonderman had made the others furious. And that young fellow with the horn-rimmed glasses, Lautermilch, was angry enough to pretend to be only amused. "I have to apologize for my fellow scientist, Steve," he said easily, "but, although a lot of scientists are coming to realize there is a lot of validity in the so-called occult sciences, you can see that there are others who haven't reached that point yet. In *The Tao of Physics*, for instance, there's an interesting anecdote—" And, wow, Sonderman was steaming over being called a "fellow scientist" by Lautermilch. What a mess. Dennis wished he were out in the bleachers with the rest of the bunch. He felt deeply depressed. Although, looking at the expressions on his comrades outside, they didn't look real happy, either. Sanders was trying to keep two of the girls from sneaking off to the McDonald's, Buck was in the first row, his face squeezed up in a grimace of thorough dislike— it was hard to tell at what, Buck had been so antsy lately. Only Afeefah, sitting primly next to her father's empty seat with a lighted candle balanced carefully on her two hands, seemed at ease.

He came back to reality. "—what?"

The host was looking at him. "I said, we haven't heard anything from you yet, Mr. Siroca."

"Oh," said Dennis. "Well— I don't know much about geology or any of that, but all anybody has to do is open his eyes to see that there's a pralaya due. I mean, it's in the Zend Avesta and all."

"What was that word you used, 'pralaya'? What's a pralaya?" Talltree asked.

"Uh, well, there's been four pralayas so far, and each time the world gets destroyed. If you go by Heraclitus, we're probably about due for the next one," Dennis explained.

"Heraclitus? The Greek? Are you telling me that Heraclitus read the Zend Avesta or whatever it was?"

"Oh, man," said Dennis, sorry for him, "what difference does that make? All those old sages tapped the same sources of wisdom. We're going to get it, Mr. Talltree, there's just no doubt of it."

The woman psychic all but reached over and patted his head. "You see," she cackled, "out of the mouths of babes and all! I just go by the word of God, personally. 'For then shall be Great Tribulation, such as was not since the beginning of the world to this time, no, nor ever shall be!' That's Matthew 24:21, and what could be clearer? There's gonna be the worst time ever—you just read your Second Timothy and your First and Second Thessalonians, and you'll see. All you *sci*-entists with your *sci*-ence's gonna be cast down into the Lake of Fire—that's Revelations, and that's good enough for me!"

"Actually," said Jeremy Lautermilch, nodding in agreement, "as a scientist I see no obstacle in accepting the revealed Word—"

"Thank you, Dr. Lautermilch, and I'm sure our listeners are going to want to hear more about that," the host cut in, nodding to the engineers. "And you'll be talking about that very subject at the Myst-O-Rama on Wednesday night, won't you?, but right now we have to take care of some business. . . ."

Somehow Dennis got through the hour, wishing every minute of it that it was over, sneaking out every time there was a commercial break to mellow up with a couple of quick hits in the men's room. But it didn't get better. It got worse. Just at the end Tommy Pedigrue showed the stuff he was made of, hogging the camera to say, "Of course, our scientific panel has not yet made its findings public. But certainly we don't want our good people of California panicked by irresponsible rumors. So let's all cool it until we have some *facts*." He sat back, beaming. And as he had learned how to use the medium and had kept his eyes on the clock, there was no time for anyone else to get a last word in; Talltree gave his final credits and close, and they were off the air.

And not a moment too soon. Dennis was the first one out of the door, almost colliding with Pedigrue's girl friend, Myrna, as she went to congratulate him on his performance. The Jupes rose to go, all but Buck, who sat grimly staring at the emptying studio. "Come on, Buck," said Dennis. "Let's go home. Saun? What'd you think, did it sound all right?"

Saunders Robinson finished blowing out his daughter's candle and took her arm. "Well, Dennis," he said, "I'll tell you. Like you didn't have no chance to do no better, you understand what I'm saying, so it wasn't so bad, you know?"

"Yeah," said Dennis dispiritedly. "I was afraid of that. Let's get the troops out of here—Buck? Where the hell'd Buck go?"

Robinson looked up. "He's going into the studio. You, Buck, what you doing? Come on—" He stopped and his eyes got round. "Oh, sweet holy Jesus," he said softly.

Dennis turned around, and there was Buck, not going into the studio exactly, no, but heading toward the door with something in his hand. And out of the door Tommy Pedigrue was coming, leaning to listen to what his girl was saying in his ear, and he glanced idly at Buck coming toward him, and saw what Buck had in his hand; and he ducked aside—behind the girl—and Buck's hand followed, and the little gun popped, not very loud. The girl gasped a long exhalation as bright blood began to slide down the pale blue front of her blouse, and she fell to the ground, leaving Tommy Pedigrue shieldless behind her, staring at Buck with the eyes of a trapped fox.

THE STORM

The rain had spread all up and down the coast. In Marin County, north of San Francisco, gusts made the roads slippery and the visibility poor, and five teenagers in a Toyota failed to navigate a curve.

Just off the road was a nine-foot boulder with a curious history. It was not related to any of the rock formations near it. Long ago it had been part of the California subduction zone, had been dragged twenty miles down into the earth, churned about, squeezed, and abraded. Then, over millions of years, it rose slowly back to the surface, in time to receive the full force of the car at seventy miles an hour. The flaming wreckage scorched it, but with nothing like the heat it had already endured. More than enough, though, to char the five teenagers to indistinguishable pods of ash.

Saturday, December 26th. 8:15 PM.

Since he was a Pedigrue, the police gave him every care. Lieutenant Kwiatkowski took his statement in the lieutenant's own office, sitting at the lieutenant's own desk. There was a thick motel tumbler of good Scotch on one side of him and a plastic airlines cup of hot coffee on the other, and two of the family's lawyers were sitting by the wall listening to every word. It didn't take long.

It would, actually, have taken quite a lot longer if the lieutenant had not hurried it along so. He was not impolite. Not to a Pedigrue. Just anxious to get the bare facts, and not much else. The curious thing was that Tommy could remember every detail, the color of Myrna's blood on his cream linen jacket, the expression of the murderer, the absolute hush for a second after the flat smack of the pistol shot. He had been supercool, Tommy had, receiving every vibration. He still was. He noted the muddy trickle of rain at the corner of the lieutenant's window, the lock on the telephone dial, the American flag lapel pin on the blouse of the woman sergeant who was taking it all down. He sipped absently from either the Scotch or the coffee at random, taking time to be sure he got every particular exactly right. Even so the whole thing was over in fifteen minutes. The lawyer on the right came over close to him. "We'll stay with you for the identification, of course," he whispered, but Tommy shook his head. "You're sure? As you wish, Thompson, but please remember you're in shock. Please simply say nothing at all, to anyone. Certainly you should not volunteer anything about the young lady's, ah, personal life."

Tommy waved him away, and then the lieutenant, too, courteously left him alone in the office—"to rest"—for no more than twenty minutes before they went over to the medical examiner's place for the really bad part.

But even the bad part was made as nearly painless as it could be. They had put Myrna's body on one of those rolling trolleys. It was in a little room by itself, none of those file-drawers of corpses you see on television. None of that smell of faint decay you imagined. No smell at all, and no sound. And no movement. The sheet was pulled back below her chin and her eyes had been closed. And the identification was only a formality anyway. "That's her," Tommy said, and was allowed to go. The lieutenant supplied a cop and a police car to drive Tommy wherever he wanted to go.

But there wasn't enough gas in the tank to take him where he wanted to go. Tahiti, maybe. The Gobi desert. The South Pole. Somewhere where no one knew him, and where he didn't have to speak to anyone.

On the other hand, he *wanted* to talk. The policeman was trying to be polite, but he had a little transistor radio going besides the regular police calls. It was almost all weather. There was a flash flood watch for all coastal and mountain areas, water was pouring over the spillways of the San Gabriel dam, traffic was blocked off on Topanga

Canyon. "Bad storm," Tommy observed. "Sorry to take you out in it."

"That's all right, Mr. Pedigrue," the cop said, slowing down and observing with professional interest the flares and the slickered cops waving them around a three-car pileup.

"I guess you get used to this kind of thing," Tommy said, staring. If there were any mutilated bodies he couldn't see them. "It was quite a shock to me, though. And a real tragedy. She was a beautiful woman, Myrna."

He stopped himself then. He was being unnaturally talkative, and knew it, and knew that some of the things that were trembling in the back of his throat to be said were in bad taste. But he wasn't embarrassed; he was rather proud of himself for taking it so well. Still, who knew who this cop might talk to? "They've got the man that did it, anyway," he observed, and the policeman reluctantly switched off the transistor radio to humor this important person. Yes, the perpetrator was under arrest. He hadn't been charged yet, but there wasn't any doubt. He was crazy, sure. He'd been assigned a public defender at his request—he wasn't *that* crazy. He was probably being interrogated right now. It was not clear whether any of the other witnesses would be charged as accomplices, but some of them were still being questioned too. Not just about the shooting. Most of them disappeared long before the police arrived, but half a dozen had hung on, and the officers had found a little of pills and joints all over the floor, among the benches. So there was the narcotics angle, too. And, oh, sure, Mr. Pedigrue, most of them had records. Nothing really heavy. The tall black one had two felony convictions and had done time. One of the women had an active parole violation, but what it looked like to the cop, it was just another nut case. Like all those other nuts, you know? Squeaky Fromm and Sirhan Sirhan and Lee Harvey Oswald . . . although, if you wanted the cop's opinion, that wasn't just a nut. No, sir. There were some pretty high-up people involved in that, stonewalling every investigation, and we probably wouldn't really *ever* get the truth on that one. You dig into those high-level politicians and you find they're just as goddam— At that point the policeman was happy to turn into the driveway of the Pedigrue estate, because he had just remembered who he was talking to. He put the floodlight on the door, and watched Tommy Pedigrue run through the rain until he was out of sight. If he had any wondering to do about his passenger it had to be deferred, because as soon as he had signed on again he had his orders. There was a man reported in trouble in Malibu Creek. It was going to be a long night and a wet one.

Tommy told the housekeeper he had to change out of his wet clothes and would see his father in the morning. She didn't question the fact that he was going right to sleep. She obviously didn't believe it, either, but that was not important. Tommy skinned out of the soggy linen jacket and realized that the dirty chocolate-bar smudge over the pocket was, actually, still Myrna's blood. He hurled it into the bathroom hamper and found a robe to wrap around his shivering body.

Maybe it had been a mistake to come here instead of going to his own home, but he didn't want to face his own home that night. This room was comfortable—this suite, rather—actually, this part of the children's suite that he had shared with his brother until Townsend went off to prep school and then into the world. His own closets were almost bare, so he wandered into Townsend's old room to find slippers and socks. His brother's room had been kept in strict tradition, with his Yale banner on the wall and his half-dozen Apollo blazer patches stitched to the bedspread and the one real basketball trophy be had ever won by the window. Tommy's own room was bare; he had cleaned it all out. But what remained, because it was not only a souvenir of his own childhood but Towny's as well, was the common playroom between, with its cupboards of rainy-day puzzles and games and its still marvelous HO model-train layout. Tommy had tried to get the train for his own kids, but Townsend would not hear of it; and then, of course, when Tommy's marriage came apart there didn't seem to be any point.

The housekeeper knocked. "I thought you might be hungry, Mr. Tom," she said, wheeling in—what? A *gurney*? No. A cart with hot plates, sandwiches under a napkin, a pot of baked beans. "Your father's coming up to see you," she said as she retired. But she didn't have to. Tommy could hear the slow tiny elevator, and then the whine of his father's chair.

"You handled this very well, Tommy," he said.

Although Tommy was standing up at the dinner cart and his father sitting in the wheelchair, the old man dominated the scene. Not unusual; he always had. "Thanks, Dad," Tommy said gratefully.

"Has the woman got a family?"

"Myrna. Yes, there are some people back east. She had a husband, too, but they've been separated for a couple of years."

"I don't want trouble with her family," his father remarked.

"Her name is Myrna Licht, Dad."

The old man studied him for a moment. "You've had a very difficult day," he announced, explaining to himself his son's small resistance. "We're going to have to clean all this up. All of it, Tommy. I've arranged an investigation of this Danny Deere's connection with those crackpots—privately. And I want a full report, complete with conclusions and recommendations, from those scientists of yours Monday morning."

Tommy had been filling a plate with baked beans and cole slaw; he put it down to express himself better. "I don't think that's possible, Dad!"

"Make it possible."

"You know how scientists are. They say they haven't completed their research yet. They don't have enough information—"

If his father had still had a foot, he would have stamped it. "Damn it, Tommy. For a million years people have been having to make decisions without knowing all the facts. That's the nature of the beast. That's what politics is all about. If they can't do it, we'll get somebody from the foundation to whip it together."

191

Tommy hesitated a moment, then resumed filling his plate. "I guess you're right, Dad."

"We'll talk about it in the morning." The old man spun his chair around to leave, then paused. "It's good to have you home for a night," he said.

"It was the weather, Dad. Half the canyon roads were closed because of the storm."

His father nodded. "Thank God. The rain'll be making the headlines, not you and your women."

Tommy ate half of what was on his plate, but he wasn't really hungry. He wasn't sleepy, either; the adrenaline was still charging his veins. He made himself a drink and went into the playroom.

The playroom was a good size, twelve feet by eighteen, or almost. One loop of the model train layout climbed up the side walls and completely circumnavigated the room; other loops were on folding shelves that completed the circle of track around the engineer's post. Tommy checked the controller to make sure everything was still connected, then let down the arms. The tracks still joined perfectly. From the marshalling yard he selected a Santa Fe hog pulling four Pullmans and a club car and sent it creeping across the bridge, then up the long grade to make the circuit of the room at molding level. Tommy had always enjoyed his toys. He had always owned a great many of them. Still did, although, as he had just discovered, some of his present toys bled on him when they were destroyed. He watched the string creep along the shelf of track absently, contemplating a thought he had been fleeing from. The bullet that broke the Myrna-toy, of course, had not been intended for her. It could have been himself, not Myrna, who was right now lying in the medical examiner's file drawer. By rights it should have been. By rights his life at this moment should be over.

On Mount Palomar an astronomer left the darkroom to peer out at the sky. His budget of observing time had been rained out for six consecutive nights. Now, shivering in the mile-high air, he saw Jupiter and Saturn glowing through a break in the clouds, and wondered if the cluster of galaxies he was concerned with would show up yet that night. It didn't much matter. He wasn't going anywhere. Down below the clouds, rain was still soaking the Pauna valley. Little creeks like Frey and Agua Tibia ran a quarter mile wide, and the roads were under water.

Sunday, December 27th. 1:30 PM.

Danny Deere didn't own a pair of boots, but Maria had insisted on lending him her husband's. Or nephew's, or son's; at any rate, he was dressed for the weather. Joel took no chances, however. He was out of the car and at the door, with an umbrella over Danny's head while he escorted him to the door. "You sure you want to do this, Danny?" he chattered. "It's no day for a drive in the country."

Danny didn't answer, except to tell him to get the umbrella out of his face. It wasn't doing any good; the wind was as bad as the rain, and the drops came horizontally into his eyes and down the collar of his trench coat. Danny jumped into the car and began removing as much as he could of the rain gear while Joel ran around and started down the driveway.

Joel was watching him in the mirror. "He didn't seem like that bad a kid, Danny," he offered. "Uptight, sure. Messed up. But I never figured him for a killer."

"Watch the road!" Danny ordered, drumming his fingers on the armrest. He glowered at the condo as they turned into the freeway. It didn't look any better in the rain. The great crane hung idly over the near side of the building, two loops of cables swinging beneath it in the wind. There were no windows in the building yet, and the scaffolding that ran up one side showed just how far the work had got. Too far. It wasn't going to go away.

"Would you like me to turn on a little heat?" Joel inquired.

"Will you shut up?" Danny demanded, but his heart

193

wasn't in it. He leaned back and closed his eyes, hoping Joel would think he was asleep. He wished he were. He didn't want to listen to the radio, because the part that wasn't about the lousy weather was about the lousy fink, Buck. He especially didn't want to think, because everything he thought was even lousier.

The trouble with pretending to sleep was that you sometimes went ahead and did it. Danny roused slightly as the car turned off the Hollywood Freeway and began to move carefully through the drenched, almost empty city streets. But be didn't come fully awake till he felt Joel slam on the brakes and cry, "My God, Danny, look at that!"

"What? What?" Danny barked, but then he saw. They were slowing down as they approached the ashram, and it was a mess! Shards of glass spangled the sidewalk. The sign over it had been pulled down and swayed crazily in the wind. The black man, Robinson, was boarding up the shattered windows while a little girl in a poncho too big for her was handing him nails.

"Somebody really had himself a time," Joel marveled, pressing the button that rolled the side window down as he slid in toward the curb. Danny jumped up.

"Close that goddam window! Keep going. Don't stop! Right on by, you hear me?" He cowered down out of sight, but it wasn't necessary. The little girl looked at him with absent curiosity, but her father's attention was firmly focused on the boards he was nailing.

"You don't want to stop, Danny? I thought you said you wanted to talk to—"

"Will you for God's sake keep going?" He lifted his head and peered back. From a distance the damage looked even worse than it had close up. He tried to tell himself that the storm had done it, but he knew better.

"Go where, Danny?"

"Just keep driving! Let me think a minute." God, how rotten everything had gotten, and how fast!

For the first time in years, Danny wished he had someone to talk to. *Really talk*. Joel wouldn't do, nor his lawyer, nor any of the women he scored in that big elevated bed when the mood moved him. None of the people he knew would do, because they were all wimps; what he needed was a friend, and he didn't have one.

The thing was, he had made some mistakes. Maybe a lot of mistakes. Maybe the worst of them was tipping his hand to that Keating woman. But who knew there was going to be a shooting? If it hadn't been for that— There was no point in thinking in that direction; it had happened, and the shit had hit the fan. There was a time to cut your losses, and it was getting close to that time.

"I could just keep on driving like you said, Danny," Joel called, "but the driving's pretty hairy. Why don't I just park for a while?"

"Park, park!" Danny barked. "What do I care if you park? Just shut up, will you?" He looked around. They were on Wilshire, in the middle of the Miracle Mile, and there were very few cars in sight in the driving rain. Danny realized it wasn't just the weather; my God, it's still Christmas weekend! He wrenched his thoughts back. Cut your losses. How? He had a little time, he realized; this Christmas stuff wasn't a bad thing, because no business was being done anywhere. If the scam was irreparably damaged it would be a day or two before it could be felt. And a lot could be done in a day.

If you had the cash.

"Joel," he yelled. "Head for the freeway."

"Sure thing, Danny. Are we going home?"

"No, we're not going home! Just shut up a minute." He was thumbing through his private address book for a number he had never really intended to use. "Yeah, okay, here it is. Out Brentwood way. And move it, you hear me?"

The security was everything that Danny's own pretended to be and was not. The gate across the driveway had the same voice communications and electric lock as his own. It also had more. It had a closed-circuit television system— no, it had two of them! Two separate cameras! One peered inside the car while the other swiveled down to check the license number. A voice said something, and Danny gave his name to the air.

There was no answer, but after a moment the gate slid into its housing to let them in. Watching everything, it was not lost on Danny that four rows of tire spikes retracted themselves into metal plates on the roadway at the same time. Now, that was *security*. You could break through the gate, maybe. But you couldn't get much farther.

But what a house! Danny wrinkled his nose at the simple ranch house that appeared at the bend in the driveway—a two-bedroomer, one fifty, one seventy-five tops. It wasn't until he was inside the building that he realized this could not be Boyma's home. A place for admitting visitors, maybe, especially visitors Boyma didn't specially want. No doubt the place where Boyma actually lived lay farther within the estate, and no doubt Danny Deere was never going to see it.

No one frisked him, but the man who let him into the living room did a good job of looking him over. He was kept waiting for twenty minutes, then admitted to what had obviously been built as one of the bedrooms and was now Boyma's office. The mobster was behind a desk, but not sitting down; he was standing, seesawing up and down on his toes, his hands clasped behind him. "You saved me a trip, Deere," he said approvingly. "That's nice, for a friend."

"You were coming to see me?" Danny wet his lips. "Oh, about my source into that committee? Well, that one dried up, but I, uh, I'm working on a new one. What I came for, I want to borrow some money."

"Oh, you want money?" Boyma nodded, playing with the zipper of his maroon jogging suit. "How much?"

"A lot, Mr. Boyma," Danny said. His lips were very dry and he looked longingly at the wet bar at the side of the room. "Maybe as much as half a million dollars." It was easier to say than he expected it to be, but still—half a million dollars! He had never thought of asking anybody for that kind of money before.

"You got big ideas," Boyma said, letting go of his zipper. "You know what that would cost you? I got to go for ten points, you see."

"Ten per cent a *week*?" Danny yelped.

"It's inflation, Deere. You heard of inflation. I could put the money in the bank and get what we used to get on the street. Not counting you're a bad risk. First there's your guys shooting women—"

"No, Jesus, really, Mr. Boyma! I had nothing to do with that!"

"—then there's this other thing. I wanted to be friend-ly, Deere, but look what my friends found in that joint of yours." He opened a drawer and passed over a white flyer, letter-size paper, with a picture of the very condo-minium that blighted Danny's life every morning he looked out the window.

"Jesus, Mr. Boyma, I didn't know that was yours," he said, rubbing his throat.

"Nice little circular, right? But the units haven't been moving the way they ought to be, and what I found in that place of yours was this one. Somebody stole like two hundred of them and fixed them up, see?"

He passed over another, identical circular, but someone had mimeographed over it in green ink. It was now an underwater scene. Green fishes were swimming in and out of the upper stories, and wavy green lines overhead told the story. Across the bottom, in the same blurred green ink, a legend read: *Don't you know IT'S OVER?*

"I didn't know you were in it," Danny said desperately.

"Oh, yeah, I'm in it. I'm in it twenty-six million dollars worth, Deere."

"I'm sorry. Look! I'll go right down to the ashram now and tell them to lay off—"

"You won't have to do that, Deere, because I already had my boys put them out of business. No. You can forget about them. What we're talking about now is you. You're going to quit depressing the real-estate market. It isn't good for business, Deere, and it isn't good for you personally."

When natural gas is found with oil in remote parts, it is often flared off in immense, permanent flames. The only way to save the energy is to freeze the gas to -260° F. and ship it as Liquid Natural Gas, or LNG, to where it can be used. The first LNG plant was built in Cleveland, Ohio, and in 1944 the storage tanks turned brittle from the extreme cold. They cracked. The liquid gas spread quickly into gutters, sewers and cellars. Eventually it reached a flame. The firestorm that followed cremated 128 people and incinerated three hundred acres of the city of Cleveland. The present LNG plants are very much better constructed than that in 1944. They are also very much larger.

Sunday, December 27th. 7:00 PM.

It was not only gritty, grimy weather, it was a gritty and grimy world, and how suddenly it had become that way! Rainy Keating pushed the vacuum cleaner over the rug, with one eye on the window, and sometimes one eye on the telephone, and her thoughts grimier and grittier than anything else around. It was over an hour since Tib had called to say that he was coming over. She wished he would get there. It was not a reasonable wish, because she only had to look out the window to see what was keeping him. But she wished. Failing that, she wished the phone would ring, even if it was only Tinker. But not even Tinker had called her that evening.

Rainy hadn't known Myrna Licht at all, really. Not as a human being, anyway. Only as a subject for offhand gossip, like any other of Tommy Pedigrue's girls. And then, when the shooting happened, she had been much too astonished to feel anything for the young woman whose life had been terminated. It was like any prime-time cop show. It was not a thing that happened to real people. It was a TV series, full of uniformed police and plainclothes detectives and ambulance orderlies and all sorts of stock characters from the casting offices. There had been no sense of personal involvement. Certainly none of fear—though the murderer obviously was not going to give any further trouble, with that black man sitting on him.

Nevertheless she was feeling this sense of loss, and it

was not the loss of Myrna, it was the loss of a kind of innocence. And not just her own. Los Angeles was an itchy sort of city at best, too big to be a community, too sprawling to unite on any ground except the common contempt for everyone who had not had the wit to move there. It was itchier than ever now. Not terror. Not even belief, in spite of the hundreds of people you saw walking around with smudges of black on their foreheads, copying the Jupes. They were not really believing, just displaying that itchy, resentful concern. Rainy put the vacuum cleaner away and began to fill the mister for her plants, wishing Tib would get there so she could talk to him about it.

When the doorbell rang she was more astonished than pleased; how had he got past the doorman?

But it wasn't Tib. "Good evening, Mrs. Keating," said the taller of the F.B.I. men, "may we come in?"

He didn't wait for an answer, just brushed past; of course, they hadn't let any doorman deflect them from the swift completion of their appointed rounds! "Come in," she said to their backs. "You know, I was kind of hoping I was through with you guys."

"Not just yet, Mrs. Keating," the short one smiled, shaking off his raincoat on the rug she had just vacuumed.

"You could have called first."

"No, we couldn't, because your phone's out. And we do have a few questions."

"Didn't you get my message? I passed on the citations about the Einstein effect—"

"Yes, you told us that," he nodded, "but you haven't told us about your relationship with a Soviet national, one Lev Mihailovitch." He reached out without looking, and the taller one put a gray-bound folder in his hand.

Rainy sat down, feeling more baffled than ever. "The cosmonaut, sure. I met him once."

The F.B.I. man looked at her quizzically, then referred to the folder. "At least once, yes," he agreed. "You were in his company for approximately three hours here in Los Angeles, at which time you are reported to have discussed what you termed 'secret police' matters with him."

"Oh, my God, what nonsense! We had a few drinks."

199

The agent turned over a sheet, then nodded. "Yes, quite a few," he confirmed. "Furthermore, he has telephoned you on a number of occasions within the past few days."

"Absolutely not! No, that's all wrong, believe me."

"I'm afraid we have information that it is so, Mrs. Keating." The agent took out a Kleenex and wiped his nose before reading from the list. "Let me see. Three times on the twenty-third of December. Then at nineteen hundred hours on the twenty-fourth and several times on the twenty-fifth."

"Now, that's absolutely untrue," Rainy argued. "You've made some dumb mistake. I wasn't even home most of that time!"

The agent waited patiently, looking at her. "Oh," she said, "wait a minute." She remembered the infuriating messageless beeps on her answering machine. "I suppose it's possible that he may have tried to call my *number*, but I wasn't there so he hung up."

"Or alternatively," said the agent, "when he finally found you in he went to an outside phone to make his call, in order to defeat any, ah, monitoring of his own telephone in the hotel in Mexico City."

"Is that where he was? I didn't know—well, maybe I did, but anyway I certainly didn't speak to him!" She took a breath, and then anger broke through. "And how dare you tap my telephone! That's against the law!"

The agent regarded her frostily. He glanced at his colleague, and then said, "If you feel your civil rights have been compromised you have the right to make a complaint to the supervising agent. The number of our Los Angeles office is two seven two, six one, six one. Alternatively, under the Freedom of Information Act—"

"Oh, shove your Freedom of Information Act!" She was angry at herself as much as at the F.B.I. man, even angrier at the whole grimy world. "Listen. If Mihailovitch called me, I didn't know it. I haven't seen him or spoken to him since the ASF meeting, and I don't expect to, ever. Do you have any other questions before I throw you out of my house?"

Her cheeks were flushed, and behind the huge glasses her eyes were misting with anger. The F.B.I. man studied her for a moment before he glanced at his colleague. They exchanged a little smile; they had seen this sort of display many times before.

He put his raincoat back on. "If we do," he said, "we'll certainly come back to ask them. And do have a Happy New Year."

There had been many times in Tibor Sonderman's life when he had not known what to do next. Not surprising, in someone who had become an orphan at ten in Yugoslavia, desperate for an education and a place in the world in a country that was seeking both for itself. But he had always known what to do in order to find out what to do next. You study, you ask questions, you read what other people have written on the subject. Now he had not even that knowledge. He was stuck in dead center.

He was dithering. Upstairs to fill a cup of instant coffee from the kitchen sink; into his bedroom to glower at the rain; back down behind the fake bookshelves to sit before his computer and wonder what commands to give it. It was maddening. It was maddening in the literal sense, that the thought crossed his mind that he was going mad. He did not know what he wanted.

He ordered up the latest series of reports from the center for the study of transient phenomena—aurora sightings, a red tide, an ultra-violet nova in the constellation Ursa Minor—and when he had them did not know what he wanted with them. He stared at the neat typing on the CRT, uncomfortably aware that this logged-on time was costing money. Not his money, to be sure, since he was charging it all to Pedigrue's committee. But to charge it to the taxpayer was even worse. . . . Although you could argue that, he thought, because it was simply diverting tax money to a useful scientific purpose, i.e., subsidizing the database people, at no cost to himself . . .

He swore out loud. That was exactly the sort of meandering substitute for thought he had been guilty of all day! He should have given it all up and gone off to Rainy's when she called. Or he should have told her that the weather was simply too bad for driving and there would certainly be no cabs; either one, but what he had done had been to postpone decision by telling her he would come over later.

Firmly he picked up the telephone and dialed her number, to tell her that, after all, he would not be over.

But even that definite act was denied him. There was no answer, only a weird quavering signal. Perhaps her phone was out of order because of the storm.

He groaned, turned off his computer, turned off most of the lights, struggled into his raincoat and left the house. Now he had no choice but to go, and he would be seriously late.

He would be *very* late, he discovered, driving along the rainswept streets toward the main avenues, because the storm was even worse than he had expected. Tib disliked driving and did it as seldom as he could; in moments of self candor he conceded that his preference for public transportation had almost as much to do with his driving skill as with his morality. With his little car skittish on the slippery streets and buffeted by the winds, Tib felt wholly inept, and not merely as a driver.

The difficulty with being a geologist was that, although a great deal was known about the structure of the Earth, not much of it seemed useful in predicting events. Plenty of instrumentation was deployed. Delicate strain gauges measured the forces between the sides of geological faults. Theodolites and lasers gauged the almost invisible tilting of the ground as it humped itself up into wide domes . . . and then, sometimes, relaxed again; and, other times, exploded in tectonic violence. That great bloat in Palmdale had been rising and falling like a sleeping man's diaphragm, and every lift and fall had been metered for decades. But what did it mean? Could he, or anyone else alive, say that there was going to be a shattering earthquake along the San Andreas fault? Of course they could!—as long as no one asked embarrassing questions about time. It would surely happen. There was simply no question about it. But you could also say that about almost any point on the surface of the earth, even where no faults existed: sooner or later Chicago and Minneapolis would feel the ground shake beneath them and their structures sway into rubble, although it might be tens of millions of years in the future. For Southern California it would surely not be millions of years, and might not even be tens; but the social clock ran so much faster than the geological that pinpointing it within a few decades was not close enough to be of any help. Even less help in estimating damage. The best federal study had guessed at a major quake within thirty years, probably, with a loss of life in the tens of thousands, most likely, and property damage in the hundreds of millions. At least.

And no one had listened.

At least, no one had listened—he fumbled for the word he wanted—had listened *purely*. The only ones who had heard were the ones who had polluted the message with their own poisons, the quacks and the charlatans, the politicians and the greedy pirates like Danny Deere.

Why would no one hear what he had to say?

He slammed on the brakes, swearing to himself.

He had been deep in his own thoughts, and had not seen what was going on. A mile back slickered emergency crews had warned him that he was proceeding at his own risk, and now suddenly he saw how great that risk was. Just ahead of him, on the canyon road that led to Rainy's apartment complex, the road seemed to be in the process of closing itself. A delta of glistening red-brown slime was building up on the roadway itself, and the gutters along the sides had become mud rivers.

And something worse was very near to happening.

Up on the hill was someone's estate. They had obviously had experience of mud slides before, and so they had taken steps against them. They had built a cement tennis court, anchored to piles sunk into the hillside, to protect its border.

But it hadn't worked! Now the wash from the hillside had undercut the cement. The reinforced concrete beams that held it together were visible in his headlights, and they were bare. All the earth had been washed away, and only the pillars held it. One of the pilings, once eight feet deep in the ground, was now not touching earth at all; it hung in air over a gulley. Tib swallowed and eased the car past, watching the pillars for movement. He didn't stop shaking until he had reached Rainy's apartment, passed the doorman and was actually standing at her door.

And, wouldn't you know it, she was agitated about something herself, and obviously not very interested in what was agitating him. But what was agitating him should also have agitated her, so he spoke over whatever it was she was saying: "They're closing off the canyon road. They only let me in because I said I was going to evacuate my mother."

She stopped, regarding him. "Your mother?"

People who have been told that their senses of humor are deficient dislike explaining their jokes. Tib was annoyed; it was not a *big* joke, he conceded to himself, but it wasn't a *bad* one. And for this he had driven eighty-five minutes through the worst weather of the year!

But he could see that Rainy was deeply disturbed. "It does not matter," he said, taking off his wet coat. "Please tell me what is the trouble."

"Those F.B.I. people! They've been here again and, listen, you won't believe this, now they think I'm in some sort of conspiracy with the Russians!" She repeated the conversation with the agents, and waited for Tib's response. He sat with his rubbers in his hand, not noticing that he was dripping mud on the new rug. His face was gray. "I thought you might think it was funny," she said. "I mean—I didn't. But I was hoping you'd talk me into it."

He sighed and put the rubbers in the bathroom. "Naturalized citizens from Eastern Europe have trouble thinking such charges are funny," he said. "I am sorry. It is not funny. It strikes me that everything is getting terribly unfunny at once."

In a trailer on one of the access roads to Yellowstone Park, a U.S. Geological Survey scientist pondered a question of timing. His observations showed that the park was swell-

ing like a balloon, as liquid rock squeezed its way up to the surface. Rock cores revealed that the entire Yellowstone area had erupted in the past in scores of immense volcanic explosions, scattering ejecta over millions of square miles; there had been major eruptive outbreaks every few million years, and it had been several million years since the last one. Clearly, another vast eruption was due at any time, geologically speaking. The question in his mind was, did "any time" mean within the next million years? Or the next hundred? Or next week?

Sunday, December 27th. 10:40 PM.

Although Meredith was really sick with anger and pity, when she allowed herself to think about it, her old man was taking it harder than she. He had been a day and a half alternately raging and grieving, and his emotional binge seemed to grow stronger, not less. To be sure, there was always a way of soothing him down when upset, equally good for herself; but it had worked three times already, and only temporarily.

Maybe food? While Sam took his mood off to exercise it on the telephone she considered making him something to eat. Something hearty. Something he liked. She opened the refrigerator and peered into the snowfield that was her frozen food locker. Of course! She took out a frozen package of creamed chipped beef, scraped off the frost and puzzled over the instructions on the package.

Even by Meredith's own standards, she was not concentrating on cooking tonight. Her concerns were both personal and professional. Personal: Sam Houston Bradison had been the light of her life since they were both twenty, a long time ago, and she had never seen him so upset. The death of Myrna Licht had hit him hard. Not only because she had been his own student; because she had been a good one; because she had wasted her skills with those conniving Pedigrues; because, most of all, she had died of it in the long run.

And professionally, the storm was looming ever larger

in her mind. The radio was full of it—when it was not full of stale details and gossipy speculations about the death of Myrna Licht. There was nothing really unusual about heavy rains and mud damage at this time of year. Almost every year it happened. Almost every year the media went into a flap and a largish number of Californians went through a season of misery, and then it went away. It was like everything else about Los Angeles. Los Angelenos knew that car exhaust was strangling them, but they kept their cars. They knew that earthquakes were inevitable, but they built homes under earthfill dams. They knew that brush fires took an annual toll, but they moved into the chaparral. And they knew that every winter the rains came. This was no worse than other years, really. Not as bad, so far anyway, as, say, February of 1980; and that not nearly as bad as some of the real destroyers. There had been a winter way back during the Civil War when a warm hurricane from the Pacific struck and stayed. The combination of the downpour with the snow melt from the warm winds had filled the entire valley with water from mountains to mountains—what would they say if *that* happened again?

She wished Sam would get off the phone so she could check the latest reports from the Weather Bureau, just to reassure herself that this storm was only a normal winter rain, maybe a little early, but not unprecedented; and certainly nothing to do with Jupiter!

She realized she was standing there with the frozen chipped beef in her hand and the refrigerator standing open as Sam came morosely back into the kitchen. "Your friend Tib doesn't answer, and Rainy Keating's phone is out, and the governor is supposed to be coming down here to 'inspect the emergency'. So I can't get anybody at all. What the devil are you doing with that stuff?"

Guiltily she closed the fridge. "I thought you might be hungry, dear."

"I'm too mad to be hungry." He snapped on the television set irritably, switching from one newscast to another without listening to any. He was wearing the hapi coat she had brought back for him from a conference in Japan, and his bony knees were bare; after the last time she had applied her sovereign remedy for stress it had not seemed worthwhile to dress again. "I've got political IOUs to pick up all over this state," he declared. "I'm going to see that the governor does something!"

He plucked a Christmas card off the tree and began scribbling on the back of it—names of his protégés and allies, the political family he had built up over forty years of teaching and working. There were four former students in the state legislature, and a dozen more in government jobs. At least as many more in the even more powerful position of lobbyists or special-interest pleaders. "I'm not going to let this pass," he said, and then, "Now who the hell's that?"

It was nearly midnight, no time for the doorbell to ring. Meredith peered through the spyhole anxiously before she opened the door, but of course there was nothing to be seen but formless wet shapes on the patio. A muffled voice called, "Hello, Grandmerry."

It was Dennis, and there was someone with him—good heavens, that black man from the Jupes; good heavens again! and with a little girl holding his hand. She opened the door and, without entering, her grandson asked, "Can I ask you for a favor?"

Sam got up and peered to the door. "Come inside and ask it, boy! You're going to drown out there."

They came in, Dennis looking worried, the black man self-possessed and wary, the little girl even more self-possessed and not wary at all. "I wasn't sure you'd let me in," Dennis told his grandfather, who grunted without answering. "But that place we've been living in is no good now—"

"It never was any good!"

"—anyway, we can't leave Afeefah there now. They've been asking for emergency volunteers on the radio, and Saun and I want to go out and help. So can we leave Feef here for the night?"

"Well, of course you can!" cried Meredith, smiling at the little girl, who studied her thoughtfully before allowing her a small smile in return.

Saunders Robinson patted his daughter on the head and steered her toward the woman. "We appreciate that a lot. And, look, I'm really sorry about what happened at the TV station. We had no idea."

Sam Houston Bradison was not a person to hold a grudge. "It wasn't your fault, although—" He stopped himself and changed what he was going to say. "If you two are going out to dig ditches you'll want better clothes than you've got on. Come on, let's see what we can find."

Meredith felt her heart warm toward her grandson. Was it a sort of penance Dennis was paying, for having been part of that lunatic bunch? If so, she approved it. And she realized what it meant: they would be out all the night, building dikes, cleaning runoff channels; no fun for anyone.

"What you got to do is, you got to put it in the boiling water, you know?"

Meredith realized she was still holding the packet of frozen chipped beef. "My mind was wandering—Feef? Am I saying it right?"

"My name is Afeefah, and it means 'chaste'. But you can call me Feef."

"I thought I'd better make you something to eat."

The little girl shook her cornrows. "We ate. We been eating, one place or another, last couple hours, nowhere else to go."

"Sure you had a place to go, Afeefah. You're very welcome here! How about a glass of milk?"

She shook her head again. "Black people can't 'tabolize milk," she said seriously. "Anyway, there's somebody in your driveway."

"Oh, really?" Meredith peered out the kitchen window, but there was only Dennis's car to see. Still, she could hear a motor. "Somebody lost and turning around, I guess. Well! Let's make up a bed for you, shall we? I bet you're tired, this time of night."

Afeefah corrected her politely, "I most usually stay up later than *this*." But she trailed along happily enough as Meredith pulled out clean sheets and pillowcases. It was really very pleasant having her around, poor little thing! They could hear the men moving around in the mud room, finding boots and heavy-duty pants, but Afeefah did not seem anxious to be with her father, or worried about staying all night with total strangers—white strangers, to boot. And helpful, too. She stretched across the bed to catch one side of the sheet and carefully tucked it in, then, without being told, began stuffing pillows into the cases.

Meredith sought for a compliment. "How pretty your hair looks."

The girl acknowledged the validity of the remark. "I done it myself," she pointed out, in the interests of accuracy.

"You did it beautifully. Are you sure you wouldn't like something to eat?"

It took only a moment to establish that Afeefah was really fond of Twinkies, and of course there was always plenty of that sort of thing in Meredith's larder. It was good having a child in the house again, Meredith thought after she had told Afeefah where to find the junk food. At least twice a month she and her husband had debated getting rid of this house and moving to something smaller, now that there so seldom was anyone to occupy any of the children's, or later the grandchildren's, rooms; but at times like this she was grateful for them. She switched on the bedside radio, not so much for company as to make sure it worked in case Afeefah wanted it, and, of course, got a weather report. She paused with the coverlet in her hands to listen. The wind was from the south at fifteen to twenty-five miles an hour, pumping up moisture from the sea; the system was stalled. But at least—for the first time in many days—there did not seem to be another storm waiting its turn out over the Pacific. There was a worrisome low far out past the International Date Line, but with any luck at all it might not hit. At least, the coast would have a chance to dry out a little.

So the governor might make it through in the morning after all—sometime tomorrow, anyway. And then Sam would have a chance to—to do what, exactly? Her husband's discipline was political science. It was a good enough thing to study, but it led you to assume that everything wrong in the world could be made right by the right kind of election or the right kind of laws. And was there really any way to make storms and earthquakes illegal? Or was he just out for the blood of the Pedigrues?

She pulled the coverlet straight—more or less straight—and then stood up. Had that been the doorbell? Again? At this time?

Afeefah was there before her. As Meredith was hurrying to answer it Feef met her with a soggy brown-paper package in her hand. "He didn't want to come in," she said. "He just says to give this to this lady—" pointing to the name on the envelope.

It said in crabbed, foreign-looking printing: MRS RAINEY KETING PERSONAL. "How very strange," said Meredith. Outside she heard a car door slap tinnily closed, and when she looked out the little sports car was backing carefully out into the streaming street.

Lev Mihailovitch looked up at the house as he turned toward the freeway, hoping he had done the right thing. Was this Mrs. Dr. Bradison a black person? If not, was this child her maid's, perhaps?

But he didn't have any choice; the document was not truly of sensitive importance, but there were persons somewhere who thought it was. He could not simply mail it. And he had been turned away from the road to Mrs. Dr. Keating's apartment, and her telephone had not seemed to work—it did not matter; it was done. He concentrated on driving. This weather was unpleasant, although Moscow's winters were of course far worse. The car was even more unpleasant. At the rental place at the airport it had looked enough like the special-order car they had made for him at the Togliatti works in the Soviet Union to tempt him, but it was not the same; the shift did not operate in the same way, the windshield wipers were automatic instead of being turned with one hand while he drove with the other; all of its parts were strange. In any case, driving in Los Angeles was a terror.

He paused at a traffic light to look again at the map, and confirmed his belief that he was going the best way. The Ventura Freeway. Straight over to the San Diego, then down Century Boulevard to the airport. In decent weather, no more than forty minutes. Today— One could not say, but surely before his plane was due to take off. If any planes were taking off. Even if they did not, it had been irregular for him to leave the airport at all between planes, and it was best not to keep his "companion" waiting at the check-in counter.

Of course, Lev Mihailovitch had much less fear of "companions" than any ordinary Soviet citizen. He was not ordinary. He was a cosmonaut, and cosmonauts were next to God. Cosmonauts were allowed to order special little sports cars and drive them at eighty kilometers an hour all over the city, with the traffic militiamen waving them on. Cosmonauts got five-room apartments on Gorky Street; cosmonauts got to buy at the best of the special stores. It was not a bad life, being a cosmonaut. It was even permitted for a cosmonaut to disappear from his party for a little while, now and then. Even if some attractive young capitalist woman was involved—cosmonauts, after all, were men!

For someone whose mother had been a Jew, Lev Mihailovitch had done well. Even his internal passport had "Russian" stamped on it, not "Jew", and he was welcomed at the best clubs in Moscow. A cosmonaut had all sorts of privileges . . . but not, Mihailovitch thought with some concern, the privilege of failing to show up when he was supposed to. It could lead to unpleasant consequences. It would surely lead to the asking of questions he did not want to answer.

Perhaps, after all, he would regret the impulse toward chivalry that had brought him here. Mihailovitch craned to see his watch, failed, muttered to himself and turned on the radio to see just how late he was.

Of course, now none of the stations chose to give a time hack. He divided his attention between the radio and the road, not quite able to deal with either. How fast the radio announcers spoke, in this shorthand idiom that was so hard to understand! He made out that two house trailers had been swept away, and several cars, but could not make out where. (Along the ocean, surely? Surely not here!) Flood control channels were filling with silt; yes, fine, what did he care? And then he made out that something bad had happened, or was about to happen, to the Pacific Missile Test Range. Dikes had broken, but whether that meant that the range was washed out he could not tell. That touched him more nearly. At least it might put his companion in a good mood! Mihailovitch himself, not so good. After all, the astronauts were comrades in the space experience. He wished them no harm. He had had many a good drink with the moonwalkers and the veterans of EVA experiences so like his own. Although the Pacific Range was not at all like the Cape, was a part of the space program with which he had no more to do than his astronaut buddies—spy satellites and even worse!—still the people in California, too, were in some sense his family. *They* would understand his chivalry.

He reached irritably to switch off the radio, could not find the unfamiliar knob, took his eyes off the roadway for a moment.

Mihailovitch did not see the van that skeetered across the freeway in front of him until it was broadside to his lane. His reflexes were instant. He swerved the wheel and missed the van.

At the last minute he knew that he could not, however, miss the divider that kept southbound traffic from north. He struck it and caromed off, winding up clear back across all four lanes, with two wheels up against the retaining embankment and the steering wheel in his lap.

When he realized that, though the car would not move again, he was hardly even bruised he was extremely grateful; on second thought, grateful twice. Grateful that he had formed the habit of fastening seat belts whenever he drove. Ten times more grateful that now there was a clear and unarguable reason to be as late as he liked. No questions would be asked of a simple car accident in a storm!

At a hearing on offshore oil leases an environmental scientist testified that carbon dioxide in the air trapped heat, and that the more fossil fuel was burned the more carbon dioxide would be in the air. He cited studies showing that in the century from 1850 to 1950, atmospheric CO_2 increased from 268 to 312 parts per million, an increase of 16%; and he quoted from a study by Siegenthaler and Oeschger to show that burning as much as ten per cent of known *fossil fuel reserves*, even if spread out over several centuries, would raise the CO_2 by 50% or more, a highly probable danger level. The commission listened patiently, and then voted to approve the leases anyhow. All those empty gas tanks wanted filling.

Monday, December 28th. 6:20 AM.

When Joel de Lawrence was a contract producer he owned a stucco California ranch house, a sports car, a mistress, and a drug habit. The habit was sleeping pills. The reason he needed them was the insomnia of fear, the fear everybody on the studio lots always had that the front office would rise up one morning and pass a whim, and all that would melt away. As indeed it had.

That time in his life was decades past. Now he slept like an angel. There was no nagging late-night fear of loss to keep him thrashing about. He had very little to lose. Each night he drank two mild Scotch-and-waters while he watched the late news, and as soon as the last map of the weather report was off the screen he went to sleep, and dreamed better than he ever had in his life. The dreams alone were almost worth the loss of the hacienda and the starlet. It was Norman Mailer in the dream this time, scuttling into de Lawrence's elegant office with a cigarette hanging from his lip and a thick bundle of manuscript under his arm. "It's yours, Mr. de Lawrence," he said. "I've already talked to Redford, and he'll do the male lead. Bo Derek's eager to do Cynthia. And I won't let anyone but you produce it." "Why me?" asked the dreaming Joel—not out of modesty, simply to understand the facts before deciding whether to grant the petition. "Well, Mr. de Lawrence, you won't remember me, but I've always admired your work. When I was here back in 1946, writing *The Deer*

213

Park, you let me come on the set one day. My mind's made up. If you won't take it I'll withdraw the script. . . ."

There was the faintest hint of muddy light at the window. De Lawrence squeezed his eyes tighter and turned over. "I like your style, Mailer," he told his pillow, "but I'll have to think about it. . . ."

But the dream was over. Mailer disappeared, and Joel de Lawrence opened his eyes to peer at the orange digits on his bedside clock. It was time to get up.

By the time he had finished showering and shaving the dream had vanished completely; he did not remember Mailer or the studio or any of the conversation. But his body remembered. He felt pleasantly relaxed, as though he had been making love. The coffee had brewed itself, and he had a cup while he dressed, peering out of his window. The pleasant lassitude began to slip away. The weather was really bad, the worst of the year anyway. From his window there was little to see except for the gardening shed and a corner of the four-car garage, but what he could see was wet and worrying. The earth could not absorb the rain as it fell. Rivulets were streaking the expensively laid turf. He worried about the driveway, which needed grading every month anyway, and was particularly vulnerable to rainstorms; the shock absorbers on the limo were his responsibility. He wondered if the Mexicans' repairs had fixed those annoying little roof leaks; should he take a look before Danny got up?

But Danny was already up. The phone from his bedroom rang peremptorily, and kept on ringing until Joel got to it. It was very unlike Danny to get up before seven-thirty; what was stranger, he was apparently dressed and ready to go. "*Now*, Joel, you know what I mean 'now'? So get your clothes on—"

"Oh, I'm ready, Danny. But have you been listening to the radio? A lot of roads are closed."

"So we'll take the ones that're open!"

What Joel had not been able to appreciate from the window was the wind. It was blowing hard; between his door and the garage he was soaked, in spite of poncho and boots. The driving was going to be even worse than he had thought. So, no matter how much of a hurry Danny was in, Joel took time to make sure he was ready for it. The tires were all at pressure. The gas gauge said three-quarters full. When he opened the trunk the jack, the emergency flashlight, the flares, and the spare tire were all in good shape. He thought for a moment, and then shuffled around in the back of the garage where he kept things that he could see no immediate use for, but were too good to throw out. One of Danny's brief loves had briefly persuaded him to keep a kitten. The animal had lasted less than a week, but there was a sack of Kitty Litter, nearly full, on top of a stack of For Sale signs. Joel lugged it to the trunk. Sometimes you could put that stuff under a wheel when there was thin, slippery mud and it would get you out.

All this delayed him, and by the time Joel got to the front of the house Danny Deere was hopping from one foot to the other in anger. "What the fuck's keeping you, goddam it?" he yelled through the rain. He was wearing the poncho and rain hat again, but not the boots; and he was carrying his big dispatch case with the combination lock. Joel did not know what had happened between Danny and Buster Boyma; Danny hadn't said, and Joel hadn't asked. It wasn't good, that was obvious. Danny had been explosively silent all the way home. This was not a good morning to cross him.

"You never go downtown this early," Joel apologized, starting the car down the driveway.

"Today I do! Move it!"

Joel nodded without speaking, keeping his attention on the washboarded road. The driving was as bad as he had thought it would be, but Danny didn't comment. Didn't say anything when they passed the Mexicans, all staring out at them from the shelter of their gatehouse porch; didn't even speak when they came to the condominium. Danny's attention was all inside the car. He seemed to have trouble knowing what to do with the dispatch case. First he kept it on his lap. Then he put it behind him. Then he put it on the seat and put his poncho over it, and finally he put it on the floor and leaned forward so that he

215

was half sheltering it with his body. Joel recognized the pattern. It was the money syndrome. Every time Danny carried large amounts of cash with him he was antsy . . . but never, in all the years, as antsy as this.

According to the radio there had been seven inches of rain in the past four days, and the stagnating storm that was drenching the freeway now might dump another six inches. Might dump more. Along the sides of the freeways there were now little streams.

Since there was no more room for water between the particles of sand and grit and clay, every drop that fell from the sky rolled down the slopes. There was a trickle down every bank along the freeways, a stream flowing down each canyon. On the steep declines the rushing water picked at the dirt and carried it along. Because the gravel multiplied the force of the running water, the Los Angeles Flood Control authorities had stretched chainwire catchment fences along every likely spillway. They stopped the solids and let the water harmlessly through.

But seven inches of rain was close to their design limits. Every catch-fence was now full. Rubble brought the levels behind the fences up to the fence tops. If new floods came, the water would spill over. Each catchment fence would become a six-foot cascade, and as the water struck the base of the fence it would erode the supports, and the fence would go down, and all the tons of uncompacted aggregate, mud and wood, rocks and gravel, would batter down toward the next.

It hadn't happened yet, but Joel de Lawrence's face was pinched as he watched the banks and roadways. There weren't many cars yet; that was good. There might not be very many at all this Monday morning, even after a holiday weekend, because anyone with any sense would stay home if he could. Some slopes looked safe enough—the old cemetery near the on-ramp of the freeway was heavily grassed, because no one had mowed it in years; that was good. Some were already a jelly of mud, like the landscaping around the condo construction. And there were worrisome features he had never paid attention to before, the great rock that as long as he could remember had been embedded in a hillside a mile from Danny's home. Only now it was no longer exactly embedded, because the water had carved much of the dirt away from its base. As they inched past, Joel de Lawrence could see an emergency crew toiling up the hillside toward it.

Even worse, the whole Southland was beginning to stink. Joel could smell someone's ruptured drains even with the windows closed, and according to the radio there was worse. Down in Orange County nine million gallons of raw sewage were pouring out of San Juan Creek every day. Another quarter of a million gallons sluiced through Loma Alta Creek to the sea, after a mud slide had ripped a hundred-foot gap in a main. When Joel tried to talk to his boss about all of this the little man ripped his head off, so he concentrated on his driving and his thoughts.

In a way, it was very exciting—almost even pleasurable. It gave a special focus to Joel's thinking. The inside thinking. The part that was as private as his dreams. He had trained himself to drive and respond to Danny with the outer layers of his mind, while inside he was busy with the skills he had tried to keep alive within himself for twenty years. Camera angles, special effects, casting, lights: not of films that he was going to produce, because he did not really believe he was ever going to produce any. But the films that he *might* produce, if the impossible occurred; even the films that he might have produced a quarter of a century past, back in the days before the studios had all gone into the hotel business and Joel de Lawrence had had a steady job. He could have done more! He could have gone just a little farther! He could have been the one to innovate that special saturating Francis Ford Coppola sound, or that Kubrick wash of color; he could have— He could have done many things, but he did not. He had shot pages of script and gone home at five o'clock, and it was no wonder he had wound up no better than this.

Yet—one picture could put it all back for him. And pictures were everywhere. What a film this storm would make! Not expensive, either; a simple story, with all this for background. Maybe a cop story? Maybe a bank robbery? The crooks getting away with the money, but somehow trapped in the mud—that could be a great car chase, the fleeing felons and the L.A.P.D. black and whites struggling after each other at fifteen miles an hour, because the roads were so bad? He didn't need much. A script. A couple of bankable actors. A camera crew; not much else, because if he had a crew right now he could get all the background footage he could use, and there was the film! It was all so simple.

It was also fantasy. Twenty years of fantasies had taught Joel de Lawrence to know them. It *could* happen; but it wouldn't, and the reality of his life was this limousine, and this little man yammering at him from the back seat, and this miserable, blowing, soaking rain. When they finally got onto Sunset Boulevard it had taken them an hour to go a twenty-five-minute drive, and it took them another half hour on the Strip itself. Traffic barely crawled along, as half the motorists paused at every southbound intersection, peered worriedly at the steep inclines leading down toward Santa Monica and Wilshire, and then drove along to seek a gentler slope. In spite of the early start, it was past nine when Joel finally let Danny Deere out at the back entrance of his building, and went to park the car.

Joel trudged back through the rain, rather content with his life. The fantasies were still there to be tapped when he wanted them. Listening to the horns of the cars on Sunset Strip he heard them as a musical score for the film he would (he knew) never make—not a score, but background—maybe linked with some of those electric tonalities, by somebody like the Barrons (were they still alive?). And perhaps you could get a theme out of it, and the theme could be a hit single, and . . .

The sound of Danny yelling dispelled the reverie.

Joel got rid of his sopping coat and tracked the sound to the telephone room. Danny had been in a bad mood ever since he came away from that mobster, Buster Boyma; so mad that sometimes he was even silent, nose pinched white with suppressed fury; not a time to cross him. Now he was not silent, simply inarticulate with rage. He stood in the phone room with that dispatch case cradled in his arms, yelling at his secretary and at the one telephone seller who had managed to get there that morning. All the desks should have been filled by now! But that was not the worst. The electricity was flickering worrisomely, and the one telephone seller was holding a phone pleadingly toward Danny Deere. There would be no soliciting from the office of Danny Deere Enterprises that morning. All the phones were out.

Hundreds of billions of dollars have been spent on dams, levees and other projects to reduce damage from flooding over the past few decades. Nevertheless, the losses from flood damage increase at a higher rate each year in the countries which have implemented flood-control measures than in the countries which have not.

Monday, December 28th. 8:20 AM.

The fifth or sixth time Tib woke it was daylight. If you could call it daylight; the light was a greasy gray, and he could hear the rain still falling. He slept poorly with another person in the bed, that had been a truth for all of his life, but there was more to it than that. He could not sleep because his churning mind would not allow it.

Slowly and quietly Tib turned the covers back and let his feet down to the floor. It was a pity really that they had spent this night in her home rather than his. His own home was certainly not large, but at least there was a place to go—a very good place; he could have gone down to his workroom. He could even have worked . . . assuming, of course, his fluttering mind had settled on a course of work to do. But at least he could have thought, without the distraction of another person in the room.

He risked turning the light on in the bathroom, with the door almost closed so that only a sort of artificial moonlight came into the bedroom/living room/dining room that was all there was of Rainy's apartment. Moving slowly, barefoot and noiseless, he eased a chair around so that he could watch the rain splashes on the window and, at the same time, see the outline of Rainy under the covers less than ten feet away.

He had set himself for thinking. But the thoughts were stale. What kept coming back into his mind was geology, because geology was what he knew. But the problems were not scientific! They were moral. Tibor Sonderman had never been a religious man, but he had always had a great consciousness of sin. Sin was all around him. If it was not his own—not *all* his own—he shared the communal guilt, because he did nothing to prevent it.

The sins that troubled Tib Sonderman had nothing to do with theology, and not even much to do with sex. They were social sins, and this city he lived in was Sodom itself by those lights. Los Angeles was a city of three million in a place where there was no reason for it to exist at all except for climate, and it was destroying that. It did not have water, but needed to steal it from the north. It did not have good communications, and so had to pave itself over with noxious freeways. It did not even have land to build on! It had only the valleys—which were not enough, and in any case should not be built on because they were capable of growing food—and the hills, which certainly should not be built on because inevitably, sometime, something would shake down what you built. Especially in California! Viewed in the long time-scale of geology, California thrashed about like a frightened snake. Its string of volcanos popped one after another, like fireflies; the whole state twitched like a horse's hide in fly season with earthquakes. It was not merely that it was certain that a vast earthquake would occur. What was certain was that there would be an endless series of them! forever! or at least for the next ten million years or so, until some great new cycle of fire began in some other part of the world. But by then Los Angeles, and everyone in it, and no doubt the race that had built it would long since have disappeared!

The risk was always there, no risk but a certainty; but there were times that were worse than others. Today was one. The rain exacerbated the geology.

How many days a year like this were there? Perhaps as many as ten? And how often did damaging shocks, say Modified Mercalli VIII or higher, occur? Maybe one every five years? Tib wished for his calculator, but the probability computation was not too hard to do in his head. Say the odds against a damaging earthquake on any particular day were 1800 to one. Say the odds against that day being one when the ground was saturated and ready to be shaken into thin soup—as happened in China, with half a million dead; as happened in Alaska, when buildings toppled into the gruel—were 36.5 to one. Then, cumulating them, once every 65,700 days, say 180 years, the lethal combination should strike.

Once in 180 years did not seem like much. But Los Angeles was over a hundred years old; it was halfway there.

Rainy stirred in the bed. She lifted herself on one elbow and spoke to him; her eyes were open, but she was still asleep and in a moment she put her head down and closed her eyes again. Tib sat immobile until her regular breathing resumed. And he saw his error. Two errors! First, the city of Los Angeles of a hundred years ago was not the city of today, with split-levels and ranch houses dug into every hillside. The second error was more serious. He had been thinking geology again, and the question was still moral.

He was certain of that. But the precise formulation of the question eluded him. His orderly mind was crumbling in disorder; Tommy Pedigrue and the Jupiter Effect, the death of Myrna Licht, and the wickedness of Danny Deere were all spinning around in his head, and tranquility was not even a hope.

"You look," said Rainy from the bed, "like somebody who can't find his car keys." This time she was wide awake, and had been watching him without moving.

"What I think I've lost is my mind."

"Maybe you left it in the bed? You want to come back and look?"

"Oh, my God," he said, "how flattering you are." He came over to sit on the edge of the bed, kissing her good morning. All the turmoil in his head receded to a distant pinwheel whirl, no longer an obsession. "You do cheer me up, dear Rainy. I have noticed that since you got the federal police off your back you have been in a real good mood."

Rainy lay back, regarding him. "Think so? Um." She considered for a moment. "I would point out, my dear colleague, that, first, they are not entirely off my back; they were here last night; so your theory is not sufficient; and, second, that two things happened at the same time, i.e., it also happened that you and I became lovers. So it is not necessary, either; and a theory which is not both necessary and sufficient is no theory."

Tib gazed down at her. "It is funny that that should sound so strange to me. Is that what we are, lovers? Not 'dating' or 'going with'?"

Rainy picked up his hand, lifted it to her mouth and touched the fold of flesh between thumb and forefinger with her tongue. "It's what I would like us to be, I guess," she said. "Now! Your endless sexual indulgences have made you smell like a goat. Come shower with me."

It was not a thing Tib Sonderman had been used to doing, and he was awkward with her at first. Not for long. It turned out to be about as pleasant, in a gently sexual way, as anything short of intercourse, and marvelously relaxing as well. It even stimulated conversation, and he found he was telling her his perplexities and puzzlements. It brought them no nearer solution, but it seemed to bring Tib and Rainy closer to each other, while the water of Mono Lake and the Colorado River splashed over them and into the drain and Tib did not give it even a thought. In spite of the considerable sexual indulgences of the past eight or ten hours they might easily have wound up on the convertible bed again if Rainy had not heard a sound imperceptible to Tib, excused herself, wrapped herself in a towel, and disappeared.

Reluctantly, Tib turned off the shower. She had closed the door behind her, but he heard an exclamation, then sounds of scrambling around the room, then a brief low-voiced conversation of which he only caught one word, but that word was one he had not wanted to hear: *Tinker*.

He stood on the fluffy pink mat with the towel in his hand and a whole scenario unrolled inevitably before him. The name of the skit was Returning Husband Discovers Wife's Lover, and he was playing one of the leads.

How very embarrassing, he thought. Now, what were the traditional stage directions? Under the bed, in a closet, out the window? But none of those were available; not even his clothes were available. No. Of course they weren't. They were exactly where he had left them, namely draped across the kitchen chairs.

He might have gone on drying himself indefinitely, but he heard the door close, peeked out and saw Rainy, all by herself, wrapped up in a robe she had grabbed from somewhere, the towel turbaned around her wet hair, staring thoughtfully at Tib's trousers. She looked around. "That was Tinker," she said. "He said he was worried about me. He said the back road is open now, so we could get out if we wanted to."

Tib nodded. Her face was so blank that he could not tell whether she was closer to laughter or tears. In the event, there was neither. She moved into the kitchen to start water for coffee. "He's really a sweet man," she said. "But we're really not married any more, and now I guess he understands that."

About seventy million pieces of solid matter strike the Earth's atmosphere every day. Fortunately, all but a few of them are extremely small, of the order of a billionth of a gram. But any person who spends much time walking, sunbathing or playing golf is, on average, "struck" by several of these micrometeorites each week—with so little force by the time they reach the Earth's surface that they are indistinguishable from ordinary atmospheric dust.

Monday, December 28th. 11:40 AM.

Saunders Robinson got up from the canvas cot where Dennis was sleeping to get his fifteenth cup of coffee. He didn't even drink coffee. But he didn't want to sleep, not covered with mud, not in this high-school gymnasium with the canvas cots all over the basketball court. They had been up all night, shoveling mud into potato sacks up along Mulholland Drive for three hours, then back here in the emergency shelter for nearly another three. The Red Cross woman handing out the coffee had a radio going, turned down low in case any of the five or six families who had elected to try the shelters were really trying to sleep—few of them were—and reports were coming in from what seemed like the entire world: Mandeville Canyon, Rustic Canyon, Montebello, Pacific Palisades, all over the Santa Monica Mountains, Mount Olympus, the San Gabriel foothills, Encino, Monterey Park. The Pacific Coast Highway was closed (surf); so was the Ventura Freeway (slides). Malibu residents were ordered to boil their water. The governor had been asked to declare a state of emergency, and the Naval Air Station at Point Mugu was flooded.

There was not much loss of life. Quite a few highway deaths, but that was not unusual for a Southland Monday morning, where you could almost always count on one or two motorists winding up guillotined in a windshield, or with an engine in their laps. But the property damage! Half of Los Angeles had leaking roofs. Another half was worried about its houses slipping down the hillsides, and some of them were seeing it happen. The black family in the shelter had an unusual story: they had been burned out in the middle of the night, when their cellar flooded, silently and without fuss. The water had risen to the base of the natural-gas hot-water heater, half a foot a minute. It covered the jet, but the flame did not go out: the gas bubbled through the rising water and burned in spatters of flame at the surface. When it came close to the two-by-sixes that held the floor of the living room in place, they began to smolder. The smoke alarm woke the family in time to see their house burn from the inside, with all the water in the world surrounding it on all sides.

Robinson realized his fifteenth cup of coffee was empty, and wandered back to the urn for number sixteen. There were not many people in the refuge. Most threatened families had refused to leave their homes—or been afraid to. Of the forty people in the room that could have sheltered five hundred, more than two dozen were volunteers like himself, from the Red Cross lady at the coffee urn to the handful of Tree People and casual volunteers who had responded to the radio appeal. Most of them were silent, staring around as though they were wondering what they were doing here. Robinson wondered that too. It had been his idea to volunteer, and the word "penance" stuck in his mind when he suggested it; but he knew he had beaten Dennis to the point of making it articulate only by moments. He debated trying to call Afeefah to tell her he was all right—mostly to see if she was—but the nearest phone was in the school office, and the effort seemed considerable.

A man came in from the rain. He didn't trouble to take his rain hat off, or even to close the door. He would not be that long. "Okay, troops," he called. "Saddle up."

They could see little outside the canvas top of the National Guard six-by-six, but there wasn't much to see. Dennis craned past Robinson's shoulder to peer out at the rain and the hillsides, accepting the penalty of blown drops in his eyes; it was nearly seventy degrees outside, and a lot hotter than that inside the truck. They were barely crawling along, on a stretch of the freeway that had been closed to all but emergency traffic for the past twelve hours. The driver didn't seem to know where he was going. Twice he started on a down ramp, stopped, muttered with the L.A. County Flood Control engineer in the seat beside him, and then grindingly backed onto the freeway again. It was lunch time, and Dennis was beginning to be very hungry. He had slept through the sandwiches at the high school, and now he regretted it.

On the hillside just ahead of them the slope was rather gentle, and there were no split-level houses to dam and channel the water. The rain soaked in where it fell and did no harm. As long as it could. Until the ground was saturated, and the soil would not accept one more drop. Even then it only flowed gently down the gentle slope. It did not channel scabland trenches into bare soil, because the

225

soil was not bare; it was once dense turf, now grown to weeds and tangles but all the better able to hold itself together because of that. And it did hold, through the first four-inch downpour, and the three days of lesser rains that followed, even through the three inches that had fallen overnight; but by that time on Monday it was no more firm than Jell-O. Worse. The structural integrity had been violated. All along the side of that hill, row on row, over a period of decades, holes had been dug. They were quite uniform holes, each one of them eight feet long, forty-two inches wide, and seven feet deep. The hillside had been perforated like the stub of a check.

At the farthest corner a wedge of dirt slid suddenly into the shoulder of the freeway.

Moments later, a hundred feet up the slope, the bonds that had held the soil together had lost all their strength. They surrendered to the gravity of the slope. A crack three hundred feet long zipped itself open, and the entire slope dissolved into mud, pouring thickly over the lip of the concrete abutments onto the freeway. The flow carried with it the rusted old flowerpots, the marble markers that had headed each hole, and the contents.

The first Robinson knew of it was when the truck slammed on its brakes. "Jesus, would you look at that?" somebody cried from the front seat. Robinson and Dennis pushed back to the crack in the truck's cover and peered out. It was hard to see anything, because they were down in a cut; far ahead they could see the construction work that they had been supposed to be heading for, with a huge crane vibrating in the wind. But they could not see just what was on the side of the road. There was an off-ramp marker, but there was no ramp. There was not even a shoulder. The truck had moved gradually over into the center lane, then even into the fast lane . . . and Dennis saw wonderingly that the other lanes were gone.

The road was completely blocked. The entire north-bound section of the freeway was filled with mud, a slide that went up twenty feet on the right to join the slope of the hill and filled all three lanes to the concrete divider on the left. "Back it up, dummy! Back it up," somebody

226

squawked from in front, but the gears ground and the wheels spun, and the truck would not move. The mud had the car. "Oh, shit," yelled the engineer. "Now you've done it." And then, louder, craning toward the back, "Everybody out; from here on we walk!"

The dozen men in the truck looked at each other, then sprang from the tailgate. They barely made it. They slogged through the quicksand-flowing mud to the hillside and found it was coming to meet them. The only way was back, along the freeway, to a point where a retaining wall still held, and then they turned to look back.

The river of mud had already filled the inside of the truck. It was cresting over the top, like slow-motion surf, and riding the top, like a sort of surfboard, was a huge mahogany box, earthstained and crumbling. As they watched, the side ripped open, and the contents, staring emptily at the storm, slid out.

From the hilltop a quarter of a mile away Manuel could not see the earthslide, but he saw the sad remaining cypress dip and bow. He crossed himself, not sure he had actually seen it.

Manuel was not a stranger to hard work, because you could not grow up to child-rearing age in the Sierra Madre without tens of thousands of hours of it; but in Aguatarde it had been his own land he fought for. Not Danny Deere's. Especially not this real-estate corporation who was hiring his family today.

Especially not when any man could see that it was all useless; the walls would stand or they would not, and what foolishness they tried with sandbags and plastic sheets would make no difference. In any case, the five men of his own family and the fourteen construction workers, all who had shown up at the job that morning, were not enough to make a difference. From his great car on the road the fat boss had been sending orders here, there, everywhere, some on the telephone in the car, some by his narrow-eyed men who plowed up through the mud in their narrow shoes, destroying their cream-colored slacks and spoiling their pale trench coats forever. Manuel knew he had been demanding help from the county for many hours, but he was not the only one demanding. Meanwhile, a man had to think of himself. The young men were out there; Manuel had found a spot on the second floor of the building, where the rain came in only in driplets from the canvas-covered windows and where, if anyone should appear, he could make a great show of putting the canvas back where he had prudently ripped it loose an hour before. It would be worrying if the person who came, if anyone came, should observe that his poncho was dry, so Manuel was careful to stand by the open window every now and then to soak it a little.

All this would pass. Everything always had. All the same, Manuel was not at ease in his heart. There was a worry he had never had before, and he could not know if it was real. He inclined to think that it was only a filthy imagining of his nephew Jorge's cousin Pilar, the puta. Against his orders, she had sneaked into his house in his absence, not once but often. Always she brought disgrace on the family, not to mention the sickness of the privates that his nephew and even his sons could not be persuaded to fear. She had been one of those people on television, with the shoe-blacking on their faces. Manuel himself had seen her on the six o'clock news, being chased by the doorman of a great hotel in Beverly Hills. Yet she had seemed for once in her life sincere! Was it possible? Was it true, as she had once told Jorge and Jorge Manuel himself, that those little nuisance earthquakes that happened any time—one never even noticed them until one saw the reporter joking about it on the newscasts—these tiny shudders, with the ground so wet, could be serious indeed? He did not know. He did not want to know. He had nearer concerns. He had left the women with instructions to move everything of value to the back of the truck, and to drive the truck for high ground at need. The Danny Deere might believe that his home was safe from natural disasters, but he was a man who could afford to be wrong; a poor man could not. Yet who knew if the woman would remember? Or if she could drive the truck without destroying it? There were many worries!

He observed that he was truly not needed, because at last the fat man's bellows had been heard; eight or ten new men were slogging up through the mud toward the work crews behind the project. That was good.

But not altogether good, Manuel perceived, because he was not there; and with all those men there would be a need for an underboss. Who better than himself? And an underboss could almost certainly demand more than the three dollars and fifty cents an hour that was all these scoundrels would pay for the risk of a man's health and life. It would be necessary to get very wet again.

But it was worth it. Manuel looked around at the room, sighed and left the building to climb toward the top of the hill. Just in time.

Buster Boyma had not set foot outside his car the whole time he had been there. It hadn't saved him. His russet-brown jogging suit was spotted with water and mud, the carpeting in the car was filthy, even his hands were smeared with soil. It gave Boyma pain to have his hands dirty; they felt dry and cracked. It was just one more thing to make him furious. For this he had failed to show at a grand jury hearing! His lawyer would smooth it over, no doubt, that was what he was paid for; but his lawyer would expect to be paid accordingly. And for what? His whole purpose in being here was to make sure his property was safe, but what good was he doing? He had kept the car phone busy with appeals to everyone in California for help, and where was the help? Fourteen volunteers were supposed to be on the way, but what good would fourteen men, shovels and bare hands, no earthmoving machines, no engineers even, do against this rain?

Somebody would pay for this! He had already marked a dozen somebodies, three or four of his own men, a lot more of the people in government who *owed* him. He yelled for his driver, off taking another message to the handful of workers on the hill—actually the same message, *Do something!* But the storm made it impossible to be heard, of course. . . .

The storm and something else. Something new was

happening. Even over the sound of the rain and the wind, he could hear shouting.

Chapparal had once covered the hillside, but it had been ripped out to get the ground ready for sodding in planting. In two months it would be a handsome park, to compensate condo owners on the convex side of the curve for missing the ocean view on the concave—would be if any of it remained for two months. But the water was seeping under the plastic. Each drop carried one grain of dirt an inch or two. Many drops had carried much earth, and the cohesion of the soil was almost gone.

In spite of the best efforts of the men frantically battening it down, the wind lifted a corner of the plastic. Five men rushed to fight it back where it belonged; the wind tugged at the places they had left. It bellied the edges between the stacks of cement blocks and the drums of wall-finishing that weighted the plastic down, and the plastic tore; and the whole hillside began to slide. A crack opened. One of the men saw it and yelled; the others saw it, and ran. None of them was caught, but the hill was on the move.

The foundations had gone down to bedrock, and they held. It did not matter. All they accomplished was to create a holding pond for the fluid mud. Earth and plastic, barrels and cinder blocks all slid together. They filled the lower floors of the condo with gluey mud and spilled over to block the freeway cut.

The workmen stared, astonished, at the building still standing and the giant crane poised over their heads. Each one was certain that it would fall, but it did not.

But in the dammed freeway cut, a pool of water was forming.

Boyma stared, paralyzed with fear. He thought the crane was his enemy; he did not notice the row of temporary power lines. The crane swayed but remained erect; but the mud pulled the lines down with a rattle of artillery fire and great flashes of light.

"Now they've done it!" Boyma shouted. He was beside himself with rage at "them"—whoever they were—at everybody! There was no one to yell at. Even his driver was gone, ordered to carry orders to the top of the hill. Boyma wanted to get out of there, to his comfortable home where he could change his clothes and plan his retributions—and wanted it soon, because he saw that a pool of water was forming along the freeway. He opened the door of the car to yell for his driver.

The men on the hill saw him and waved madly, but Boyma paid no attention. He shouted furiously as he stepped down into the water. The fallen power lines lay no more than twenty yards away in that same stream; and when he stepped into it he died.

The most violent earthquakes in the history of the United States stopped clocks in Boston, set bells ringing in Norfolk, Virginia, created large, permanent new lakes in Missouri, Arkansas and Tennessee and destroyed 150,000 acres of forest. The epicenter was in New Madrid, Missouri. There was not many human deaths. There were not many human beings in the area, and especially there were no large buildings to fall and crush them, since the shocks began in December, 1811. Now millions of people live in the affected region. Many live and work in vulnerable high-rise buildings, and almost none of them have any idea that they are at risk.

Monday, December 28th. 5:50 PM.

What Rainy had expected to find at the Bradison house had not been very clear. The phone had rung, to signify that it was working again, and it was not Meredith but Sam Houston Bradison himself, demanding they come over to see the governor. He sounded peremptory and hurried. He'd been trying to get through for hours, he said, and did she know where Dr. Sonderman was so he could come too? At that point there was some slight embarrassment in Rainy's mind at how to explain that she knew very well where Dr. Sonderman was, and she had failed to get clear just why the governor was going to be at the Bradison home. Nevertheless, they obeyed, driving with as much speed as they could manage with caution, and as much caution as they could afford with speed; the rain was only occasional now, but the streets were still as likely to be flooded as not.

By the time they got there it was late. She half expected the governor would have been and gone by then, but apparently he was having his own troubles with the storm. What was happening was that a young black girl was dusting end tables while Meredith was straightening the books on the shelves. Sam Bradison himself let them in through the kitchen, where he was busily washing dishes and putting them away. Obviously the governor had not yet arrived, and, obviously, what Rainy found herself doing very soon after that was pushing a vacuum cleaner over somebody else's carpet. It was not what she would have chosen, not least because Tib had been drafted into the kitchen with Sam Bradison, and she could not hear what they were saying to each other.

Not that she could hear much of what anybody else was saying, over the noise of the antique Hoover. She was not even aware that Meredith had left the room at first—no doubt to flap over the bathrooms or the halls. The little girl was talkative enough, but not directly informing. She did not appear to know who the governor was, much less why he was coming. She managed to convey that her daddy was asleep somewhere in the house after a hard day of shoveling mud, along with Meredith's grandson, and that she didn't think much of Meredith as a housekeeper, but Rainy had already formed her own opinions of that. She pushed back an armchair to get at the accumulated pencil stubs and cigar ash underneath it, reconsidered, and carefully pushed it back again. By the time she had gone over all the exposed surfaces Meredith was back.

"I guess we're as ready as we'll ever be," Meredith said, surveying the room with satisfaction. "You're really sweet, Rainy—and Afeefah, of course!"

"You would have done it for me," Rainy lied. "You don't get the governor coming every day. Speaking of which—"

"Yes?"

"Well—what is this going to be?"

Meredith sat down on the couch, pushing a scrap of paper Rainy had missed underneath with her foot. "It's all Sam's idea," she said. "I don't always understand Sam's ideas. Afeefah? That's good enough, honey. Why don't you just sit down and rest for a while?"

The little girl frowned. "Got to do the windowsills yet," she said. "Lady? You going to give the lady the thing that came for her?"

"Oh, good heavens, thank you, Afeefah. Of course! Now where in the world did I put that?" She stared around the room as though it were someone else's, then disappeared down the hall. Rainy sighed and got up to help Afeefah with the windowsills.

By Rainy's calculation the governor was now more than an hour late for whatever it was he was late for, and she was beginning to get hungry. Or else she was about to start her period. Or, most likely, both.

Rainy was uneasy in her mind, and she hoped that was the reason; she was not sure just what she was uneasy about. Her—she said the word to herself again to get used to it—her lover, the Herr Doktor Sonderman with his middle-European ways, was probably not the reason. He had been very silent all day, and withdrawn except when they were making love; something was on his mind, and it was trying to be on hers too, if she had only known what it was. She relished the chatter of her housecleaning associate because it took her mind off that unfocused concern. Afeefah was seven years old and in her last school she had been in the top ten in her class. She didn't know what she would be in her new school, because she didn't yet know where they were going to live, but she wasn't worried. She was going to be a nurse when she grew up, that was why she was so good at cleaning, because that was mostly what nursing was, wasn't it? Unless if she got a scholarship, she explained, which she probably would do, in which case she would be an obstrician and help people have babies. And it was all right that Rainy was white, although her dad didn't like her getting too close to white people, because that was mostly because her mom had

233

been white and she tooken off. It seemed unlikely that any seven-year-old really had that much to say about her life, but Afeefah showed no sign of stopping until Meredith came back into the room. "I'm sorry," she said, "but I put it away where I wouldn't lose it, and I forgot where. But here it is. Goodness! Are those sirens?"

She wandered off to peer out the window while Rainy unwrapped the little envelope. She recognized the name on the envelope as her own, but who it was from was obscure; even more obscure after she opened it, because all it contained was a Xerox—no, not even a Xerox, one of those oily thermo-copied things—of a typewritten paper. The difficulty was that the typing was in Cyrillic characters, totally opaque to Rainy.

Since the only Russian she had had any contact with was the cosmonaut who was of so much interest to the F.B.I., she supposed it might have been from him. But that did not solve the problem of what was in it.

The sirens were growing louder, very *much* louder, and then abruptly, right in front of the house, they cut off. "It's the governor," Sam Houston Bradison called from the kitchen. "Do let him in, someone."

Meredith was already at the door, holding it open while the governor's party sorted themselves out in the driveway; besides the governor's own car there were two black-and-whites and one drenched policeman on a motorcycle. Tib joined Rainy at the window to watch. "Look what I got from, I guess, Mihailovitch," she said, handing him the stapled sheets. "Do you have any idea what it is? It's all Greek to me."

Tib unfolded the slick sheets and glanced at the heading. "Yes, I think I can translate—perhaps after we are through with this meeting. It is not Greek, of course, but Russian—but I also read a little Greek, you know."

It took Rainy all the time until the governor was there, introductions had been performed, and they were all seated before she made up her mind that that had been a small joke, or at least a pleasantry; it was good to know that his mood allowed pleasantries! Tib seemed quite interested in what was going on, studying California's trendy governor with his dove-gray, soft leather shirt and his mid-calf boots. But his interest did not extend to taking part in the conversation. He shook the governor's hand politely when they were introduced and retired to a straight-backed chair between the governor's secretary, or whatever he was, and someone who seemed to be a Los Angeles city councilman. He maintained a polite expression while the governor and Sam Bradison told each other how well they remembered each other, and while everyone else in the room told what they thought of the storm, and while Sam Bradison explained what he wanted the governor to do. Which led to Rainy's being asked to recount her experience with Danny Deere, and Meredith to repeat some of the things her grandson had told her about the Jupiter Fulgarians. The governor listened attentively, frowning in the direction of his secretary. "Have you got all that, Jake? I want the A.G. to get on that right away. The only thing, Meredith," he added, turning back to his hostess, "I don't see what this has to do with the storm."

"Not a thing, Governor," Meredith assured him, but her husband was shaking his head.

"It does, you know. There's a climate of fear in this town, and it's been deliberately whipped up by people who make a profit out of it. Not just Danny Deere or the Jupes. I hold the Pedigrues responsible for a good deal of it. The whole committee was a fraud in the first place; there's no way to know whether the so-called Jupiter Effect is real or not, and the publicity given to it is dangerous. *Really* dangerous. I'm going to send you drafts of three bills I think you may want to offer the legislature, Governor. One to make spreading false warnings a criminal offense; one to make people who do that civilly liable for damages; and one to create a bona-fide commission to examine the risks of catastrophe of all sorts, and recommend appropriate building and zoning ordinances."

The governor nodded slightly. "You do that, Sam. I'll be looking forward to them. What about you, Dr. Sonderman? Everybody else has had a chance to talk."

For the past ten minutes Tib's eyes had been in his lap,

turning over and over the sheaf of papers Rainy had given him without really looking at them, deep in thought. He looked up. "Yes," he said. "Thank you."

And then he was silent, pursing his lips thoughtfully, until Rainy began to fidget and the governor's slight smile grew strained.

"You see," Tib said, "I wish to disagree with most of what has been said here. Not as to facts, but as to implications." Afeefah was passing around the room with a plate of salted nuts, and Tib absently reached out for a handful. "For example," he said, "Dr. Bradison, the Dr. *Sam* Bradison, concludes that you require better licensing arrangements so that, for example, no one will build a skyscraper that will fall down, and that in my opinion is useless. Nearly useless. One should build well, but it is impossible to build any structure so that it cannot be destroyed." He chewed thoughtfully for a second, and then went on.

"I wish to try to do something that one does not usually do in public, that is to speak to you in truth in the strong sense. That is to say, not only the absence of untruth but the entire conceptual statement, and with no attempt to manipulate the listener. Do you understand me? I will not tell you what I want you to hear because I have come to certain conclusions of my own and want you to take certain actions. I will tell you what I believe to be objective fact, and then I will tell you the conclusions I, myself, have drawn. What you then choose to do you must decide for yourself. I am open-minded about this," he added fairly, "because I have little expectation that anything you do will matter.

"In the first place, you see, all works of man are transient; nothing survives. Even the pyramids will go within a certain not very large number of thousands of years. They will be survived by a few artifacts, for a time—abandoned open-pit mines, let us say, or radionuclide waste dumps—but in a finite time even those will be subducted down into the magma and cease to exist as organized matter. This is a geologist's point of view; I am speaking, obviously, of the very long term. But it is important to understand this principle, because in the short term it is nearly completely true as well."

The governor's secretary opened his mouth, but the governor shook his head without looking at him and Tib went on. "So to try to achieve permanent safety is impossible over time. The only question is, how much time? While I have been sitting here, I have been trying to calculate some rough risk assessments. I have taken very round numbers to make the mathematics easy, but I think they are not orders of magnitude wrong, at least.

"There is a general distributed risk attached to anything on Earth: a dwelling may burn, or be struck by a nuclear weapon or some other instrument of war, or someone may destroy it in a riot or out of vindictiveness, or it may be destroyed by a large meteorite, or annihilated in many other ways; and all these events may occur regardless of what building codes you enact or what caution the owner displays. I have given a number to this general risk, point zero one, one chance in a hundred of being destroyed in any particular year, so that, on average, one can expect any given building to survive for one century of useful life. I do not know that this estimate is correct, but I would suppose that if anything it is, on the average, quite high.

"But let us now move this hypothetical building to a new location. Say, one of the Hollywood hills. Let us say its back yard is covered with chapparal, like my own house, and subject to the Santa Ana and to mud slides, also like my own house. In certain areas, at least, we can estimate the danger of fire at, again, one per cent per year; and the danger of mud slides also at one per cent a year, and now do you see what has happened? The danger is now three times as great, and the house has now a useful life expectancy of thirty-three years four months. Add to that the risk of earthquake, which I will put at one per cent for certain areas: life expectancy has now been cut to twenty-five years. Add to that that this particular house is, let us say, built in the flood channel of an earthwork dam, and we now have a house which in all seriousness cannot expect to survive until its mortgage is paid off.

"And for some hundreds of homes in this area, perhaps for quite a few thousands, such calculations can be made and this is the result. To own such a house is to play Russian roulette.

"Similar calculations, of course, can be made for other risks, and for loss of life or health as well as of property; I have not attempted to do this, since I have no expertise in these last areas.

"I believe that is all I have to say," he finished.

The governor's secretary looked nervously at the governor, seeking to learn whether he should laugh, swear or applaud, but the governor took his time giving him an indication. He too had been hitting Afeefah's party foods, and he finished chewing before he said seriously, "I appreciate what you're saying, but I'm not sure just what action government can take."

"You have understood me exactly," Tib said, nodding. "I, too, am not sure that there is any."

The governor sat back. He was a man who had made his reputation on understanding what the general run of politicos did not, counter-culture people, artists, scientists, doomsayers, idealists, and the like. "Thank you, Dr. Sonderman. Now. Before we go, Sam, would it be possible to see your grandson and this young lady's father for a moment?"

Tib got up and came over to Rainy's chair. "I think they have no further need for us. May we go home now?"

He seemed sunk in gloom in the car. The downpour was now only a sort of greasy drizzle, and Rainy felt secure enough to watch him out of the corner of her eye as she drove. "I think you confused them quite a lot," she offered.

He sat up. "Yes." He looked out the window for a while before adding, "I must work this out for myself."

"Shall I take you to your house?"

"No—not unless you wish to be alone," he said. "My car is, after all, still at yours. Oh," he added, "I forgot your paper. Let me see, can I turn on this little light in the glove compartment?" He leaned forward, peering at the first page. "It appears to be a scientific paper by a T. T.

Khrembullin from, how would you say this, from the Institute for Theoretical Astronomy in the Kazakh Soviet Socialist Republic. I do not know his name, but he is an academician, therefore important. The title you would call 'Second Order Gravitational Focusing Involving Major Planets'. There are a number of equations which I imagine you will be able to read as well as I, since they are not in Russian but in mathematics."

Rainy started to smile, to show appreciation for another pleasantry—the second attempt at humor in only a couple of hours!—and then what he said struck her.

"Major planets!" she cried. Tib turned to look at her inquiringly. "Yes, major planets! The planet Jupiter, for instance! Fasten your seat belt, Tib, I want to get home and read that!"

A wind gust of twenty-five miles an hour can turn your umbrella inside out. The highest velocity ever recorded in a hurricane in the United States was 183 miles an hour; there were higher velocities, but not recorded, since the wind blew the instruments away. Since the force exerted by a wind, and therefore the destruction it can cause, increases as the cube of the velocity, peak hurricane winds are not merely seven or eight times stronger than a stiff breeze, they are nearly four hundred times as damaging.

Monday, December 28th. 7:10 PM.

The best thing that happened in a bad, bad day was when they were stopped on the freeway and shunted off to city roads. Good things come in disguise. It looked at first like just one more disaster, and Danny Deere met it as he met them all. "Oh, shit, Joel, now what? Can't you for God's sake just get me home?"

"Sure thing, Danny," Joel said over his shoulder, "but the road's blocked. Looks like that whole condo development's down the tube."

"Down the tube," Danny repeated in sudden delight.

Well! You always get a little something for a consolation prize, and this wasn't a bad one. Anything that saved his view and bitched that bastard Boyma at the same time couldn't be all bad. He chewed the news over, tasting every crumb, because it was a hell of a lot better than thinking about the rest of his day.

Which had been a bummer from the minute he woke up. He drummed his fingers on his attache case, which still contained exactly the $87,950 he had put into it when he awoke and emptied his living-room safe. No business was done that day. By the time the fucking phone company got the fucking phones working, the first call he got was from his fucking lawyer, and it was all bad news. He had made a bad mistake talking to the Keating woman the way he did.

"We got to go clear around up the hill, Danny," Joel called. "See, a lot of the freeway cut got flooded, and I have to—"

"So do it, for Christ's sake!"

"Sure thing, Danny. Danny?"

"What?"

"Are they going to pull your license, Danny?"

"Just drive! Drive! Let me worry about that!"

But there wasn't any point in worrying about it, because either they would or they wouldn't, and the fucking lawyer just spread his hands and said there was a lot of heat, oh, yes, a *lot* of heat. The whole Pedigrue family was out to get him personally, and even old man Bradison had been making phone calls all over the state.

Danny sighed, and stared out at the unfamiliar side roads. He opened the dispatch case just a crack to feel the neatly banded bills, thinking it might soothe him. And actually it did. When you had money, what did you care? He had plenty! The worst they could do would be to put him out of business maybe, maybe eat him up with a few hundred thousand in fines and lawyers, maybe make him look bad—so what?

"Now what, for Christ's sakes?"

Joel was slowing. "It's Manuel and his boys, Danny, they're waving to us."

240

"Forget Manuel! Just keep going! I want to get home!" They were at the top of the little crest above his property now, on the old access road that the trucks had carried avocados along before the freeway was built. Danny glanced at the woebegone wet Mexicans contemptuously. Whatever they wanted, they were no problem. Or no problem except to themselves, because likely enough he'd have to fire all their asses right off the land—so what again? Let the goddam trees go. Joel could handle everything else around the house. Of course, they'd have to recalculate Joel's salary—

He lunged forward as Joel slammed on the brakes. "Oh, my God, Danny, look!"

And Danny looked, down at the muddy lake that had been his estate, where the slide into the freeway had blocked the runoff, where the old avocado trees rose out of three feet of water, where his house itself was awash to the middle of the first floor and the basement completely submerged, where all the chalks and canvases and pigments of all the paintings and sketches and playthings that were his treasure were now sodden trash, not much different in appearance from the mud along the roadside, and not much more valuable.

A supernova explosion of a star close enough to greatly damage or even wipe out life on Earth occurs about once every seven hundred and fifty million years, according to Carl Sagan. About six have occurred in the time since the formation of the Earth. About nine more will occur before our own Sun makes life on Earth impossible.

Monday, December 28th. 8:10 PM.

As soon as they were inside her apartment Rainy flung her coat at a chair, spread the Russian-language typescript on the kitchen table and took her calculator out of its case.

Although Tib was convinced he had made a fool of himself in front of the governor, he felt peaceful. The storm outside was coming to an end, and so was the storm within. Nothing had really happened. Certainly nothing to compare to the people you heard about on the radio, trapped in cars, pinned against their own bedroom walls by avalanches of mud, carried away in storm drains. Nothing like Rainy, who now had some fascinating data to play with, or even like Sam Bradison, who at least had a new crusade. And yet he felt a sense of release. He moved over to the kitchen table, admiring Rainy's blind concentration as she worked with calculator and pencil, scribbling notes to herself on lined yellow pads. He brushed against the orrery on the windowsill, sending the planets clashing against each other, and Rainy looked up, eyes unfocused behind the huge glasses. "Give me the pages you are not using," he said, "and I will make an abstract for you in English."

She nodded, and pushed most of the sheets toward him. He put them in order, captured one of the yellow pads and studied the handwritten notations at the top of the first page. "This is interesting," he said. "This paper was withdrawn from publication by the author, on instructions from someone who signs only initials."

Rainy nodded absently.

"I suppose that was why Mihailovitch smuggled it to you, then. I think he took some risk."

She looked up. "Could we hold that down for now, Tib? I'll just be a little while."

He pursed his lips and shrugged. It took him only a few minutes to make a quick synopsis of what the paper had to say, mathematics aside, and occupied only a small part of his mind. When he was finished he amused himself by spinning the orrery with one finger, while the greater part of his mind continued its slow circling toward some sort of decision, until Rainy sat up, her eyes glowing. "Oh, Tib," she said, "this is great. Here, look at this."

She sketched quickly on a lined yellow pad. "Remember the drawing of the sun as a lens? That was right—up to a point. But what this person Kerfloozilim, or whatever his name is, says is that Jupiter too did some focusing. Here!"

She pointed to the sketch:

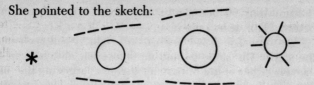

"On the left we have the star that was the source of the radiation, then comes the sun, gravitationally focusing the radiation, *then* old Jupiter! Remember? We know Jupiter and the sun and the spacecraft were in an exact straight line, because we were about to observe a transit! So the focusing effect became a real telescope, not just a magnifying glass, with a second lens!"

"I see," Tib said, watching her face instead of the diagram.

"I wonder if you do," she said, but she was smiling. "The focusing was really tight! Not just the radio and light but everything, X rays, infra-red, ultra-violet. My poor old Newton-8 got clobbered with a heat ray!"

Tib tried some focusing of his own. "Ah, yes. I do see," he said, "but I don't understand all of it. If this works, why doesn't it happen more often? For instance, why don't we see flares on Saturn and Uranus every time they go by Jupiter and happened to get in line with some star?"

Rainy shrugged. "I don't know. Because they're too big? They're very large heat sinks, and if a couple dozen square miles at the top of the atmosphere got hot we'd never notice it. Mostly because they're never in a line! All the planets go around the sun in the same general plane, the ecliptic, but each one's orbit is tilted a little compared to the others—and 'a little' means anything up to millions of miles. . . . Tib? Are you listening to me?"

He said heavily, "They thought I made a fool of myself, didn't they?"

"You mean the governor and all? Certainly not!"

He shook his head. "I think I did. I forgot KISS."

She looked puzzled, but offered her lips. "Yes, thank you," he said, kissing her and then smiling for the first time in some while, "but that is not what I meant, I meant K-I-S-S, the acronym: Keep It Simple, Stupid. Put simply, I should just have said I will sell my house."

Rainy took off her glasses and sat back to look at him better. "Tib, dear," she said, "—KISS? Even KISS-er?"

"Yes, I realize I am obscure. All right, I will spell out the steps. The slope behind my house has always been a danger, either of fire or of mud. It is not surprising that no one will listen to what I say when I myself live without regard to risk. I see that I have been deceiving myself. I have tried to set an example in, for example, limiting energy consumption, but it is not enough."

Rainy was staring at him, shaking her head—not a negative; it was wonder. "Are you planning to set yourself up as a model for the human race?"

Tib considered. "Yes," he said at last. "Exactly, although I know it sounds vain. But it is also Kant's categorical imperative."

"And you think people will listen to you?"

"No," he confessed, "I do not. Let me admit to you how much vanity I have: I was thinking, while we were driving here, that I might retain a publicity agent, so that I could appear on more radio and television shows. Or write a book, or in some way find an amplifier for my own voice. . . . But those are fantasies, of course. So I will settle for less. I will sell my house. To be quite consistent," he said, looking suddenly troubled, "I should sell my car, too, and that means I should not live in Los Angeles, should I?"

"Oh, now wait a minute, Tib," said Rainy, feeling suddenly threatened. "Your job's here."

"There are other jobs."

Rainy pushed the papers together thoughtfully. "I'll miss you if you leave Los Angeles," she said.

For a moment they sat silent, and then Tib said, "I think I've made a fool of myself again. Please excuse me, Rainy. I think I will go to my own home now."

The moon shows about 30,000 meteorite craters; the earth, which has about 50 times the cross-section capture area of the moon, presumably would have nearly a million and a half visible signs of something large striking it from space if it were not for the fact that air and water erase the traces. Even so, some traces remain quite visible, like the Barringer Crater in Arizona, and others are suspected. A few astronomers think Canada's Hudson Bay is a drowned meteorite crater. Even fewer suspect that the entire Indian Ocean may be. North America would not survive another impact like that which may have created Hudson Bay; the earth would not survive another Indian Ocean. An impact like either of those is quite unlikely in any given million-year period; but it is not impossible; and it is not the only impact from space that could greatly affect human activities.

Tuesday, December 29th. 5:10 AM.

When the telephone rang, Tib was not in his bed, and was not at first sure just where he was. There was no light, he was fully dressed, he was alone. As he fumbled for the phone he realized that he had fallen asleep in his workroom. Since there were no windows he had no idea of the time.

He said hello, and the voice that answered was Rainy's, queerly strained, almost jubilant. "Did I wake you? That's a silly question, of course I did. I haven't been to bed yet myself. I'm at the Lab."

Tib found the reading light and snapped it on, and the familiar tiny room appeared around him. He was not yet fully awake. "The Lab?" he repeated.

He could hear the smile in her voice. "Just listen, okay? Are you awake?"

"No—oh, my God." He had just discovered what time it was. "Rainy, believe me, I would listen better if I had some coffee. Let me call you back in a few minutes."

"Just listen!" she cried. There was a scraping noise on the telephone, a wait, another scraping noise. Then silence.

Tib said tentatively, "Rainy, are you there?"

Her voice came from off the microphone, and impatient. "Hang in there, will you? . . . Ah, there it goes."

There was a second of tape hiss and then a blast of

245

sound. Tib yelped and pulled the phone away from his ear, half deafened; even at arm's length he could hear perfectly what was coming out of it. What it sounded like, more than anything else, was some sort of motion-picture sound effects, the cry of a computer about to decide to wipe out the human race, or a mad scientist's laboratory. It clicked and beeped and rattled, and it went on for a full thirty seconds.

Then there was a click as it was switched off, and Rainy came back on the phone. "Did I get it too loud for you? I'm sorry; I guess I'm kind of fatigued. Do you know what you were listening to?"

"No, should I? Or wait—" Tib pursued a vagrant memory, then pounced on it. "Your spaceship? The noise it made when it blew up?"

She said with satisfaction, "You're very quick, old Tib. Exactly. The noise my spaceship made when it blew up, although I've slowed it down by, let's see, I guess this one's about eight hundred times. And do you know what it has, Tib? It has structure!"

"Structure?"

"Oh, wake up, man!" she cried. "Don't you understand what I'm saying? I've been up all night playing it, slowing it down, playing it again, and I'm *sure*. I put it on an oscilloscope and measured it, and it's regular . . . *and it doesn't repeat.*"

He stood up and switched on the wall lights; this was not an occasion for shadows. He was wide awake now. "If I understand what you are saying, Rainy, it is—it is that you believe this to be a—message?"

"A communication," she corrected.

"I do not see the difference."

"A message would be directed at us. I doubt it was. The focusing focused everything, light, heat, X rays—and radio; and so we heard a broadcast that otherwise would not have been detectable in any way. I doubt very much that it was intended for us, and I don't know what it was. A love letter, a warning, a weather report, a navigation beacon—I don't know. But it's definitely an artifact, and *it comes from another star*. I've even located the star. It's a

246

K-6, not visible to the naked eye; it doesn't even have a name, but it was in line with Jupiter and the satellite and the sun . . . and it was where the communication came from. Tib? The human race isn't alone any more."

They were both silent for a moment, and then Rainy finished, "So come on up here, Tib! I want you to help me announce it."

"Me? What would I have to say, Rainy? I'm not an astronomer."

"No. But you're a person who was saying just a little while ago that you saw no way of being heard, and now there's a way."

Tuesday, December 29th. 11:25 AM.

The noise in the Von Karman Auditorium was extreme; people were still coming in, summoned at the last minute, and for each new batch of TV and press, of scientists from JPL itself and all the surrounding schools and laboratories, the tapes had to be repeated, and Rainy had to answer the same questions again: "How can you tell?" and "Is this really proof?" and, over and over, "Are you *sure*?"

But of course no one was sure! In science one was not sure, one merely made an assumption and then contrived tests to see how nearly it was true. And of course Rainy was trying to explain that, as politicians and press, scientists and scholars whispered to each other and wondered.

Sonderman gazed at the list he had been doodling before him. It was headed "Childish vices", and it said:

Nuclear war.

Waste of irreplaceable resources.

Lack of prudence.

Failure to learn.

And that summed them up, he thought, and the last was the worst of the four.

The tape came to its hissing, moaning end for the tenth time and Rainy, eyes blinking against the lights, tired but still on her feet, held up her hand. "That's enough of that," she said. "Now I would like to introduce my collaborator in this work, Dr. Tibor Sonderman."

Tib rose and walked slowly to the podium, giving the audience a chance to sort themselves out. The press conference had been arranged on short notice; there had not even been time to set up chairs, and the people staring at him were moving around in knots and clusters. Strobes flashed, TV lights burned his tired eyes, and the buzz of talk did not die down. He cleared his throat and said:

"I have nothing to add to Ms. Keating's report as to the receipt, for the first time in human history, of a communication from an intelligent race other than our own. I wish only to comment on an implication of this fact.

"To discover that intelligence can arise is not in itself surprising, for we already knew that this is possible. It has happened here on Earth. What is surprising is to discover that an intelligent race can survive its technology. We now know that at least one other race has. It has passed the point of being able to destroy itself, as we are able now, and has gone on to some further stage; and that is new. This fact gives us hope. And it also gives us a purpose, and certain obligations. For what we know now that we did not know before is that the human race is not necessarily under sentence of death, and so certain childish and dangerous follies can be abandoned."

They were looking at him in perplexity and surprise, but not, at least, in hostility. And the TV cameras, those remarkable amplifiers of the voice, were rolling. What he said would be heard. "So we may now set behind us the kamikaze society," he said, gaining confidence with every word, "and now, with your permission, I will tell you what it appears to me we must do, in order to survive and take our place in this congeries of cultures that we now know to exist among the stars."

ABOUT THE AUTHOR

FREDERIK POHL is a double-threat science fictioneer, being the only person to have won this field's top award, the Hugo, as both a writer and an editor. As a writer, he's published more than 30 novels and short story collections; as an editor, he published the first series of anthologies of original stories in the field of science fiction, *Star Science Fiction*. He was, for a number of years, the editor of two leading magazines, *Galaxy* and *If*. His awards include four Hugos and the Edward E. Smith Award. His interests extend to politics, history (he's the *Encyclopaedia Britannica's* authority on the Roman Emperor Tiberius) and almost the entire range of human affairs. His best known novels include JEM and MAN PLUS.

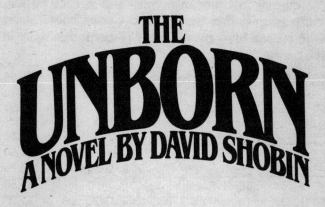

FANTASY AND SCIENCE FICTION FAVORITES

Bantam brings you the recognized classics as well as the current favorites in fantasy and science fiction. Here you will find the beloved Conan books along with recent titles by the most respected authors in the genre.